A FRESH START FOR THE COUNTRY NURSE

KATE EASTHAM

Boldwood

First published in Great Britain in 2025 by Boldwood Books Ltd.

Copyright © Kate Eastham, 2025

Cover Design by Colin Thomas

Cover Images: Colin Thomas and iStock

A CIP catalogue record for this book is available from the British Library.

Paperback ISBN 978-1-83656-206-1

Large Print ISBN 978-1-83656-207-8

Hardback ISBN 978-1-83656-205-4

Ebook ISBN 978-1-83656-208-5

Kindle ISBN 978-1-83656-209-2

Audio CD ISBN 978-1-83656-200-9

MP3 CD ISBN 978-1-83656-201-6

Digital audio download ISBN 978-1-83656-202-3

This book is printed on certified sustainable paper. Boldwood Books is dedicated to putting sustainability at the heart of our business. For more information please visit https://www.boldwoodbooks.com/about-us/sustainability/

Boldwood Books Ltd, 23 Bowerdean Street, London, SW6 3TN

www.boldwoodbooks.com

For Ann Hall (1936–2023)

Keep your face always toward the sunshine – and shadows will fall behind you.

— WALT WHITMAN

PROLOGUE

BROCK FARM, INGLESIDE VILLAGE, JULY 1936

Lara Flynn rapidly dismounted her bicycle, grabbed the leather medical bag from the basket and ran through squawking, flapping hens along a rough track towards the barn. Throwing herself to her knees on the hay-strewn floor, there was no time to remove her district nurse's hat or don her surgical gown. The baby was coming right now.

The birthing mother – a farmer's wife – lay propped against a stack of hay, wisps of dark hair plastered to her reddened, sweating face. She was pushing uncontrollably as a massive contraction racked her body. At the peak, she emitted a deep, guttural sound, one Lara instantly recognised as indicating her patient was about to deliver.

Lara spoke rapidly, still catching her breath. 'Hello, Mrs Haworth, I'm Nurse Flynn, the new district nurse and midwife from Ingleside surgery.'

'I don't give a bugger who you are,' she growled, 'as long as you can help me.'

With no time to scrub up, Lara reached for her medical bag and pulled out a pair of surgical gloves. Not taking her eyes away for a second from the glistening, dark shape of a baby's head appearing between the woman's thighs.

'You're close now,' she urged. 'I can see the head, so with the next pain, push as hard as you can.'

The woman tried to reply but grunted instead, and her face contorted as another huge contraction hit.

Lara donned her surgical gloves, then gritted her teeth. 'That's it, push. Keep pushing... You're doing so well.'

She felt her heart clench with expectation as the baby's head began to crown. In awe of the miraculous moment which had had her in its thrall ever since she'd witnessed her very first delivery as a student midwife.

'I can see the head,' she called. 'That's it, well done! Now pant,' she instructed as the child's face began to appear – forehead, eyes, nose, and mouth. The first sighting of a brand-new human, fresh to the world, was her privilege as a midwife.

Swallowing hard as she checked for the cord around the baby's neck, she spoke gently to the mother. 'Your baby has lots of dark hair; looks like he or she is going to be a bobby dazzler.'

The woman tried to reply but groaned instead as the next contraction hit. She uttered an ancient sound that seemed to come from deep inside and pushed hard.

As the head rotated, Lara expertly delivered the shoulders and the infant shot out in a gush of blood and amniotic fluid.

'It's a girl!' she cried.

'A girl,' the woman laughed, then sobbed. 'A little girl... I've got three boys; I've always wanted a daughter.'

The baby sneezed, then took her first breath.

Lara turned her onto her side to let the amniotic fluid drain from her nose and mouth. Then came that first cry, the one that always made the hairs at the back of her neck prickle. And with

her body still buzzing with adrenaline, she reached for her bag. 'I'll cut the cord, then you can have a hold of her.'

Knowing exactly where to find the newly sterilised clamp and scissors wrapped in a white surgical cloth, she grasped the instruments expertly. Then, once she had the cord secured with surgical thread, she cut the infant free. Skilfully swaddling her in a clean white cot sheet, she felt the tiny body writhe against her. Then shuffling her knees over the rough, hay-strewn floor, she held out both arms to give the baby to the farmer's wife who still lay amid the hay, swiping away tears and laughing all at the same time.

'Thank you, nurse. Thank you,' she croaked, then gasped, then sobbed.

Moving into position, Lara sat back on her heels and waited for the afterbirth to be delivered. Basking in the glory of the mother cradling her child, she remained, as always at this stage, vigilant for any sign of haemorrhage. With amniotic fluid soaking into her uniform skirt, her hands sticky with mucus, strands of hay prickling through her regulation black stockings, all she could do now was wait for nature to take its course.

Observing the detail of her immediate environment, she noted a basket of eggs tipped over on its side, one or two cracked and leaking yellow yolk. All around her, hens were pecking unconcernedly among the hay. She heard the lowing of a cow in the cobbled yard she'd run through, stepping in manure which still clung to her black, lace-up shoes. Then, she watched as a proud red and brown cockerel mounted a pile of straw and stretched its glossy neck. In the next second, the creature emitted an ear-piercing cock-a-doodle-doo.

She screamed, clutched her chest.

'I take it you're not a country girl then, Nurse Flynn,' the farmer's wife laughed.

'Most definitely not,' Lara gasped, her heart still pounding. 'I've only been here a few weeks; I was born and bred in the city of Liverpool.'

'You'll soon get the hang of things out here in the sticks, especially if you carry on getting stuck into the work.'

Still startled by the crowing cockerel, Lara snapped right back into action when the afterbirth began to emerge. 'Push, keep pushing,' she urged.

Clinging to her baby girl, exhausted as she was, Mrs Haworth did the work, and the final stage of labour was completed.

Glancing up to check her patient, Lara saw her teary once more. 'Are you OK?' she asked gently.

'I'm just fine,' the woman croaked, offering a wobbly smile. When she spoke again, her voice was husky with emotion. 'I know you're not from round here, and no doubt it'll take a good while for you to feel settled and be accepted by the local folk. But just so you know... you'll always have a special place in my heart. You brought my precious baby girl safely into this world... and there's not much more any woman could do for another.'

Lara felt her heart squeeze, an *'it's all part of the service'* response on the tip of her tongue. But given this was one of the few times so far she'd been instantly accepted by a member of this tight-knit, rural community, she swallowed it back down and took the compliment. Desperately hoping it might be the beginnings of feeling more at ease in this remote place which felt so far removed from the city of Liverpool where she'd grown up and trained as a nurse that it seemed like a whole different world.

1

Four Months Earlier

'So, this is the birthday surprise,' Lara breathed as she walked into an impressive, high-ceilinged space dominated by fluted pillars, ornate arches and crystal chandeliers glittering with rainbow light. Pulling the man on her arm even closer, she felt pleasure piqued with excitement. 'I know you said our evening was going to be luxurious, but this is beyond all expectation.'

Patrick made a satisfied noise at the back of his throat. 'So glad you like it, Nurse Flynn.' He leant in close to murmur in her ear, 'And seeing you so decidedly out of your nurse's uniform, I don't think I ever want to see you in anything other than a silk evening gown.' The smell of his cologne, the feel of his breath on her neck made her arms prickle with goosebumps.

Pulling back a little, he reached to tuck a strand of her white-blonde hair neatly behind her left ear. It felt slightly awkward; she'd deliberately let the curl fall so she'd feel different with her hair up, not for work this time but for a special night out to celebrate her twenty-eighth birthday. The moment gave her pause, especially since over the past few weeks, she'd been increasingly irritated by his supposedly jokey comments about her dowdy nurse's uniform. But in the next second, when he turned to offer one of his enchanting smiles, it was easy to overlook the recent niggles she'd had. After all, they'd been seeing each other for a while now and just when she'd thought the early glow was beginning to wear off, here they were at the Adelphi Hotel.

She linked his arm and as her heels tapped on the marble floor and her borrowed evening gown brushed against her silk-stockinged legs, she felt a frisson of expectation ripple through her body. As soon as they were in through the door of the impressive dining room, a slick uniformed maître d' showed them to their table. She saw the confident set of Patrick's shoulders, the practised nod of his head, and knew he was in his natural setting here.

And as they settled into their seats around a candle-lit table, she felt as if they'd moved way beyond the day they'd first met on the streets of Liverpool when she'd dropped her purse, and he'd stooped down to the pavement to retrieve it. Flustered by the quickness of his response, she'd gasped a thank you, grabbed her purse and immediately dropped it again. He'd laughed as he'd stooped to retrieve it for a second time and then he'd apologised for startling her, and he'd been so charming, she'd readily agreed to join him for coffee at the Kardomah cafe. As they'd chatted, she'd felt uneasy at first, putting it down to him being so handsome. Could a man be too good-looking? She'd heard her nurse friend Fiona's voice in her head: *No, of course not, you idiot, stop questioning everything... he's gorgeous.* Not that she usually listened to Fiona. Her friend's own history with men was testament enough to how flawed her decision-making could be. And being 'strong-willed' as her aunt had called her, Lara always made her own mind up.

They'd chatted easily enough; he was witty and engaging. He'd told her he was a solicitor working with wealthy business clients. On its own, she wouldn't have been impressed by that but by the time he was ordering their second cup of coffee, she'd begun to feel relaxed enough to know that if he asked, she'd go out with him on a date – of course she would.

And now, after months of regularly seeing each other, here they were in a fancy French restaurant at the Adelphi Hotel. And despite having said yes to an urgent request from Matron to do an early shift the following morning, her world felt like pure bliss as Patrick raised yet another glass of champagne. She knew already that she wouldn't be going back to the lodgings she shared with Fiona and two other nurses. Patrick had booked a suite so they could enjoy the whole night together and as it stretched tantalisingly before her, she knew she was going to make the most of it.

After the meal, when coffee had been served and he'd leant back in his chair, he reached inside his jacket pocket and pulled out an antique-looking, red leather case. She knew immediately it had to be a birthday gift of jewellery, and it made her breath catch because she didn't feel quite ready to receive something so extravagant. But his smile was irresistible and when he told her it was nothing really, just one of his grandmother's necklaces that had been left to him in her will, she felt she had no choice but to accept. But as she clicked open the case and saw a large, flower-like cluster of emeralds surrounding a circle of diamonds on a heavy gold chain, she knew this was no small gift. It was a valuable antique.

'No, honestly, it's too much,' she murmured.

'You have to take it.' He smiled. 'It's a perfect match with your gown, your alabaster skin and those beguiling blue eyes.'

She felt her cheeks flush; never good at receiving compliments, these seemed wildly effusive. But she could see the earnestness of his expression and didn't want to unsettle their evening together.

'Thank you,' she breathed, as he removed the necklace from its leather box with a flourish and got up to stand behind her to fasten it around her neck. Feeling suddenly vulnerable as he took charge of the fastening, she felt an empty sensation, a pinch of unease in her stomach. But once he was back in his seat reaching for the bottle of champagne to top up her glass, the uncomfortable moment moved on.

Groaning awake in the early hours of the morning, having never meant to fall properly asleep, she felt the warmth of Patrick's body next to her. She rolled onto her side, realisation dawning... *Oh no, what time is it?* Reaching groggily for her wristwatch on the bedside table, she squinted in the pale light of an overly ornate gold lamp. It was 5.30 a.m.... Audibly exhaling, she rested her throbbing head back down on the soft pillow. She had plenty of time to walk back to her lodgings and get ready for her morning shift. She groaned again; why had she ever agreed to work on the day after her birthday, for goodness' sake? Rolling over to face Patrick, she saw him spreadeagled with his mouth dropped open. He looked more unconscious than asleep and although she'd known him all these months, just in that moment, he seemed as mysterious and closed off as a stranger.

Slipping carefully from between the silk sheets, she collected her discarded clothing from various locations around the room. The pink, satin cami-knickers and her new petticoat were by the side of the bed. The borrowed evening gown lay in a crumpled heap, entangled with her new silk stockings near the door. Walking back towards the bed, she perched on a velvet padded chair and expertly rolled each stocking up to her thigh, then snapped her suspenders into place. Then shaking out the gown, she stepped into it, nimbly zipping it at the side. Gazing briefly in the mirror, she gathered her hair, twisted it, and fixed it with a clip. It made her smile when that one curl fell naturally into its rightful position on her cheek. But she was ready to go and still he hadn't stirred. Whenever they'd slept together in his flat, he'd roused as soon as she'd moved and pulled her back into his arms, and she'd almost had to prise herself away. It felt a little sad to see him so unaware. But then he had consumed a large amount of brandy last night, on top of all the champagne.

* * *

Over the next few weeks, she needed to work extra shifts to cover a district nurse off sick, so beyond a couple of meetups for coffee at the Kardomah, she hadn't seen Patrick properly for a while. But one morning, as she cycled past the Adelphi on her way to a new antenatal case, she saw him emerge through the door of the hotel. Instantly, she slowed and pulled her bicycle over to say a quick hello. Excited to see him, she was already holding up her hand, but he was distracted and seemed to be waiting for someone as he held open the door. She waited patiently, assuming he'd just had one of his business meetings with a wealthy client. And when a tall, slim, young woman with neatly coiffed, chestnut hair emerged, she saw him offer a warm smile. Still, Lara thought nothing of it. But the moment they began to descend the steps and Patrick put his arm around the woman's waist and pulled her close in the exact same way he did with her, she knew this was no business client.

She felt completely stunned as she sat astride her bicycle,

unable to move. Breathless, she watched as the pair walked towards Lime Street station, still entwined. And as her thoughts spiralled, white-hot anger began to pulse through her body. Shocked by an urgent car horn behind her, she cursed out loud, her voice instantly swallowed up by the rumble of a passing truck. Pushing off on her bicycle, she pedalled furiously, her heart lurching when she saw Patrick kiss the woman full on the mouth in the exact same way he always said goodbye to her.

Her breath quickened, rasping in her chest.

'Patrick!' she shouted as the woman walked away. His body twitched for a second and she knew he'd heard her but clearly, he was pretending otherwise.

Rapidly dismounting her bicycle, she pushed it roughly against a lamppost. And the moment he turned with a smooth smile, she saw him for the liar he'd always been.

'Lara. Darling,' he crooned.

'Don't even try,' she growled. She covered the distance in a few strides. 'I saw you coming out of the hotel with that woman. I saw it all.'

'She's just a friend—'

'No,' she shouted. 'Don't give me that.'

He tried to reach out to her then, but she spat, 'Stay back.'

Aware they were drawing attention from other pedestrians, she saw him narrow his eyes. 'You're making a scene, Lara,' the sharp, outraged edge to his voice only serving to enrage her further.

'*I'm* making a scene! *You* are the one who caused this. And I think most of these people passing would think I had just cause for taking you to task.'

He looked uncertain then and dropped his head, began to mutter a mixed-up collection of excuses. But the moment he glanced up and she saw the insolent jut of his chin, something snapped inside her.

'How could you do this? We were there together in that same hotel for my birthday.'

His dark eyes hardened then and he almost smirked. 'Maybe what we had together wasn't as special as you thought it was, Lara. I mean, you can be so uptight, and you are very naïve... For example, when we stayed at the Adelphi that night, I didn't even pay for the room... A wealthy American client of mine booked it for me because we had a business meeting the next day in the hotel lounge.'

A wave of fury and hurt swelled in her throat, but she could see by the tilt of his head and the glint in his eyes that he was goading her now. And in that split second, her anger dropped as quickly as it had risen. There was no more to be said. Whatever this had been, it was over.

'I never want to see you again,' she growled.

He opened his mouth as if to reply but then shrugged and walked away, leaving her completely alone, deserted in the street with people streaming by on either side.

Steaming with anger at how naïve she'd been to trust such a man, and knowing she should have taken the niggles she'd had about him seriously, there was nothing she could do now but get on with seeing her patients. Her hands were still shaking as she retrieved her trusty bicycle and pushed back into the stream of traffic. She didn't even see the dark-grey van to her left until it was too late. Startling with shock at a high-pitched screech of tyres, she felt a hard, metallic, deadening impact. And as a blood-curdling scream came from someone close by, her world went completely black.

2

INGLESIDE VILLAGE, LANCASHIRE, JULY 1936

Lara felt hot and flustered as she stood on the smooth-worn flags at the door of the doctor's surgery with her leather travelling case gripped tightly in her right hand. Just as she reached up to use the brass knocker, the green-painted door swung open abruptly. Sucking in a sharp breath, she caught a whiff of carbolic as she politely stepped aside to allow an elderly woman with white hair bound in a neat chignon to descend from the double-fronted property. Undoubtedly a patient, the woman paused for a moment to steady herself with an ornately carved walking stick. Then she narrowed her eyes and fixed her with a watery blue gaze. The moment stretched out uncomfortably, forcing Lara to blurt out a hurried response to an unasked question. 'I'm Lara Flynn, the new district nurse.'

The woman raised both pencilled eyebrows. 'You don't look much like a nurse to me, and you're not from round here.'

Lara left a beat of silence as her travel-exhausted mind struggled for a suitable response. But the elderly woman's gaze had already shifted to the white summer hat with its band of bright silk flowers that had seemed appropriate when Lara had bought it in Lewis's department store in Liverpool, but now felt frivolous and wildly out of place. At least her navy-blue cotton jacket and matching skirt were suitably demure.

She could feel her blouse sticking to her back as she made every effort to keep her voice pleasant. 'No, I'm not local, I'm from Liverpool. But once I'm in my uniform, I'll look much more like a district nurse.'

'Humph, maybe.' The woman twisted her mouth then turned to make her way to the cobbled street which ran through the centre of the village.

Not letting herself feel too thrown out, Lara was about to access the still-open door when she was confronted by a haughty-looking, middle-aged woman with bobbed black hair and a long, pale face. The woman glanced at her up and down, then by way of greeting, she said crisply, 'You must be Nurse Flynn. I'm glad you're here at last; we're absolutely snowed under.'

Flushed with heat and just desperate to get in through the door, Lara fought to stay calm.

The woman opened her mouth as if to speak again but nothing came.

Lara held her ground. She knew without asking that this must be the housekeeper, Mrs Hewitt. She had been mentioned in a letter sent by Dr Henry Bingham, the senior physician at the village practice who had interviewed and appointed Lara by telephone. It felt like a reprieve when Mrs Hewitt switched her gaze to Sam Collins, the local butcher who had used his work van as a taxi to collect her from the railway station and was now struggling to unload her trunk. The ride along narrow, country lanes, tightly confined in a vehicle smelling of raw meat, had been a shock to the system. Especially when they'd encountered a lively herd of cows heading straight towards the van. It had felt daunting, given she'd never seen a cow up close, never mind a whole bunch of them with their intimidating pointy horns and swollen udders. The butcher had cursed and sworn, then rammed his van in reverse and lurched violently back to a passing place. And once the cows had filed past, he'd muttered and grumbled and revved his engine, then they'd splattered their way through numerous fresh cow pats. The pungent smell of manure mixed with the metallic edge of raw meat from the back of the van had offered a unique introduction to country life.

Still waiting at the door, she felt relieved when the house-keeper finished her loud, jocular conversation with the butcher and turned back to her. 'Well at least you've got a sunny day for your arrival. We get more rain round here than anything else,' she offered with perhaps the twitch of a smile. Then her eyes were scrutinising Lara's new white hat with its band of silk flowers.

Something clicked inside Lara's travel-weary brain and she had to fight to control her urgent need to be in through the door. When her voice came, she tried to soften it but her words were clipped. 'Please can you show me to my room?' was what she said, but by the woman's affronted reaction and the way she thrust both hands in the front pocket of her spotlessly clean blue pinny, it felt as if she'd made an outrageous request.

She saw Mrs Hewitt purse her lips and knew that if there was a wrong foot to get off on, she had just achieved it perfectly.

'This way,' the woman called curtly, propping the door open with a large, cast-iron doorstop before turning on her heel and striding briskly ahead down a polished, green-tiled corridor.

Lara followed determinedly; she'd worked with enough ill-tempered ward sisters to not be intimidated. But this felt nothing like the warm country welcome she'd envisaged, and it made her feel a little sad. Then the jagged scar above her left temple began to throb, and she reached up to check that her neatly coiffed hair was still in the correct position to conceal the wound. It was infuriating to be so regularly reminded of Patrick and what had happened that day of the accident.

Further along the corridor, she noted a seating area with at least half a dozen people in flat caps and summer hats smoking and chatting as they waited on wooden benches. Most of them fell silent and gazed straight at her as she approached, but after ten years of nursing, it didn't daunt her; working as a district nurse in a busy city, she'd got used to being scrutinised ages ago. She nodded a hello and offered a smile but didn't get anything in response, so she switched her attention to some chairs where an elderly man with a bandaged head and a pregnant young woman with a fractious squirming little girl on her lap were sitting.

The housekeeper paused beside the young woman and spoke surprisingly gently. 'Hello there, Lizzie, it's good to see you... It shouldn't be long before you can take Sue in to see the doctor.'

The little girl of about three years old had light-brown hair gathered into two neat bunches and she glanced at Lara with big eyes and bright-red cheeks. In the next second, her mouth turned down at the corners and she began to grizzle as she pressed her little hand to her left ear. Despite her fatigue, Lara's medical brain remained fully switched on and she instantly diagnosed a case of otitis media – a middle ear infection.

As the child's mother glanced up with a weary smile, Lara noted dark smudges of exhaustion beneath her pale-blue eyes. And in the dimly lit waiting area, the upturned oval of her face seemed to be appealing for something, and it triggered an intuitive thought. She'd had moments like this with other patients –

sometimes, they'd turned out to be nothing, but she was sure she'd just spotted the shadow of a fading bruise along the woman's collarbone. She made a mental note to pursue Lizzie's case and she'd be asking if there was a clinic for pregnant and nursing mothers like the one where she'd worked in Liverpool. Unbidden, the words of the senior midwife who had led the team came to her: 'Assess your patients as soon as you clap eyes on them. It's amazing what detail you can pick up, even in the waiting room.'

Mrs Hewitt was on the move again so Lara followed, and once they were out of earshot of the patients, she asked for more information about Lizzie. The housekeeper stopped abruptly, turned to face her. 'She's struggling because Sue is a fractious little lass who's crying with earache every five minutes, so nobody in that house is getting much sleep. It's a good job they live in a cottage just across the road because they're always in here.'

Instantly distracted by another wail from the child, the housekeeper glanced back, her eyes flashing with what looked like concern. Then she was shaking her head. 'We're running way behind this afternoon... Dr Bingham's only just got back from the cottage hospital in Ridgetown, and he had to go straight into the consulting room. And our junior doctor and district nurse are covering a very long list of house calls.'

Lara opened her mouth to offer a supportive comment but something about Mrs Hewitt's stern brow and the set of her mouth gave her pause. The housekeeper was either hard-pressed or simply bad-tempered, and right now there was no way to work that out. So Lara kept quiet.

Abruptly, a large, black telephone on its own gate-legged table at the foot of the stairs began to ring violently, and the urgency of it shocked her. Mrs Hewitt picked up the receiver and spoke clearly but in a rather formal, clipped voice. As she nodded her head and continued to listen to whoever had made the call, she gestured in the direction of the broad staircase. It felt difficult to interpret what she was trying to convey so Lara held her ground until the housekeeper covered the receiver and hissed, 'Go up the stairs. Your room is second on the right, opposite the bathroom.'

'Thank you,' Lara whispered.

Before she set foot on the staircase, she gazed at the oblong of bright sunshine at the still-open front door and fleetingly felt the urge to run towards the light. She smiled to herself then because although she'd received a frosty welcome, she knew it would take much more than a seemingly ill-tempered housekeeper to stop her from making a fresh start. And as she climbed the plush, red-carpeted stairs, she felt delight as the house opened above her with its high, stuccoed ceiling, embossed wallpaper, and a tall window with rose-patterned glass. It felt more like a country manor than a doctor's surgery and it pleased her, given the cramped, rather down-at-heel accommodation she'd shared with her two fellow nurses in Liverpool. In due course, she'd write to Fiona with all the detail, and she'd also send a letter to another close friend, Maeve, who had crossed the Atlantic to nurse at the Bellevue hospital in New York. Maeve's letters described working hard on the wards but on days off, she was sightseeing and spending her evenings in the cocktail bars of Manhattan. After the accident, Maeve had urged Lara to consider New York, but the noise and the crush of another city had seemed too much to take on, especially with the intensity of the flashbacks from the accident she'd been having early on. And she'd struggled when at last she'd gone back to work, so much so that she'd applied for this post.

As she pushed open the door to her new room, a strong

smell of mothballs mixed with fresh paint hit her head-on, but the high-ceilinged space was very clean and instantly pleasing. An iron bedframe set on a square of red-patterned carpet dominated the space, but there was also a solid oak wardrobe with a matching chest of drawers and a mirrored dressing table set at just the right angle to catch the light from a tall sash window that looked out onto the street. A small fireplace with an inset of blue and yellow patterned tiles sat on the far wall and there was a white porcelain sink in the corner. She also noted an ornate, cast-iron radiator beneath the window so at least she would be warm in winter – that's if she stayed long enough to find out. Placing her leather valise on the brightly coloured patchwork quilt covering the bed, she removed her hat, slipped out of her cotton jacket and hung them neatly side by side on the shiny brass hooks behind the door.

Walking to the sink, she ran some cool water to sponge her face and neck, then glanced in the mirror to check that the newly healed scar on her forehead was still hidden from view beneath a carefully positioned lock of hair. Her cheeks were flushed bright red with the heat, and the pink line of scalp at her centre parting made her seem vulnerable somehow, a feeling compounded by the grey smudges of exhaustion beneath her eyes. She knew it was due to poor sleep since the accident, and she hoped that coming out to the countryside would help to break that cycle. And already, now she was here in her new room with its bright bedspread and freshly painted walls, she sensed the potential for finding the peace she craved.

As if to undermine that thought, the scar began to throb and, with trembling hands, she pulled a white towel from the hook by the sink and pressed it there. Just as she began to undo the top buttons of her blouse so she could splash some cool water on her face, a heavy knock sounded, the door swung open, and the portly frame of Sam Collins the butcher huffed through, dragging her trunk. His face was purple with exertion and he looked ready to collapse.

Swiftly, she refastened her buttons and moved to assist him with positioning the trunk at the side of the bed. The physical effort seemed to steady her, and she was instantly more concerned for the butcher, who stood slumped and gasping for air. When he was sufficiently recovered, he pulled a large hand-kerchief from his jacket pocket and mopped his brow. Then he wheezed, 'Well, Miss, no doubt I'll be seeing you out and about on your bicycle in due course. We're in desperate need of another nurse with Nancy Beecham retiring, and then the one we had lined up to come, she gave back word. So it's all down to you now.'

'Oh,' she said; she hadn't realised she'd been second choice but why would she? And of course, it didn't make any difference. The moment she'd seen the job advertisement in *The Liverpool Daily Post*, she'd known it was the opportunity she needed.

She was about to thank the butcher but he interrupted her. 'I hope you're soon settled, Nurse; I've only been to Liverpool once and it frightened the living daylights out of me. I was lost as soon as I got off the train and with all those folk milling around, it was terrible. So no doubt you'll feel like a fish outta water till you get used to village life. But just so you know, most of the folks round here are the kindest you'd ever wish to meet. Mind you, that doesn't mean to say I haven't had my share of run-ins with one and another of them – quibbling over the price of sausages, complaining about my butcher's boy riding too fast on his bike. But they're the salt of the earth, these folk, and if you look after them, they'll look after you.'

Still reeling from her interaction with Mrs Hewitt, Lara

found it difficult to relate to what he'd just described but she offered a tentative smile and said, 'I'll do my best, Mr Collins.'

He cleared his throat noisily and she thought he was going to say goodbye, but then he furrowed his brow and spoke again. 'I think you'll come up to scratch, but you'll have to work hard at it... I mean, our Nurse Beecham was like a ministering angel. I used to say she could deliver a baby with one hand and whip up a bread poultice with the other.'

Instantly, she felt a tickle of amusement at the image he'd conjured. She fought to contain it as he finally said his goodbyes because she didn't want him to hear her laugh and think she was ridiculing him. It's just that she'd never heard anyone, ever, give such a florid description of a district nurse. The issue hit home though because she already felt daunted by the reputation of her esteemed predecessor whose name had been mentioned many times during her telephone interview with Dr Bingham.

She knelt then beside her trunk to unpack her belongings and retrieve her district nurse's uniforms, her medical bag and the summer dresses she'd brought for her off-duty time. Hanging them neatly in the wardrobe, she stashed the rest of her essentials in the matching chest of drawers and dressing table. At the bottom of the trunk, she found the turquoise, silk gown she'd worn to the Adelphi: the one she'd borrowed from Fiona, who'd told her she could keep it. She'd brought it with her out of sheer stubbornness, and she was hoping to reclaim it somehow in this new setting. Right now though, it triggered thoughts of Patrick, so instantly, she shoved it to the back of the wardrobe. Then, as she reached to tidy the few items left in the trunk, she noticed the red leather case containing the emerald necklace. Wishing now she'd sent it straight back to him, she grabbed the box but then couldn't think of where to put it in her new room. Nowhere seemed appropriate so she threw it back into the empty trunk and shoved the whole thing under her bed. She'd return it to him, of course she would, but right now, she just wanted it gone from view. She still wondered why he'd ever gifted her such a precious necklace, and the only conclusion she'd been able to reach was that it was part of the image he'd wanted to create of himself as a successful solicitor, a man about town.

When a sharp knock sounded, she jumped up to open the door and found Mrs Hewitt there, her face pinched. 'I've just taken an emergency call and with all the staff otherwise engaged... you're the only one we've got.'

Humph, thought Lara, *I'll have to do then, won't I?*

'Who is the patient, what's the diagnosis?' she called, forcing herself to override her difficulty with the housekeeper. Already, she was walking to the wardrobe, grabbing her nurse's hat off the shelf and slipping her uniform from its hanger.

'The patient is Miss Celia Dunderdale, an elderly spinster living outside the village at Brook House. She's telephoned to report terrible pain in all her joints, and she's fallen over this morning more than once.'

'I see; it does sound urgent.'

'You'll have to take one of the bicycles, but Brook House isn't far out of the village... I'll tell you how to get there when you come down.'

Quickly, Lara changed into her uniform and pushed her brimmed nurse's hat firmly on her head. As soon as she'd descended the stairs, Mrs Hewitt handed her a glass of cool lemonade to drink while she told her where to find a bicycle in the shed behind the surgery, and described the location of Miss Dunderdale's house. Fortunately, she'd always had an excellent memory for directions – an essential when it came to working on the district. Unlike Fiona who often cycled many streets before she realised she was going the wrong way, she was very adept at finding a new address.

Pushing her leather medical bag in the wicker basket of the shiny, black bicycle with white mudguards, she noted immediately that apart from the dried buttercups caught in the back wheel, it was identical to the one she'd used in Liverpool. The front tyre was a bit soft, and the bicycle pump was missing, but given the urgency of the call, there was no time to report it. Wheeling it down the side of the surgery and onto the stone-flagged area in front, she noted in passing '*Dr H. J. Bingham*' inscribed in gold lettering on the window. She wondered when she would meet the senior doctor. In her head, she'd imagined handshakes and a warm, effusive greeting from a distinguished country gentleman wearing a smart tweed suit. But apart from the well-spoken, rather sharp voice she remembered from her telephone interview, she had no inkling of what to expect from her new boss.

Straddling the bicycle, she waited for a horse-drawn cart laden with milk churns to pass before she pushed off down the street. And as the skinny black horse plodded steadily by, it turned its head as if to say hello and the thin, sallow-cheeked driver tipped his cap. It felt instantly quaint and met all her expectations of what it would be like to work in a country practice. In the next breath, she wasn't quite so sure; the cobbled street was rougher than she'd expected, and she felt every jolt through the leather bicycle seat as she rattled her way down towards a humpbacked bridge. Moving at speed, she glimpsed some ancient-looking stone steps that led up to a spired church, then a butcher's shop with Sam Collins's van parked outside. There were quaint, stone cottages on either side and as a bright-red pillar box flashed by, she noted fleetingly a small shop and post office. Picking up more speed, she completely misjudged the sharp incline of the bridge and almost took off over it. Wrestling with the handlebars, she fought to control the bicycle and managed to right it, hoping none of the villagers had seen her careering out of control.

She was leaving Ingleside now and turning left into a narrow country lane bordered by dense hawthorn hedges. The road was uphill and no more than a rough track, and she needed all the power in her legs to pedal over such rugged terrain. But once the lane levelled out, she found herself amid open country with grazing cows and sheep in lush, green fields bordered by drystone walls.

Despite the urgency of the call, she felt thrilled by her proximity to plants and trees, and she delighted in the earthy smell of the land. In preparation for her relocation, she'd borrowed books from the library on wildflowers and already she'd spotted pink campions, purple foxgloves and frothy white cow parsley. It felt pleasing to identify the flowers; she'd imagined it would take ages before she could actively use her new knowledge.

The further she pedalled away from the village, the more pitted the roads became. She needed even more strength to keep the front wheel straight and, in her haste, she'd forgotten to bring a macintosh. Only an hour ago, the sky had been a perfect, duck-egg blue, but now black clouds had built and out of nowhere, big spits of cold rain had begun to fall. Hearing a rumble of thunder in the distance, she gritted her teeth and kept going. Even if she arrived looking like a drowned rat, she knew a vulnerable patient was waiting, so she had no choice but to push on to the emergency call.

In seconds, the rain was heavy and right away, she felt her nurse's hat sagging on her head and damp seeping through to her skin. Noting the particularly sharp bend ahead described by

Mrs Hewitt, she knew she was approaching her destination, and with rainwater stinging her eyes, she made out the whitewashed walls of a large Victorian dwelling and knew it had to be Brook House. Feeling the urgency of the call, she pushed hard against the pedals and with a skid through a puddle and a scrunch of gravel, she pulled up abruptly in front of the house.

This was it, her first call as a country nurse, and she was drenched to the bone.

3

As Lara hopped off the bicycle, she felt her black Lisle stockings saturated and chafing her heels, and her sodden, navy-blue uniform dress sticking to her body. Whipping a soggy handkerchief from her pocket, she attempted to dry the worst of the rain from her face, but damp tendrils of hair still plastered themselves to her skin. Quickly propping the bicycle against the wall of the house, she pulled her trusty leather medical bag from the front basket. As she knocked firmly on the front door and stood listening for any sign of life from within, she noted patches of flaking paint on the walls of the house and a tangle of nettles and weeds in the overgrown front garden. The house was completely silent. She knocked again, calling her patient's name – once, twice, and then when no reply came, sensing the worst and knowing that this was an emergency call, she pushed at the door and found it open.

'Hello,' she called firmly as she walked through a stone-flagged entrance. 'Miss Dunderdale... I've been sent from Ingleside surgery; I'm the new district nurse.'

Still nothing but the loud tick of a grandfather clock in the cluttered hallway.

Feeling deeply concerned now, she continued to call her patient's name, opening doors to rooms off the hallway as she proceeded. The first revealed a dusty, cluttered parlour, the next a dining room with a shrouded table and mismatched chairs. She felt a shiver run down her spine and knew it wasn't just from being soaked with rain. The house felt chilly as if there were no life to keep it warm.

She was sure she could hear a snuffling noise from the next door along, then came an unmistakeable groan.

Her heart surged. 'Miss Dunderdale?' she called as she pushed open a stiff, creaking door to reveal a dark kitchen. Instantly, she noted a small, Formica-topped table with the remains of a meal congealed on a china plate.

'Who are *you*?' a voice croaked from the other side of the room.

Her breath snagged when she spotted a grey-haired woman in a thick, plaid dressing gown lying on the floor at the far side of the room. The woman lifted her head, a deep frown etched between her dark, piercing eyes.

'I'm the new district nurse,' she replied, already assessing her patient's condition.

'From Ingleside surgery?' the woman enquired, leaning up on one elbow.

'Yes, I'm Nurse Fl—'

'I don't care what your name is, I don't want you; I need to see Nurse Wright or Dr Bingham... *You* won't be of any use to me.'

Miss Dunderdale was sitting up now, two spots of bright pink burning on her pale cheeks.

'I'm very sorry, Miss Dunderdale, but the rest of the staff are busy in clinic or out on visits and given you made an urgent call... I'm all you've got.'

'Well, I don't want you!'

The woman was struggling to get up from the floor now and as Lara moved to assist her, she shouted, 'No, get off me. You're all wet!'

'I got caught in the rain on the way here. Did you not hear the thunder?'

'Of course I heard the thunder; I'm not deaf,' she spat.

Steadying the woman now, Lara noted her rapid breathing and the pallor of her skin. This patient might be trying to turn her away, but she did look poorly, which meant she had an urgent duty to perform a thorough check.

As she pulled a chair out from the table and assisted Miss Dunderdale to sit, she was still assessing her condition – the woman was pale, breathless and appeared agitated. For all she knew, the latter might be the woman's resting state but without any prior knowledge of the patient, she couldn't risk dismissing a disturbance of mood that might be an indication of poor circulation of blood to the brain. On this her first day, she couldn't leave anything to chance.

'Is it all right if I ask you a few questions, Miss Dunderdale? Then I need to check your pulse, breathing and temperature.' She spoke politely, using her most soothing tone of voice.

'No questions, no checks!' The woman scowled. 'And when you get back to the surgery, tell Dr Bingham I need to see him as soon as possible.'

She was surprised by the aggressive edge to her patient's voice, but she stayed calm and maintained her own gentle tone. 'Given you've just sustained a fall, it's important that I check you over.'

The woman pulled her dressing gown more firmly around

her thin body. 'I will scream if you try to touch me. Under no circumstances are you allowed to come near me. I don't know you from Adam.'

'All right, all right,' Lara soothed, knowing there was no way she was going to get anywhere near this patient. 'Can I at least make you a cup of tea before I leave?'

Miss Dunderdale glanced towards the steaming kettle sitting snugly on the stove tucked against the wall. 'Not right now,' she replied, her tone mellowing a little. 'And if you don't mind, Nurse Whatever-your-name-is... I'm in absolute agony and I want to be left alone.'

'Did you hurt yourself from the fall?'

'Like I said... I don't know you, I don't trust you, and I will only be seen by Dr Bingham.'

Lara held up her hands in mock surrender. 'That's fine. I can't force you to be examined. But could you not just let me quickly have a feel of your pulse?'

'No, most definitely not. Dr Bingham always does that for me *and* he takes my blood pressure.'

She felt very uncomfortable at leaving her patient without performing any observations, but she couldn't force an examination on the woman. So there was no choice but to comply. And given Miss Dunderdale didn't seem to be on the point of collapse and there was no blue tinge to her lips or fingertips, she felt reasonably confident that the assessment could be left to Dr Bingham.

As she gathered her medical bag, she became acutely aware once more of the wet uniform sticking to her skin. The whole event seemed like a shaky start to her new job, but hey, things could only get better.

'Maybe I'll see you again another time,' she offered politely as she made towards the door. 'And I will of course pass your request on to Dr Bingham.'

The elderly woman huffed, pulled the dressing gown even more tightly around herself and turned to face away as Lara withdrew from the room.

As she closed the heavy front door firmly shut behind her, Lara began to feel flustered by the oddness of the consultation. She recognised it was partly due to it having been an emergency call, but it also troubled her that the patient had refused intervention and despite her overt hostility, Lara had noted that there was something very vulnerable about Miss Dunderdale.

Wheeling her bicycle away, she let residual thoughts from the visit run through her head. Then came a renewed awareness of her sodden uniform clinging to her legs and the brimmed hat that sat like a drooping lettuce on her head. The ridiculousness of her situation tipped the balance of her anxiety then and made her smile at the story she would tell when she wrote her first letter to Fiona in Liverpool. They'd laughingly spoken about what she might be facing as a country nurse and her friend had said, 'Well at least you won't be drenched to the bone and cycling through strong winds like we have in Liverpool, even in the summer...' Except of course, on Lara's first day, Fiona's prediction had been proven wrong... It seemed that rural Lancashire, especially here near the Bowland Fells, might be just as wet.

Beyond the weather though, this did feel completely different and as she wheeled her bicycle and breathed the clean air that followed the shower of rain, she revelled in the stillness broken only by the tweeting of birds, the distant bleating of sheep and the gentle rumble of her bicycle tyres on the road. Maybe her reception at the surgery could have been warmer, but being here now with no other visits to perform for the rest of the day, this already felt like the escape she'd been hoping for, and despite being soaked through to the skin, she'd done it: she'd physically left behind all that had happened in the city. Hopefully now the flash-backs of her accident would recede, she would begin to feel less frantic, and she would be able to go back to Liverpool in a year or two's time feeling stronger. Then again, maybe if this post worked out for her, she would stay much longer... become another Nurse Beecham retiring after a full career as a district nurse and midwife. She imagined the satisfaction of dedicating herself to her work and living an independent life. And then, after delivering most of the babies in the local area, caring for the sick and the elderly, dealing with accidents and emergencies as they arose, she would be able to retire with the respect of the whole community.

Her daydreaming gave her a boost and despite her travel fatigue and sopping-wet uniform, her body hummed with contentment. Steering the bicycle around puddles of rainwater, she breathed the smell of the damp earth, the grass, and the hedges. And she revelled in the colour and the delicacy of the wildflowers cleared of their dust by the rain. Everything appeared vibrant, brighter than anything she'd ever seen in Liverpool. And what was that running through the hedge? The pale-yellow flowers were small, but it looked like wild honey-suckle. She reached up to run a finger over the delicate petals, then leant in to breathe the sweet scent. To be so close to nature felt divine.

Approaching a single-storey, whitewashed farm building she'd noted from her bicycle as she'd passed by earlier, her skin prickled at a deep, almost other-worldly moaning noise that could only be from some large animal in pain. Then the poor creature bellowed so loudly, she felt a painful bubble of anxiety in her throat. Ill-prepared as she was for dealing with livestock, she knew she had no choice but to investigate because it didn't feel right to walk by and ignore any creature in distress. She moved purposefully towards the building. The awful sound was still emanating but she could hear a man's voice now too. It sounded as if he were out of breath, exerting himself in some way.

With no idea what she might find, she propped her bicycle against the whitewashed wall and stepped through a low doorway. A pungent smell of manure mixed with blood and salt met her. Unable to see properly in the darkened interior, she could only make out the bulky shape of a large animal on the ground, a man beside it, soothing, then uttering encouragement.

'Hello?' she offered tentatively, 'Do you need any help?'

The man turned round instantly, a deep furrow between his brows. 'Have you seen a vet heading this way?'

'No, sorry,' she replied.

The man muttered and grumbled for a few seconds. 'I can't keep on waiting; I'm going to lose both of them; the cow and her calf.' He glanced back at Lara, looked her up and down. 'You must be that new nurse who's started at the surgery?'

She was amazed that he knew, given she'd only arrived a few hours ago, but she had no time to reply because he was speaking again. 'You should know what you're doing with this; it can't be much different than delivering a baby... The calf is wedged in the birth canal, and I need you to help me pull it out. We need to get it moving before we run out of time. I've tied a rope round its front legs, but I need somebody to give some leverage while I shift the position of its head. My missus usually helps but she's away in Ridgetown today doing some shopping.'

The brown cow was moaning again, a deep, guttural, heart-breaking sound. Lara had only ever seen cows from afar, so it felt daunting to be so close to a huge creature groaning and kicking out in pain. And the stench of manure alone was almost enough to make her gag. She sucked in a breath, steeled herself. Something clicked inside of her then and she knew she had no choice but to do what she could for the poor creature.

'Stick your hands in that bucket over there and wash with soap and water first,' the farmer ordered.

She did as she was told.

'Now, when I say pull, you heave on that rope as hard as you can.'

She could see a length of rope protruding from the cow's back end and the farmer already had his arm pushed right in there, his face bright red with exertion as he manhandled something deep inside the cow's body. The poor creature moaned in agony once more and Lara grabbed the rope.

'Pull!' he yelled.

She heaved on the rope till it dug painfully into the palms of her hands. Still, there was no movement. The cow was shifting on the straw, kicking out a back leg, bellowing with pain.

She gritted her teeth, held fast.

'Pull,' the farmer grunted, sweat pouring from his grimacing face.

She heaved on the rope again and this time, there was a slight shift.

'That's it, we've got it coming now!' he called, withdrawing his arm and helping her pull on the rope.

In seconds, she saw two small, shiny hooves emerging, followed by brown, furry legs and then the pink nose of a calf. With one more huge heave, the newborn's shoulders came and then the whole calf covered in mucus and membranes slid out onto the shippon floor. She almost cheered until she saw the creature was lying limp, not breathing. Instantly, her midwifery training kicked in; she grabbed a handful of straw and started to clear the calf's snout and then frantically, she rubbed its body. Still no breath. The farmer had a ragged cloth now, wiping out the animal's nose and mouth.

'Get more straw, tickle its nose,' he ordered.

She instantly did as she was instructed, using the stalks to stimulate each nostril in turn. With her heart pounding against her ribs, she knew they were running out of time for this little one. Suddenly, she felt a movement of air on her hand and then the calf sneezed, shooting sticky mucus over her uniform.

She was laughing now, wanting to cheer.

'Aye, that's it,' the farmer cried gleefully.

She was still laughing, completely caught up in the moment.

A voice broke through sharply. 'Looks like you don't need me after all, Tom?'

She twisted round to see a man silhouetted in the doorway. As he moved towards her, she noted his athletic build and assured gait that gave him an air of decisiveness. An assessment that was instantly undercut when she noted his unruly, black hair. He offered a lopsided grin. 'I'd heard there was a city girl in our midst; never thought for one moment that she'd be any use… but it looks like you've already got her trained up.'

He was probably a similar age to her, so maybe he thought it was all right to make a joke on a first meeting. But she was beginning to feel her travel exhaustion even more strongly now, and she felt annoyed by his teasing tone and the casual assumptions he'd made based on where she'd been born. It made her hackles rise and she shot back at him, 'I was happy to help, given there didn't seem to be a vet in attendance.'

'Sounds like you've met your match, Leo.' The farmer laughed.

'I dare say,' the vet replied, with a flash of his dark eyes.

He wasn't necessarily meaning to come across as adversarial, but she felt her skin prickle. Back in the city, she'd have taken any kind of comment – jokey or otherwise – on the chin. But right now, she didn't have anything beyond the warm smile and the gentle voice of the farmer to tether her to what currently felt like a very alien environment. She fought to quell her irritation but nevertheless, it rose through her. Thankfully, the young vet had now switched his attention to the mother cow, who was gamely trying to stand. He was at the back end with the farmer to make sure she was steady on her feet. Lara waited to see the calf stagger up, wobbly on its new legs, and as soon as she saw the cow twist her head to sniff then lick her newborn, she felt as if her work here was done.

The farmer grinned in her direction as he wiped sweat from his brow then lifted his cap and set it further back on his pale wisps of hair. 'I'm grateful to you, Nurse, for helping me out. Not many would have stepped in like that, fresh from the train.'

'Don't you go giving her too much praise, Tom,' the vet added with a mischievous glint in his eye. 'We don't want to risk giving her ideas above her station.'

That was it; she knew she was way too tired to engage in any banter with the young man. 'I'd better be getting back to the surgery,' she said, addressing the farmer only. 'No doubt I'll be seeing you around.'

'You will indeed... Tom Douglas is the name, and you can stop by the farm any time for a brew of tea and a piece of cake. Just follow the track by the side of the shippon and you'll see the farmhouse up ahead. This cow is the wife's favourite, so she'll be delighted to know you had a hand in saving her.'

She felt a flush of pleasure. 'Thank you, Mr Douglas.'

Then, casting a glance towards the newly delivered cow and her baby calf, then fleetingly in the direction of the young vet who still had an amused glint in his eye, she said her goodbyes.

As she walked towards the shippon door, her foot slipped in fresh cow dung but there was no way she was going to break her stride. She kept going and as she felt the vet's eyes on her, she knew he was smiling. Grabbing her bicycle, she wheeled it away as quickly as she could, only stopping to wipe the green, sticky manure from her shoe when she'd turned the next corner and knew she'd be out of view.

The hedges still dripped with rainwater, but the sun was shining now, creating tiny rainbows of light around the wet leaves. As she wheeled her bicycle back through a bright and glistening world, a speckled bird on the branch of a tree began to sing its heart out – she didn't know for sure which wild bird it was, but she thought it might be a thrush. Whatever its name, its song was beautiful and it filled her with joy. Damp and bedraggled with her sodden district nurse's hat in the bicycle basket, cow dung on her shoe and mud and newborn calf mucus spattered over her uniform, she made her way back to the surgery. And by the time she reached Ingleside, her black wool stockings had begun to chafe at her heels, and she felt exhausted.

As she made her way up the village street, she felt many eyes upon her, but she just kept going. At the tinkle of a shop's bell, she glanced to see two women exiting the post office, one giving the other a nudge with her elbow and nodding in her direction. She offered a weak smile, and they smiled back but she could see their heads together as they walked away.

It was good to be back at the surgery and she felt relieved to return the bicycle to the shed at the rear. And as she nipped in through the back door, she hoped desperately to gain access to the stairs and her room so she could wash and change without being seen.

'Oh, you're back, are you?' Mrs Hewitt's voice called down

the hallway and with a few brisk strides, she was there. 'What
the heck have you been doing, Nurse Flynn?'

She could see the glint of amusement in the housekeeper's
eyes, and instantly, she felt dismayed to have been caught in
such a state of disarray. Looking her up and down, Mrs Hewitt
clapped a hand across her mouth, desperately trying to stop
herself from laughing. For some reason – maybe the fatigue,
maybe all that she'd been required to do – Lara felt tears prick
her eyes. She took a sharp breath to hold them back and made
to walk by.

'Nay, lass... don't take on,' Mrs Hewitt said, her voice unexpectedly gentle, reaching out a hand.

She was taken aback, wondering if this was genuine concern.
But when she saw the warmth in the housekeeper's eyes, she
knew that it was.

'Come on, come with me,' Mrs Hewitt urged, 'I'll get you
another glass of home-made lemonade and while you're
drinking it, I'll go up and run a nice hot bath for you, and then
you can get changed into some clean clothes.'

'Thank you,' Lara said, her voice sounding small.

'That's no bother... We look after our own here. And what
you did, going out there alone on your very first day... you've
already shown you're one of the team.'

Lara offered a wobbly smile and as she began to follow Mrs
Hewitt towards the kitchen, she heard a loud click as the back
door opened, followed by a brisk, leather-heeled step on the
tiled floor.

'Dr Bingham,' Mrs Hewitt called over her shoulder, 'come
and meet our new district nurse; she's done a very good job this
aft—'

The doctor stopped abruptly in front of her, a battered,
leather briefcase held firmly in his hand. He was taller than

she'd expected, his face angular beneath a checked trilby from which grey-brown hair poked untidily. Instantly, she knew he was nothing like the image of the esteemed country doctor she'd had in her head. This man appeared distracted, slightly dishevelled, and seemed to be scrutinising the mud which she'd left on the pristine, tiled floor. When he looked up, his gaze was direct, his eyes were piercing, and she felt her breath catch as she stood in a dishevelled state with her wet uniform clinging to her body. He opened his mouth for a second as if he were about to speak, then rudely, he turned on his heel and strode away, muttering.

She blinked hard to banish tears that threatened, glad now of the housekeeper's presence as she caught her dissatisfied tut at the doctor's lack of manners.

'He can get a bit worked up over muck and mess but he's a good sort, really... He'll likely be more talkative when we have our evening meal later,' Mrs Hewitt offered before murmuring something else Lara couldn't quite catch as the housekeeper grasped her arm and guided her towards the kitchen.

She was determined not to lose face; she knew she'd risen to the challenge of everything she'd been required to do today. And if Dr Bingham was disapproving of a bit of mud on the floor created in the line of duty, or if he had deliberately set out to intimidate her, he would soon learn that he would have a fight on his hands.

4

Later, as Lara sat at the scrubbed wooden table in the large stone-flagged kitchen, she felt the oppressiveness of silence. Dr Bingham was straight-backed at the head with Mrs Hewitt to his left and Angus Fitzwilliam, the tousle-haired young doctor whom Lara had been rapidly introduced to, to his right. All she could hear was the clink of knives and forks on porcelain plates and she felt so tense, she was struggling to chew and swallow each mouthful of the nicely prepared evening meal of beef stew and potatoes. Every so often, she glanced up to see Dr Bingham with his eyes determinedly down, and Dr Fitzwilliam seemingly distracted and glancing around the kitchen as he rapidly consumed his food. She kept a steady demeanour but there was a rolling, sick feeling in her stomach. It would have been lovely to break the silence, but she was brand new here at this table and it felt inappropriate to even try after the frosty reception she'd received from Dr Bingham earlier.

Mrs Hewitt cleared her throat and glanced across at the young doctor. It felt as if she were about to ask him a question but then thought better of it. Dr Fitzwilliam appeared oblivious, and he had an air of determination as he shovelled food into his mouth without spilling a morsel on his expensive-looking shirt and red striped tie. By this stage, even though it didn't feel like her place to do so, she was seriously considering asking a question just to break what felt like an icy silence. But as she framed the words in her head, the kitchen door flew open and a breathless, rosy-cheeked young woman in a navy gaberdine mac and a district nurse's hat bounded in.

'There you are, Nurse Wright,' cried Mrs Hewitt, jumping up from her seat and walking straight to the Aga to serve another plate of stew.

'I'm so sorry I'm late, yet again,' the nurse gasped, whipping off her hat to reveal an untidy mass of black curls. Fighting to get her arms out of the mac, she almost tripped over the brown and orange striped tabby cat who had been sleeping in front of the Aga but now jumped up with a yowl and ran. 'Oops, sorry, Tiddles,' she cried, scraping her chair on the stone-flagged floor before throwing herself down opposite Lara.

Still breathless, she beamed across the table. 'You must be Nurse Flynn, my new partner. So no standing on ceremony: you can call me Marion.'

'Pleased to meet you, Marion,' Lara replied, as the excited young woman thrust her arm across the table to shake hands, dipping her sleeve in gravy along the way.

Lara felt entranced by this breath of fresh air who had sailed into the room and immediately broken the silence. Even Dr Bingham had the trace of a smile on his face and clearly, he was pleased to have Nurse Wright at the table.

In between bites of stew and potato, Marion offered a commentary on her visits: 'I was up at Fell Farm last thing to see young Lucy Taylor – it's taken such a long time to heal that leg wound but finally, she's improving.'

'I'm delighted to hear it,' Dr Bingham offered, leaning forward in his chair, his eyes alive with interest. 'Are you still using the iodine dressings? And did you check her temperature?'

'Yes, and yes. No fever... I think we might be almost home and dry. But she still needs daily visits until the wound is healed completely.'

Lara's interest was sparked. 'What happened to the girl? Did she have an accident?'

Without pausing for breath, Marion answered, 'She had an altercation with a vicious boar, took a strip of skin off her lower leg. It seemed all right at first but then after four days, she developed a fever with yellow pus oozing from the wound.'

Mrs Hewitt cleared her throat. 'Not at the table please, Marion.'

'Sorry, Mrs H.' Then speaking to Lara under her breath, 'I always get a bit carried away with the gory detail.'

Dr Bingham spoke again. 'If we hadn't got on and treated her aggressively, she could have developed sepsis. The boar was covered in manure, full of bacteria.'

'What is a boar?' Lara asked tentatively.

The whole table turned to stare at her, then they each began to chuckle.

'A boar is an uncastrated male swine,' Dr Bingham announced abruptly.

'Oh,' was all Lara could manage in response.

'Don't worry, Nurse Flynn, you'll soon get used to the country lingo,' Mrs Hewitt offered.

'Ha! Maybe the lingo, but it'll take longer to get used to the patients.' Young Dr Fitzwilliam laughed. 'I came down here two years ago, after studying at the University of St Andrews medical school which was in driving distance of my grandfather's estate.

I thought it would all be fine because I was used to the Scottish locals and established farming families. But it felt like these Ingleside villagers and the outlying community were a different breed. In fact, I've only just started to break the ice with the more hardened of the local populace.'

'That's because you, Angus, are a posh boy,' Marion teased. 'Lara might be well-spoken but she's probably not posh. And more importantly, she's a lovely district nurse and not a "wet behind the ears" junior doctor.'

Dr Fitzwilliam snorted with laughter, then carried on eating.

Marion leant forward in her chair as if she were going to reach out across the table again. 'It might take a good six months but with your lovely face and beautiful smile, you'll soon win them round. I had a head start; I was born and raised around here. So they knew where I was from and who I was, from the get-go.'

Lara understood; it was the same in Liverpool. But what surprised her was her colleague's voice had only the slightest hint of a northern accent. 'You don't sound like you're from Lancashire.'

'That's because I trained in Edinburgh and then I moved even further north to work in the Highlands and Islands... That's where I learnt to ride a motorcycle.'

'A motorcycle?'

Lara was impressed.

'I've tried teaching Angus to ride it but he's hopeless... keeps skidding off, so he always takes the Austin on his calls. But I think you might be a good pupil. So as soon as you're ready, we'll give it a go.'

Instantly, she felt a stab of anxiety. She hadn't even contemplated this other level of challenge.

'Give it a few weeks,' Mrs Hewitt offered, a crease of concern between her brows. 'Let Nurse Flynn get settled in first, hey.'

'Yes, of course.' Marion beamed. 'And she'll be doing the more local visits at first so a bicycle will be ideal.'

'Oh, she's already tried out the bicycle. Haven't you, Lara?' the housekeeper chuckled.

'Not today in that pouring rain?' Marion's eyes were round with horror. 'Not on your first day?'

Lara nodded. 'Nothing like being in at the deep end... I went out to see Miss Dunderdale. She was not happy.'

'Oh no, that's not a good one to start with... It took me a full year to even be allowed in through her door. She insisted on being seen by your predecessor, Nurse Beecham, or Dr Bingham only.'

Lara was nodding, 'Yes, she told me that very firmly once I found her in the kitchen. But she didn't answer the door and she'd made an urgent call for help so I just went in.'

Marion shot a hand across her mouth. 'How did that go?'

'Not well. She sent me packing.'

A murmur of solidarity rippled around the table.

'She's down for a visit by Dr Bingham tomorrow, after morning surgery,' Mrs Hewitt said, gazing to the head of the table. 'You'll work your magic, won't you, Doctor?'

For a second, Lara thought the doctor wasn't going to reply but then he shrugged his shoulders and offered a tight smile. 'She just needs to know that someone is there for her, that's all. It's a sad state of affairs, really, the way she lives.'

'Doesn't she have any family?' Lara enquired.

'None that will talk to her,' Marion added, placing her knife and fork down with a clatter as she finished the last of the beef stew. 'She's cut herself off completely and told her relatives they won't be getting a penny of inheritance.'

'That's sad,' Lara murmured, imagining some family tragedy or an ongoing resentment. She knew what it was like to be estranged – after her father had died from pneumonia one freezing cold winter when she was a baby, her mother had stayed in Liverpool barely six months before she'd handed her over to her older sister and eloped to New York with an American ship's captain. Nothing more had ever been heard from her, but Lara had been lucky in that her spinster aunt had been a quiet, meticulous woman who had devoted herself to her care. Aunt Matilda hadn't been affectionate in a physical or demonstrative way, but she'd made sure to place her at a decent girls' boarding school and she'd provided a lump sum of money in her will. She'd died during Lara's first year of nurse training at the Liverpool Royal Infirmary, and the small inheritance from her aunt had given her security during those early years at the hospital when she'd been hard-pressed by the intensity of the work. It had felt like a security blanket, just in case nursing didn't work out for her. The training had been extremely tough, especially on wards with the most brutal of sisters or in theatre where the juniors had been required to carry amputated limbs to the furnace. But she'd had the mettle to withstand all of that and importantly, given she was an only child abandoned by her mother, she'd found like-minded nurses who had become very close friends whom she'd laughed and cried with so openly that they were now like family.

Glancing up from her reverie, she saw Marion shrug. 'Well, I suppose it is a bit sad for Miss Dunderdale, but my way of thinking is that you make the bed you lie on. If she'd been nicer to her family, then maybe they would be there to support her now.'

'Hear, hear,' cried Angus.

Dr Bingham didn't make any further comment, but he pressed his lips together and looked thoughtful.

Mrs Hewitt heaved a sigh. 'It's hard, isn't it? But I think it's important for us not to judge. Miss Dunderdale is entitled to her own counsel, and many people have things they'd rather keep hidden. Just because she's lived here forever doesn't mean she should share what happened in her early life.'

'You make a good point, Mrs Hewitt,' Dr Bingham said, but Angus and Marion remained silent.

'Right then.' Mrs Hewitt sighed, pushing back her chair and rising from the table. 'Would anyone like some rice pudding?'

'Yes please,' they all called, and Lara raised her hand. 'Yes, me too, please.'

Once she'd taken her first mouthful of the pudding, she knew she had never tasted anything so good in her whole life – it was thick and creamy with a nutmeggy skin and delicious crustiness around the edges. The dollops of pale sludge that had been served at the nurses' home in Liverpool didn't even deserve the name of pudding after this. She scraped every speck from the sides of her dish and when she looked up, the rest of the table, apart from Dr Bingham, were smiling in her direction.

'Goodness, Nurse Flynn,' offered Mrs Hewitt. 'It looks like you might have been on workhouse rations in Liverpool.'

She felt her cheeks flush. 'Oh no, it's just that I've never tasted anything so delicious.'

Mrs Hewitt gave a satisfied chuckle as Dr Bingham rose from the table, slowly shaking his head. 'If nothing else, thanks to Mrs Hewitt, we probably have the finest rice pudding in the world, right here in Ingleside... I'll see you all in the morning, team,' he offered with what seemed like a conciliatory nod in her direction.

The air felt clearer once he'd departed and as Mrs Hewitt

poured a small glass of sherry for each of them, Lara began to feel more relaxed.

Angus knocked his back in one then jumped up from the table. Using the flat of his hand to tidy his fluffy, dark-blond hair, he muttered, 'I'm off to The Dorchester for a pint of ale. Does anyone want to join me?'

Marion was already shaking her head and murmuring, 'Not tonight, sunshine. I'm way too tired.'

But Lara was instantly puzzled by the name of the pub. 'The Dorchester?' She frowned.

Marion laughed. 'It's the local nickname for The Fleece, the pub at the top of the hill. Nobody really knows why but it's often called The Dorchester… Maybe because, just like The Old Oak further down, it's so far removed from the London Dorchester that somebody gave it a playful nickname that stuck. But it's a friendly place, good for a sing-song or a game of darts. That's if you can stand to be crammed in with lots of men.'

Lara knew instantly it was too early to experience The Dorchester with Angus, so she shook her head. 'No thank you. Maybe another time.'

'Are you sure?' he asked, already walking to the door, impatient to be off.

'We nurses need to chat,' Marion said with a smile. 'And we need to let Lara find her feet before she's exposed to the regulars in that place.'

Angus guffawed. 'Right you are… And you'll all probably be tucked up in bed when I get back. So I'll see you in the morning bright and early, ready to tend our patients and continue our good work in the community.'

'Go on with you.' Mrs Hewitt laughed. 'And if you're up first thing, it'll be the first time ever.'

Once the table had been cleared, the women sat with

another small glass of sherry. It was impossible to resist Marion's boisterous personality and lively chatter so already, she felt surprisingly at ease.

'So, how did you come to be called Lara?' Marion asked as she leant across the table. 'It's an unusual name; I don't think I've ever heard it before.'

'I'm not completely sure, but I was told that on my mother's side of the family going way back, there was a great-grand-mother called Lara whose family had been Russian immigrants into Liverpool.'

'That sounds so romantic,' Marion breathed. Then narrowing her eyes, she leant across the table to scrutinise her face. 'Yes, I can see it now. With your white-blonde hair and blue eyes, I can picture that Russian side of your family.'

'I've never heard it before, but Lara is such a beautiful name,' Mrs Hewitt sighed.

'Thank you.' Lara smiled. 'But I wish I had a gold coin for every time someone called me Laura.'

'Oh God,' Marion said, 'I get the same... people call me Miriam, Marilyn, Marianne...'

Mrs Hewitt chuckled. 'You'd think Edith would be straight-forward, especially since I've lived in this village most of my life. But I'm always getting Enid.'

Marion laughed then and raised her glass. 'Well, ladies... here's to us... Laura, Marilyn and Enid.'

'To us,' they cried, clinking their glasses.

They continued to chatter about this and that for another half hour or so until Marion began to yawn dramatically. 'That's me gone; it must be something you put in the sherry, Mrs H.'

Lara followed Marion's lead and got up from the table, and they turned together to say goodnight to the housekeeper.

'Goodnight, lasses. And in the morning, Dr Bingham has

requested that you go out together, just for the first day. He should have told you himself; he must have forgotten. But that's the plan.'

'All right,' Marion called sleepily.

But Lara felt her breath catch as something dawned on her. 'So will we be travelling together on bicycles? Or in a car?'

Marion linked her arm, pulled her close. 'Oh no, we won't need any car. I can put you on the back of my motorcycle. No problem.'

Lara's heart lurched. The country lanes were deserted compared to the Liverpool streets, but those narrow lanes and drystone walls felt daunting. And to be on the back of a motorcycle, putting all her trust in a woman she'd only just met... The scar on her forehead instantly prickled just at the thought of it.

Marion leant in. 'Don't you be worrying. When I worked in the Highlands, I once rode halfway up a mountain with a pillion passenger. It'll be fine.'

Lara swallowed hard and tried to smile. It felt as if her second day was going to bring a whole new set of challenges. She knew she was brave, and she was a very determined person, but after her accident in Liverpool, the thought of moving at speed along the narrow country lanes, with a lively fellow nurse she barely knew in charge, filled her with horror.

5
_____

Lara slept fitfully after being woken by the church bell ringing the hour, every hour, all night long. Then hearing the lively banter and tramp of clogs on the cobbled street as local folk headed to work, she felt shocked by how misguided her expectation of peaceful village life had been. But having successfully adjusted to sleeping in a dormitory at boarding school and surviving the early-morning clatter and chatter of the nurses' home, she knew she'd get used to it. And in between the noise, a special silence fell outside the walls of the solid stone-built doctor's surgery, and it instantly calmed her.

Once she was washed and dressed, she descended the stairs, expecting to hear the rest of the house stirring. But all was silent except for the clatter of pots and pans and a tut of frustration from Mrs Hewitt in the kitchen.

'Good morning,' she called brightly as she entered.

The housekeeper turned with both eyebrows raised. 'You're an early bird.'

'I suppose so. But this is my usual getting-up time.'

'Mmm, it feels like Liverpool Royal Infirmary time and

Ingleside Village Surgery time might be somewhat different. But it's good to have company in the kitchen. Sit yourself down; I'll be with you in a minute once I've got the stove fuelled.'

After a bowl of porridge with a sprinkling of sugar and lashings of cream, Lara was still alone at the table. And as Mrs Hewitt whipped up a batch of scones, she called over her shoulder to fill Lara in on the morning routine of the other members of the household. Dr Bingham always took a full English breakfast with freshly brewed coffee in his room at seven thirty sharp, while Angus and Marion ran in late to grab a cup of coffee and a slice of toast and jam.

There was no sign yet of the late breakfasters so with her stomach in a knot over the motorcycle issue, Lara made her excuses then went back up to her room to rearrange her belongings in a desperate attempt to distract herself from what lay ahead. Before her accident, she would have relished the adventure, but her confidence had been wrecked by that one lapse. Even at the thought of riding on the back of Marion's motorcycle, she felt that familiar throb of her scar. And when a forceful knock sounded on her door, she almost jumped out of her skin. She knew it had to be Marion; who else would hammer so frantically?

Her colleague stood beaming as she chewed a piece of toast and strawberry jam. 'All set?' she asked cheerily.

'Yes,' she replied, forcing a smile as she swept up her district nurse's hat and followed her colleague down the carpeted stairs, then out through the back door to the cobbled yard.

Marion turned abruptly as soon as they were outside. 'I think you're going to be an excellent pillion rider – you're tall but not too tall, strong but not fat.'

Lara gulped back the fear that twisted in her chest and said, 'Oh, that's good, thank you.'

Marion was leaning in so closely now to peer at her face that she could see a tiny toast crumb stuck to the corner of her mouth. 'And you have the bluest eyes I have ever seen in my whole life.'

Taken aback by the very close proximity of her ebullient colleague, it took her a moment to respond.

'I inherited the blue eyes from my mother... or so I've been told,' she stuttered.

'Oh, did you not know her then? Has she passed away?'

Despite Marion's obvious good humour, she didn't feel like confiding that her mother had abandoned her as a baby and now lived in America, so she offered, 'Something like that,' then said, 'Where's the motorcycle?'

'This way.' Marion grinned.

With a studied semblance of calm, she followed Marion to a lean-to shed. Spotting a battered blue Austin with muddy wheels parked skew-whiff on the cobbled area at the side of the surgery, she knew it had to have been left by – and now stood waiting for –Angus. She couldn't help but feel a little envious – with some of the inheritance money from her Aunt Matilda, she'd paid for driving lessons in Liverpool and she'd become a competent driver, but she'd been too busy with work to take it any further. The little Austin would be just right for her because from what Mrs Hewitt had said about the shiny black Rover Sports Saloon that was Dr Bingham's prized possession, she never wanted to go anywhere near anything like that.

'Wait here. I'll bring the motorbike out,' Marion ordered. And as she strode away, Lara noted the navy-blue trousers and sturdy black boots she was wearing. Glancing down to her own uniform dress and the black Lisle stockings and flat leather shoes she always wore for work, she wondered how on earth she was going to straddle a motorcycle in a way that might preserve her dignity.

After much bumping and banging, followed by a single curse from inside the wooden shed, Marion emerged wheeling a Norton motorcycle with a worn leather seat. 'This is Gloria,' she announced, beaming a smile, 'and I call her that because she is absolutely glorious.'

Lara gulped in air. She could see there was barely space for two people on the elongated leather seat and just a metal strut on either side, presumably where she needed to place her feet.

Sensing her disquiet, her colleague offered, 'It might look a bit daunting, but you can sit side-saddle if you want.'

She rapidly assessed the option and knew she would feel extremely insecure and off balance.

She cleared her throat, tried to make her voice sound confident. 'No, that's all right, I'll have a go at sitting astride.'

Marion stowed her medical bag and her folded gaberdine mac on the rack above the rear mudguard, then slipped her leg expertly over the motorcycle. Once she had both feet planted squarely at each side, she invited Lara to 'hop on'.

Her heart lurched, she snatched a breath as she attempted to mount, but there was absolutely no way she could get her leg over because her uniform skirt prevented it.

'Hoik up your skirt!' Marion called over her shoulder.

She had no choice but to pull up her clothing and expose her thick, black regulation stockings to above the knee. Clumsily, she slipped onto the leather seat, but this felt nothing like the bicycle she'd ridden yesterday and all those years in Liverpool. Preserving her dignity on a lady's bicycle had been no problem but right now, her skirt felt indecently hoisted way too high. She pulled her dress down as far as she could on either side and once she'd found the supports for her feet, it felt a little better, but she was still far from comfortable.

'We're heading out first to visit little Lucy Taylor at Fell Farm,' Marion called back to her as she kick-started the motorcycle and vigorously revved the engine. The noise was high-pitched, almost ear-splitting.

Lara grabbed Marion around the waist, grateful for her strong frame. And as they lurched away over the cobbles, she clung on for dear life. Once they were out on the road and picking up speed, she gritted her teeth and clamped a hand over her hat to prevent it from blowing off. Desperately clinging to Marion with just one arm now, she saw the stone steps to the village church flash by and uttered a silent prayer. This felt wildly out of control but with Marion oblivious in front, there was no way of communicating with her. Her colleague shouted something back to her but there was no chance of deciphering it because it was drowned out by the noise of the engine and the wild crunch of tyres on grit.

As they left the village and headed out to the country roads, her heart was hammering so hard in her chest, she was sure Marion would be able to feel it. This was lightning speed compared to a bicycle and the rough, country lanes were unforgiving as they threw the motorbike from side to side. As the hedges and drystone walls whizzed by, she sat rigid, too shocked to do anything but hold fast and pray.

If they did crash and die, bizarrely, she wondered if Patrick would find out. She'd been told by Fiona that he'd tried to visit her at the Liverpool Royal when she'd been lying unconscious, but his sole purpose had been to fish for information about the whereabouts of the emerald necklace. Of course her friend hadn't said a word, and she'd marched him straight out. But when Lara had been told that he'd turned up like that, it had made her want to hold onto the necklace a while longer. Fiona would return it to him if she did die, and in fact with her only living family being the mother whom she'd never known, it would be her nurse friends at the hospital alone who would mourn her passing.

Distracted by her thoughts and memories as the hedges and flowers and drystone walls whisked by, she suddenly realised she was already getting used to being on the back of the motorcycle. She still clung tightly hold of Marion and her heart continued to pound, but she was now far less terrified than she'd expected. Instinctively, she sensed Marion's strength and her confidence, and this felt like an opportunity to take back something she'd lost that day of her accident.

The motorcycle was slowing now as it struggled uphill through an increasingly remote and windswept landscape. Long lengths of drystone wall slid by on either side, the trees were stunted and bent to the shape of the prevailing wind, and she noted heather and yellow gorse at the edge of the road. And when at last Marion began to slow even more, she called back, 'Hold tight, we're about to go over a cattle grid and the farm road is very bumpy.'

In moments, they were rattling over metal, then bouncing over bumps and hitting potholes as they wove their way along a rough track. If Lara had been a less determined person, she'd have asked Marion to stop and let her dismount so that she could make the rest of the way on foot. But she wasn't about to lose face now, not after what she'd been through to get to this point. At last, she spied a ramshackle barn and knew that the first part of her motorcycle experience would soon be over.

The moment Marion cut the engine, it felt as if the world plunged into blissful silence, punctuated only by the bleating of sheep and the mournful cry of a single wild bird overhead.

Knowing she needed to dismount first, Lara swung her leg over the body of the motorcycle. Still feeling weak at the knees, she sucked in a deep breath and reached to pull her colleague's medical bag from the rack.

Marion hopped off the motorcycle, straightened her back and inhaled dramatically. 'It's a bit out in the wilds but I love the air up here. It's so fresh and invigorating, especially when the wind's blowing a gale.'

Lara had to admit there was something to be said for the magnificence of the landscape, set as it was against a solid back-drop of looming fells with their shades of green and russet-brown and an everchanging play of shadow and light. The view down to the green fields and scattered farms was breathtaking and when she spotted a cluster of buildings, she asked, 'Is that Ingleside?' and felt wondrous when Marion told her that it was.

'It's an incredible view,' she murmured, and as she handed the medical bag to Marion and followed her towards the barn, she felt the twist of anxiety deep inside, that had been tightly held since her accident, ease just a little. In the next breath, she came rapidly down to earth when she noted the derelict state of the farm buildings. Then shock hit her and she gasped out loud at a cacophony of squealing and grunting up ahead.

'Don't panic, it's just the pigs,' Marion shouted. A noxious smell hit Lara and the large, bristled head of one of the beady-eyed creatures shot out over a low door as the animal bumped hard against the rickety wood. When the pig emitted another ear-piercing squeal, it shocked her so much, she almost lost her footing.

'Are you OK?' Marion called. 'Sorry about that. Pigs are always noisy, but you'll get used to them.'

'I'm fine,' Lara gulped.

The path to the farmhouse was bordered by a tangle of straggly rosebay willowherb and nettles. And in a bid to keep up with Marion, Lara upped her pace and accidentally brushed her hand against a stinging nettle. Instantly, she felt a prickle of pain. She'd only ever once been stung as a child when she'd been on a Sunday School outing to the park, and the intensity of it shocked her, but she gritted her teeth and quickly caught up with Marion.

The small windows of the ramshackle farmhouse were dark, in complete contrast to the bright and sunny summer's day. As Marion knocked on the flaking, black-painted door, she glanced at Lara and offered a reassuring smile. In seconds, the door was opened by a boy of around ten years old dressed in ragged shorts and wellington boots. His face was grubby, his blond hair dishevelled, but his bright blue smiling eyes offered a warm welcome.

'Come in, our Lucy's waiting for you,' he said as he disappeared inside the gloomy farmhouse.

'Thank you, Robin,' Marion called after him, stepping through with Lara following.

It took a few moments for her eyes to adjust to the darkened interior but when they did, she saw a low-beamed kitchen with an iron stove and a solid, scrubbed wooden table where a woman with unravelling strands of brown hair plunged and kneaded a mass of bread dough.

'Hello there, Marion,' the woman called, about to wipe her floury hands on her striped apron.

'No need to interrupt your good work, Alice,' Marion offered. 'I know where to find everything and I can report back to you on the way out.'

'And who's this you've brought with ye?' the woman asked, her bright eyes looking Lara up and down.

'I'm the new district nurse,' Lara piped up, feeling as if she needed to make her mark.

The woman frowned and pummelled the bread with extra vigour. 'You don't sound like you're from round these parts.'

'No, that's right. I'm from Liverpool.'

She saw Alice Taylor purse her lips. 'Liverpool, hey.' She didn't offer any other comment but continued with her kneading.

As Lara followed her colleague out of the kitchen, she sensed more than a squeak of tension in the way Alice pounded the bread dough. It made her feel a little daunted as she climbed the narrow creaking stairs behind Marion. Arriving on a small landing with dark green, peeling wallpaper, she saw two rooms – one with the door closed, the other ajar.

'Morning, Lucy, how are you today?' Marion called as she walked in ahead, leaving Lara in the doorway with her hand still throbbing from the nettle sting. A double bed occupied most of the room and the girl was in a single bed next to a window which had a view of the farmyard. Lucy Taylor had the same blonde hair and blue eyes as her brother, but her face was pale and so thin, it appeared chiselled in comparison. But there was something serene in the way she lay in the narrow trestle bed with its spotless white sheets and threadbare patchwork quilt.

'I've brought a new nurse with me today,' Marion announced, gesturing to Lara with a nod of her head.

'Hello, Lucy, I'm Nurse Flynn.'

The girl offered a brief smile before pulling up her bedcovers to expose a left lower leg encased in a spotlessly clean bandage.

'You know the drill, don't you, my lovely,' Marion said, rolling up her sleeves and plunging her hands into a bowl of soapy water which had been left conveniently beside the bed.

'My brother Robin always makes sure I have the water and the towel ready for the nurse,' Lucy said, shyly glancing in Lara's direction.

'That's an excellent idea.' Lara smiled as Marion dried her hands on a small towel then began to set up for the dressing. She kept an eagle eye on her colleague's procedure in case she was ever required to make this visit alone. After the bandage had been removed, Marion peeled back the dressing and Lara noted the extent of the raw suppurating wound which was larger and deeper than she'd expected. It was healing now but she could see that it must have been down to the bone. The thought that this had been caused by a living creature made her shudder. She'd imagined the countryside would be more like the picture book of farm animals she'd loved as a child – neat and green with clean, friendly animals.

Lucy sucked in a breath, then stoically gritted her teeth as Marion swabbed the wound with carbolic solution, then liberally applied iodine. Clearly, she'd learned to manage the sting of the lotions, but Lara's heart twisted with sympathy at the girl having to endure this every single day. Then as Marion expertly applied the new dressing and rebandaged, she saw the girl offer a shaky smile.

'I'm giving you a brand-new safety pin today,' Marion smiled, holding up the shiny pin between finger and thumb before fixing it into position.

Then, rooting in her trouser pocket, she produced a caramel toffee wrapped in gold paper. For a moment, she held back the treat, teasing. 'Oh, this isn't for *you*, Lucy. This is for our new nurse,' before erupting into laughter and handing it over to her.

'Thank you, Nurse Marion,' the girl lilted and then with a shy smile in Lara's direction, 'Bye-bye, new nurse.'

'Bye Lucy,' Lara called as she turned to follow Marion back down the narrow stairs and into the dark kitchen.

Alice Taylor's large, earthenware bread bowl had been covered with a clean white towel and set in front of the stove to rise, and she was at the sink now waiting for Robin to pour a bucket of cold water for the washing up. While Marion sat at the table to write up her notes, Lara stood quietly observing the activity in the kitchen. It didn't shock her to see that the family had no running water; there were still plenty of houses in Liverpool that relied on a pump. But she'd imagined somehow that out here in the open green spaces of the countryside, there wouldn't be any poverty, that all the country folk would be living comfortably.

'That's the trouble with baking; it makes so much washing up,' Alice called as she added some boiling water from the kettle to the cold water in the sink. It looked like she was about to smile, but a shadow crossed her face instead and produced a bleak expression only accentuated by the dark smudges beneath her eyes.

'All's well with the dressing today,' Marion said as Alice plunged her hands into the water and scrubbed vigorously at an enamel bowl.

'Oh, that's good,' she called back, 'but like you've said before, it'll be a while before it's fully healed?'

'That's right. Great things take time. But we're on the right track, so that's good.'

Finishing her paperwork, Marion got up from her chair and walked over to speak quietly to Alice at the sink. 'And like I've said before, I don't want you to be worrying about the fees. I've spoken to Dr Bingham, and he understands that with these slow-healing cases, the costs mount up. So he's happy with a joint of pork every now and then as payment.'

Alice paused her scrubbing, her shoulders dropped and when she turned, she tried to smile but her eyes were shiny with tears. 'If some more money does come in, we'll pay our way, just the same as other folk.'

'I know you will,' Marion said, reaching out to place a gentle hand on her arm.

Once they were back outside in the sunlight, Lara heard her colleague heave a sigh. 'I wish we could do more to help families like the Taylors. Farming up here on the fells can be a desperate business. But in Alice's case, it wouldn't be half so bad if her husband Vic didn't spend every Friday night in The Fleece boozing away what little profit they make.'

'I suppose it's not for us to judge, and who knows what we'd be like if we were in that situation,' Lara offered in response.

'That's a very liberal view but I think we *do* know, don't we? If it were me or you or Alice, we'd be using every penny to fix up the farm and look after the children.'

There was no argument to what had just been said so Lara hoisted her skirt and clambered onto the back of the motorcycle. And as Marion deftly kick-started the machine into life, her stomach lurched again as they set off at speed over bumpy ground.

As they made their way along increasingly narrow lanes to visit other outlying properties, she noted once more the purple heather and yellow gorse at the side of the road. And when the hills opened out to reveal a distinctive symmetrical peak flanked by straight-topped fells on either side, all showing their summer green and brown switching and changing with light and shade, she felt contentment settle gently upon her.

The rest of their morning visits were routine – a check on an elderly farmer who had recently suffered a stroke, a dressing for a farmer's wife, a Mrs Ashworth who had a chronic diabetic leg ulcer, and a farm labourer's young son who was recuperating from a severe bout of tonsillitis. Then they were homeward bound for a quick lunch before the afternoon clinic and another list of house calls.

As they coasted back down to Ingleside, Lara began to feel even more comfortable on the back of the motorcycle. With the warm breeze on her face and the reassuring solidity of Marion in the driving seat, she felt lighter than air as they zoomed along with blue sky above and the wildflowers and green ferns whizzing by at the side of the road. It was only her second day and already, she was beginning to feel she'd made an excellent start to rural practice.

6

Dr Bingham sat hunched over his desk, his head down as he perused a patient's notes. Lara had knocked politely at the door, entered, and then been motioned to wait as he continued to glance through the notes. But as time stretched on and he still hadn't lifted his head, the tick-tick of the clock on the wall seemed to grow in intensity. Determined to stick it out, she glanced back to his bowed head and tried desperately to believe that the thinning spot of hair on his crown made him seem vulnerable. But that theory was instantly undercut by the thrust of his angular chin and the determined way he flicked through the case notes.

Feeling disconcerted, she thought back to the frosty greeting she'd received from him yesterday and wondered if she'd been summoned in relation to the mess she'd left in the corridor. But surely he wouldn't have waited to follow that up, and given Mrs Hewitt's sombre expression and the deadpan way she'd told her to go to his room, she knew it had to be something more serious than a bit of mud on the tiles.

So here she was, feeling increasingly frustrated with what

seemed unacceptably rude behaviour and wanting to get whatever was coming over with. Needing to distract herself, she
shifted her gaze to the shelves on the facing wall which held
leather-bound medical books and neatly labelled jars of
powders and liquids in precise order. Her eyes then flitted to the
corner of the room where an anatomical model stood perfectly
assembled on a polished table. As she glanced over the smooth
wooden parts – lungs, heart, liver, and bowels – she recalled the
feel of them in her hands from her days as a probationer nurse.
The way they fitted neatly into place, but only if you got them in
the right order. She thought of Maeve, cursing and swearing in
her thick, Dublin accent as she wrestled to get the anatomical
pieces into position, and it made her feel lighter.

When Bingham shifted in his chair ever so slightly, she
thought he was going to look up, but still he pored over the
document in front of him. This felt increasingly unfair, especially since she was brand new to the post and had absolutely no
idea why she'd been summoned.

At last, the doctor closed the notes, snapped the cap of his
black and gold fountain pen into place and looked up with a
steely glance. 'Right, Nurse Flynn,' he said, leaning back in his
chair and fixing her with an even sharper gaze. When he
realised she wasn't going to glance away, he cleared his throat
and leant forward. 'I've just returned from my visit to Miss
Dunderdale.'

She noted the tetchiness of his voice but remained confident
that she'd done all in her power yesterday to placate a difficult
patient. He continued to stare at her with his eyebrows raised.
She had no idea what she was supposed to say in response.

At last, he sighed heavily. 'When I examined Miss
Dunderdale this morning, I detected an irregular pulse, something I have never noted before. I asked about your visit

yesterday and she told me you didn't even check her pulse or her temperature or perform any observations whatsoever. Did they not teach you to take vital signs at the Liverpool Royal Infirmary?'

She felt a stab of anger, enhanced by the knowledge that around the table last evening, there'd been general agreement on the difficulties posed by Miss Dunderdale. She fought hard to keep her voice steady but when she spoke, it held an edge of outrage. 'Yes, of course I've been trained to read vital signs, but I cannot do so against the will of a conscious, compos mentis patient. Miss Dunderdale point-blank refused to let me anywhere near her.'

Bingham frowned. 'So, you're telling me that you couldn't find any way of persuading her to let you even take her pulse... What if you'd found her collapsed? Would you have recorded her pulse and respirations then?'

'Yes, of course I would have!'

She was indignant now, unable to temper her voice or hold back the flush of red on her neck. She couldn't bear to look at him, so she gazed at the row of glass jars on the clinic shelf. Instantly alarmed by a diseased eyeball, she had no choice but to switch her attention back to Bingham.

'Despite your impeccable references, Nurse Flynn, the incident raises a whole issue regarding your practical skills. We've never had a city nurse here at the practice and I'm beginning to wonder if I've made the right decision by appointing one. After seeing the mess you left in the corridor yesterday, and then hearing this account from a patient, I'm seriously considering sending you packing right away.'

She felt her stomach twist at the unfairness of everything he'd just said. If that was how she was going to be treated here, then she might not wait for him to 'send her packing' – she could be out through that door today. And as her steel will came fully to the fore, she felt the buzz of it through her body. When she spoke, her voice was clipped, professional. 'I'm sorry you have an issue with my visit to Miss Dunderdale, Doctor, but I did everything in my power to assess her condition. I made a judgement based on years of hospital practice and district-nursing experience. It would have been impossible to force any observations on a patient in such an anxious state; it would have caused her a great deal of distress. Therefore, as requested very firmly by the patient, I left the house.'

He narrowed his eyes, scrutinising her.

She clenched her right hand into a fist, determined to hold her ground.

The moment she saw his shoulders drop, she knew he was softening his position, at least a little.

'I'm prepared to give you a second chance, Nurse Flynn... but you will be under regular scrutiny during the probationary period. Ideally I would have liked you to be supervised by Nurse Wright for a full week, but our staffing levels won't allow for that. However, the patients and families in this tight-knit community are good at reporting back any issues, so if there is any question over your ability, I will be seeing you in this room again and a judgement will be made regarding your position here in our country practice.'

She felt incensed, but not by what he'd just said – she already knew that as a country nurse, she would undoubtedly have a learning curve, and the role would test every bit of her knowledge and experience. What enraged her was Bingham's high-handed manner. Dealing with the consultants and the matrons in Liverpool had been challenging, but she hadn't expected to find the same out here in a village practice.

She sucked in a slow, steadying breath. 'Yes, of course I

understand that there will be a probationary period,' she said firmly.

He slapped his palm down on the desk. 'Right then, that's settled. Let's review your situation in a few weeks' time... I think that's fair, don't you?'

She offered a single nod.

Then taking up his fountain pen again and removing the cap, he offered a final steady glance. 'Now, you should probably go and get yourself some lunch. Our working days here are very long.'

It was on the tip of her tongue to tell him that all days were long in nursing and doctoring, and that that was also very much the case in the city. But he was pulling another set of notes from the pile on his desk now and his head was down. As she turned to leave the room, she glanced at the anatomical model in the corner of the room again. Right now, she felt certain that she would get more understanding of her current situation from its wooden brain and neatly chiselled heart than from the senior doctor.

As soon as she clicked the clinic room door shut behind her, the scar on her hairline began to prickle. She was sorely tempted to run upstairs to her room and sponge her face with cold water, but the merry sound of Marion's laughter stopped her in her tracks.

Walking into the kitchen, she slipped into her seat opposite. It felt reassuring to be back in what was already her place at the table, and it eased her to listen to her colleague's lively telling of a funny story from the days when she'd worked in the Highlands. Despite the grilling she'd just had, she enjoyed the warmth of Marion's chuckle and it felt comforting to see Mrs Hewitt's face bright red with laughter.

When the hilarity died down, Marion fixed her with a wide-eyed gaze. 'What did his lordship want then?'

'Oh, he was just checking if I'd settled in all right,' she breathed, feeling a flush on her neck at the distortion of the truth. But as a brand-new member of staff, it felt way too soon to speak out loud to the whole team about Bingham's questioning of her professional competence. She caught a sideways glance from Mrs Hewitt, indicating that she probably knew the whole story, and maybe she too thought that there was an issue.

'He never once checked if I was OK when *I* first started,' Marion muttered, unknowingly making Lara feel worse because it meant her colleague hadn't been singled out for any questioning.

In the next moment, Angus strode into the kitchen and threw himself down onto his chair. Instantly, he reached for a chunky ham sandwich from the selection on a large, blue, willow-patterned plate in the centre of the table.

'Oi, wash your hands, *Doctor*,' Mrs Hewitt called.

He ate the sandwich in three bites before heaving a sigh and dragging himself up from his chair to scrub his hands at the kitchen sink.

'Angus, did Dr Bingham ever check that you were settling in when you first started?' Marion called after him.

'No,' he offered over his shoulder. 'But he made my life hell for a full six weeks, before reducing it to occasional hell, which is where I now exist,' turning as he dried his hands. 'Why are you asking?'

'Oh, it's just that he's been checking on Lara, making sure she's all right... Just seems a bit out of character. He usually only calls someone in if there's a problem.'

Angus looked thoughtful as he took his seat again and reached for another sandwich. 'Definitely... but I don't know how you'd know that, Marion, because you've never once been called to his room for an audience. In fact, for some bizarre reason, you seem to be the chosen one.'

'Don't be ridiculous,' she coughed, two spots of bright pink appearing on her cheeks. 'Lara is set to be in that position, just look at her... She is absolutely perfect.'

Starting to feel increasingly uncomfortable amid the banter stemming from her mistruth, Lara felt the need to change the subject.

'How was the pub last night?' she blurted in Angus's direction.

'Good, very good,' he muttered between mouthfuls. 'The usual gang were there and, Nurse Flynn, you might be surprised to learn that you are already a topic of conversation.'

She felt her breath catch and coughed a little on the cheese and pickle sandwich she was nibbling with little enthusiasm.

'No teasing now, Angus,' Mrs Hewitt warned. 'It's still only Lara's first proper day.'

'All the more amazing,' he grinned, 'that she has already made her mark with the local farmers.'

Mrs Hewitt frowned.

'Our Nurse Flynn has not only been carrying out her nursing duties; apparently, she's also a dab hand at delivering a calf.'

Lara felt her cheeks flush; she knew exactly what was coming next.

'My esteemed veterinary colleague, Leo Sullivan, was in the pub last night. And according to him, yesterday afternoon, our own Nurse Flynn was called to assist Tom Douglas with the delivery of a calf. He said she—'

Lara spoke up before Angus agonisingly stretched the story too far.

'It was nothing, I was wheeling my bicycle back from the visit to Miss Dunderdale and I heard the excruciating sound of an animal in pain. Mr Douglas asked me to help pull on a rope to deliver the calf, and that's exactly what I did.'

'Well done, Lara!' cried Marion. 'I once delivered twin lambs but never a calf... Those things are big, and they can get stuck fast in the birth canal.'

Lara was shaking her head. 'Honestly, I was just helping out; he told me exactly what to do. Anyone could have done the same.'

'Well, it seemed to have made quite an impression on the vet. Leo couldn't stop talking about it—'

'That's enough now, Angus, stop it,' Mrs Hewitt interjected, clearly sensing Lara's discomfort.

'Stop what?' huffed Dr Bingham, coming into the kitchen to take his seat at the head of the table.

Angus was straight there, and Lara felt her heart sink. 'Oh, just that our new nurse not only went straight out on a visit yesterday to one of our trickier patients, but she also delivered a calf on the way home.'

'Delivered a calf?' Bingham huffed. 'What the blazes...?'

'I was called in by a local farmer, a Mr Douglas,' Lara repeated. 'He needed urgent assistance, or the mother cow and the baby would have been lost.'

'Where was the blasted vet?'

'Mr Sullivan arrived late, just as I was leaving.'

Dr Bingham regarded her. 'Well, Nurse Flynn, clearly you have many potential talents... Let's hope your practical skills regarding homo sapiens match up to those required in the veterinary field. And I sincerely hope that in future, you will prioritise the needs of our patients above those of the local livestock.'

'Yes, of course I will,' she replied, feeling the flush on her cheeks brighten. 'I would always do that. But surely you yourself wouldn't hesitate to help any living creature in distress?'

Bingham took a breath as if he were about to say one thing, but then he shook his head as if he'd changed his mind. 'Honestly, those vets, they'll have us doing all their work if we're not careful. Things have certainly gone downhill since Arthur Sullivan let that son of his into the practice.'

Mrs Hewitt spoke firmly. 'Don't be saying that, Dr Bingham. Young Leo is a lovely lad; he always has a smile.'

Bingham made a low grunting sound as Angus desperately tried to stop himself from laughing. And Lara knew for sure that next time the young doctor was in the pub with Leo, this would all be reported back. She could already see the vet's grinning face, and when she recalled the way he had teased her after she'd delivered the calf, it made her feel even more thrown out.

'Are you OK?' Marion asked, scrunching her brow.

'Yes, yes. Of course,' she offered. 'Just wondering what we'll be doing this afternoon, that's all. I'm trying to get used to the routine.'

'You're in clinic, with me,' Bingham called abruptly down the table.

Marion offered her a brief, sympathetic smile. 'You'll be fine,' she mouthed.

7

After a rapid run-through by Dr Bingham of what her duties would be for the afternoon clinic, Lara walked out to the waiting area to see if any patients had arrived. The first two appointments were antenatal checks and that was reassuringly familiar territory. Mothers and babies had formed a big part of her work in Liverpool, and she'd done a long stint in maternity after she'd completed her midwifery training. So, despite the shaky start to this second half of her first official day, she was feeling quietly comfortable with the duties outlined. Especially since all the appointments would involve the taking of temperature, pulse and blood pressure. Having spoken privately after lunch to an outraged Marion about what Dr Bingham had accused her of, she was determined to grasp the opportunity and prove her worth. Her colleague had wholeheartedly supported her management of Miss Dunderdale, and she'd agreed there was absolutely no way any nurse could persuade that particular patient to have her pulse taken or do anything else if she refused point-blank.

And before Marion had headed out to her motorcycle for

her afternoon visits to the outlying farms, she'd said, 'Look, Lara, I've hardly spent any time with you yet, but just from this morning's visits, I already know you knock spots off most of the nurses I've worked with. So you go into that clinic with Bingham, and you show him.'

There were no patients in the waiting area yet and as she eyed the layout of the furniture, she thought it might be good to rearrange some of the wooden chairs so the space could be used more effectively. Tutting when she noted a glass ashtray that hadn't been emptied, she moved to collect it but stopped dead in her tracks when she heard a loud crash as the front door hit the wall when it was flung open. Then a blood-curdling female voice screamed, 'Help me!'

She felt it like a punch to the gut and instantly, she was running to see Lizzie, the young woman who had been in the waiting area yesterday, hurtling down the corridor with a screeching child in her arms. 'She's scalded. It was a boiling-hot cup of tea!' she shouted, her voice crackling on a sob.

Instantly, Lara saw white bubbles of blister already forming on the little girl's face.

'Give her to me,' she yelled to the hysterical mother, grabbing the child and running with her to Dr Bingham's room. She pushed straight through the door, aware of the doctor jumping up from his desk, papers fluttering to the floor.

'Lizzie's little girl is badly scalded,' she shouted across the room, already at the sink, pushing in the plug and running cold water. Grabbing a clean towel from the side, she lay it on the examination couch and placed the screaming child there to quickly strip off her jumper and vest. Bubbling, bright-red skin extended over her shoulder and down her right arm, and there were some splashes on her face and chest. She was fighting and kicking but Lara held firm, grappling with her then carrying her to the large sink and plunging her into the cold water, holding her body under and using the towel to soak up cold water to swoosh over her scalded face.

Bingham was right beside her, helping to restrain the child.

When the door clicked open, Lara saw a distraught-looking Mrs Hewitt. 'Look after the child's mother,' she shouted, her heart thudding in her chest, her teeth gritted, knowing that this first half hour of treatment would be crucial in avoiding permanent scarring for the girl. The poor little mite was writhing and screeching as Bingham used a ceramic jug to pour freshly drawn cold water over her head.

Ten minutes went by. Still the child screamed, still Lara and Bingham fought to keep going with their cold water treatment. Blisters had fully erupted now – a large one on the girl's forehead and two smaller bubbles on her right cheek. Her arm and chest were scalded deep red and peeling, but not blistered.

When enough time had gone by for the efficacy of the cold water to be negligible, Lara pulled Sue out of the sink and wrapped her in a clean, white towel. Exhausted now, the tiny child was sobbing and shivering with cold but thankfully, the blisters looked as though they'd been contained.

'Give her to me,' Bingham said, his voice gentle, threaded with emotion, as he held out his arms to take her.

Lara handed over the little girl, her hair bunches wet through and unravelled, her eyes red with crying.

'Now, Sue Cronshaw,' he crooned, starting to rock her gently from side to side, 'you've had a nasty shock but you're safe now and we're going to look after you.'

Seeing this other side to the doctor made Lara's throat tight with emotion – especially after the tense interaction she'd had with him earlier. She could only watch as he carefully carried Sue to his desk chair and then sat nursing her on his knee. With the pristine white coat he'd donned for the clinic now soaked through and his hair dishevelled, he sat rocking the little girl back and forth, murmuring to her until she fell asleep.

Lara felt as if she hardly dare breathe in case she broke the spell, but once she could see the little girl was settled, she said quietly, 'I'll go and check on the mother and then I'll assemble the materials for the dressings. We'll need plenty of vaseline gauze; do you keep a good stock?'

Still rocking the little girl, he nodded and pointed towards a tall white cupboard in the corner beside the sink.

As she exited the consultation room and walked through the waiting area, there was no sign of the child's mother, but their first antenatal case, a Mrs Rose Ryan, was sitting rigidly upright, her eyes wide. Knowing Mrs Hewitt must have taken the distraught mother through to the kitchen, she offered a smile to the red-haired young woman who had tears shining in her eyes. 'I saw Lizzie Cronshaw in a terrible state; is her wee girl all right?' she asked, her voice gentle and full of concern.

'Yes, she's going to be fine. No need for alarm.'

Rose drew a shuddering breath then placed a protective hand at the top of her baby bump. 'This is my first, but I grew up in a big Irish family with loads of children. Even so, I find it scary when I think of what it will be like to have my own wee child out in the world.'

'Don't you worry, you'll soon learn to cope,' Lara soothed, making her voice confident. But underneath her professional demeanour lay an awareness of all the terrifying ailments and potential disasters that awaited every small child. Medical science had moved on from the dark days of the last century but there were still no effective treatments for childhood infections such as diphtheria, whooping cough, and polio, and if infection took hold after an ailment or an injury, there was a real risk of it causing death from sepsis. During her work at the hospital, she'd found the children's ward especially gruelling given the number of very poorly little ones she'd sat by, knowing there was no chance of them surviving.

Indicating to Mrs Ryan that they'd take her into clinic as soon as possible, she made her way to the kitchen to find a silent, petrified Lizzie Cronshaw in Marion's place at the table. She was gazing straight ahead, empty-eyed, as Mrs Hewitt busily picked through a bowl of wild raspberries before tipping them into a freshly rolled pie crust. The housekeeper glanced up and they exchanged a nod before she vigorously rolled a pastry lid for her pie. Lara slipped into the chair opposite Lizzie and reached out to her. Suddenly, the young mother gasped as if she'd been woken.

'Your daughter is going to be fine. She has some blisters, and the skin is very red and peeling in places but with daily dressings, the wounds will heal. You did absolutely the right thing by bringing her here straight away.'

Lizzie bowed her head and began to sob. Then gasping for breath, she ranted, 'It was all my fault. I put the cup of tea too close to the edge of the table and she's been out of sorts for days with that bad earache. I should have been more careful.'

Mrs Hewitt quickly wiped her floury hands on her pinny and put an arm around the young mother's shoulders. 'You need eyes in the back of your head when they're that age. My son got up to all sorts. It's impossible to watch them all the time.'

Lizzie was shaking her head, then her face crumpled. 'I'm not a good mother; Ed keeps telling me how careless I am,' she hiccupped.

Mrs Hewitt narrowed her eyes and when she spoke, her voice was forceful. 'Your Ed doesn't know the first thing about being at home all day, every day, with a small child.'

Lizzie was still shaking her head. 'No, he's right, I'm not fit to be a mother. That's why he has every right to be angry with me sometimes.'

Lara exchanged a wide-eyed glance with Mrs Hewitt.

'You are very fit to be a mother; you are a good mother,' the housekeeper said firmly.

Lizzie's face was sheet-white, her expression mournful as she leant back in her chair and ran a hand over the seven-month bump of her pregnant belly. 'I should give this one away, give it to somebody who'll take proper care of it. A woman who can't have one of her own.'

Mrs Hewitt grabbed Lizzie's shoulders and gave her a squeeze, a light dusting of flour rising into the air as she rubbed the young woman's arm, her voice breaking ever so slightly when she said, 'Nay, lass. Don't you be saying that.'

'Mrs Hewitt is right,' Lara said softly, 'And you did the right thing when you brought Sue straight here. No mother could have done more.'

'I didn't stop her reaching for that cup of hot tea though, did I?'

'It was an accident,' she said gently but firmly, and as the young woman's head dropped, she hoped it was an indication she was taking that on board.

As Mrs Hewitt murmured more words of comfort, Lara quietly got up from the table. 'I'm going to sort out Sue's dressings now. And as soon as I have her bandaged up, you can come in and see her.'

Lizzie looked up, swallowed hard, then nodded.

When Lara got back to the clinic room, she was relieved to find Sue still sleeping on Dr Bingham's lap. As he glanced up, she saw a flash of sorrow in his eyes. He quickly composed himself, but he'd seemed vulnerable in that moment, and it softened her attitude towards him just a little.

He cleared his throat. 'As I indicated, the dressings are in that tall white cupboard next to the sink, and the trolley is there beside the examination couch.'

'Thank you,' she said, walking briskly over to wipe down the trolley with carbolic solution and prepare all the materials. 'Are you all right to keep hold of her while I do the dressings?' she asked.

He nodded and then straightened in his chair, supporting the sleeping child in a position that would allow Lara to work. Then he spoke quietly. 'I've checked her right eye and thankfully, there doesn't seem to be any damage, but there's quite a bit of swelling and it'll be closed for a while.'

'I'll need to bandage over it anyway,' she said as she scrutinised the girl's face for the correct positioning of the dressings. It was tricky to apply the vaseline gauze, a dressing pad and then a bandage without any slippage, but she managed to have it done before Sue roused up. Dr Bingham didn't utter a word all the way through, but she was sure she detected a murmur of approval as she secured the final length of bandage with surgical tape. When the child began to wake, she was crying with pain, and Dr Bingham administered a small drop of laudanum to settle her. And once she was sleepy again, he laid her tiny body on the examination couch and went to the opposite side to assist with the positioning of the bandages over her scalded chest.

'She'll need admission to the hospital in Ridgetown,' he murmured. 'I'll take her in the car once we've attended to the antenatal patients. In the meantime, now she's sleeping, let's put her in the bed in the side room and bring her mother through to wait with her there.'

Lara nodded her agreement and as soon as the bandaging

had been completed, she went back to the kitchen to find Lizzie sitting silently in her chair with an untouched cup of tea in front of her.

'Good news,' she said, 'all the dressings are done, and your little girl is sleeping. We're going to keep her here until the afternoon clinic is finished and then Dr Bingham will take her in the car to the cottage hospital.'

'Hospital?' Lizzie's eyes opened wide with horror.

'She'll need to have her dressings changed at least once per day in the first few weeks, plus some medicine for the pain, so it's best that she's admitted. But you'll be able to go and see her during visiting hours.'

Lizzie began to sob.

'There's no way round it,' Mrs Hewitt offered as she walked over to put an arm around Lizzie's shoulders. 'The nurses have to do the dressings and it's important they keep an eye on the wounds for any sign of infection.'

Still Lizzie sobbed but she was wiping her tears away now with the flat of her hand and trying to compose herself. Mrs Hewitt rooted in her pocket and produced a clean, neatly folded handkerchief. 'Come on lass. Dry your eyes and let's go and see your daughter... She's going to be fine, just fine.'

Once the little girl was settled in the side room with her mother, Lara went straight back to assist with the clinic. The two antenatal patients were dealt with efficiently, and their vital signs plus abdominal girth and fundal height measured accurately. There were two minor emergency cases but the whole clinic proceeded smoothly with no reason for anyone to find fault. Bingham didn't go so far as to say 'well done' but she could tell by his demeanour that he was satisfied with her performance. And later, when all the patients had been seen, she left him sitting behind his desk, his fountain pen gently scratching on paper as he wrote up his notes. When she checked on Lizzie and Sue in the side room, she was pleased to find them both sleeping peacefully – the little girl curled up next to her mother on the bed. She wasn't sure what time they'd be making the transfer to the cottage hospital, but she'd make sure she had all the tidying and cleaning done first, so she would be ready to leave.

Hearing Bingham emerge from his room, she left the sleeping mother and child and gently closed the door behind her. The doctor seemed distracted, lost in his own thoughts as he strode by with a frown, offering no more than a nod. She couldn't help but be taken aback after they'd worked so closely together all afternoon. Clearly, for whatever reason, he was a man whose moods ebbed and flowed like the tides. She'd worked with other senior doctors and ward sisters at the Royal who'd functioned in the same manner. She supposed it might be a way of maintaining control by keeping their staff permanently on edge. But whether it was a deliberate strategy or not, it felt exasperating. And if she'd gauged Bingham's temperament during her telephone interview, she would probably not have accepted the position.

The sound of chattering voices at the back door heralded the return of Marion and Angus. 'How did you get on with the clinic?' Marion called brightly.

'Yes, it was fine in the end,' she replied, 'but we did start with an emergency admission... Lizzie Cronshaw's little girl, Sue, tipped a cup of scalding-hot tea over herself. She's currently with her mother in the side room awaiting transfer to Ridgetown hospital.'

'Oh no,' Marion crooned. 'Poor little mite, she's such a bonny little thing. Will she be all right?'

'Yes, I think so. They live in one of the cottages just across the street, don't they, so they got here quickly. And we used plenty of cold water to minimise the damage. They always look bad at first, scalds, but they should heal up nicely.'

Marion was nodding. 'Are you OK? What an introduction to country practice... It's usually much calmer than that around here.'

'Yes, I'm fine... The training just kicks in, doesn't it?'

'It does, but bloody well done all the same.' Marion grinned, putting an arm around her shoulders and giving her a squeeze.

'Less of the chit-chat,' Bingham called somewhat brusquely as he exited the kitchen. 'I'll get the car; we need to transfer Sue Cronshaw to Ridgetown hospital. Nurse Wright, I need you to accompany me.'

Marion's mouth dropped open. 'But... Sue is Nurse Flynn's patient, surely she—'

He cut in firmly. 'No, not this time; Nurse Flynn is new to the job.'

Lara felt a painful lump in her throat, she'd wanted so much to complete her care for the little girl by doing the handover at the hospital. It was always satisfying to see a case right through. But she had no choice; the boss had spoken, and she was not going to be allowed to transfer her patient.

Snatching a breath, she spoke quickly. 'That's all right, I'll go in and check on Lizzie and Sue now, make sure they're ready to leave.'

Marion offered a sympathetic smile as Lara turned to walk back to the side room and by the time she'd heard the click of the back door as Bingham went out to his car, she'd swallowed down the lump in her throat, but it still niggled at her.

Little Sue was rousing from her sleep and her hand was already sneaking up to explore the bandages when Lara crouched down beside the bed.

'I need you to leave that alone,' she said gently, taking hold of the girl's tiny hand and easing it away from the dressing. 'It's there to make your head better.'

The girl opened her eyes wide and stared straight at her, then she nodded.

Lara smiled. 'You're such a good girl.'

'Good girl,' Sue repeated, her face starting to scrunch with a smile as her mother began to rouse next to her.

Lara straightened up from the bed and spoke to Lizzie as soon as she opened her eyes. 'We're getting ready to move Sue to Ridgetown hospital now, and of course you can go with her to get her settled.'

Lizzie's face was ashen, she looked groggy, but she nodded and gathered Sue close, twisting her body to sit at the side of the bed with her child on her knee.

'Are you coming with us, Nurse?'

'No, it will be Nurse Wright who accompanies you.'

'Oh,' Lizzie said, raising her eyebrows. 'I thought—'

'It's fine, Nurse Wright and I work very closely together. So she'll have all the information about your daughter's case.'

Lizzie nodded, readying herself.

Lara walked beside the young mother as she carried her child to the shiny black Rover that Dr Bingham had parked at the front door. Marion was ready and waiting and she helped them into the back. But as soon as the car door clicked to, she startled at the heavy sound of running feet and a man's shouting voice. A dark-haired fella, broad through the chest with a muscular build, his face flushed red from exertion, was hurtling towards the car, his clogs sparking on stone.

'Stop right now!' Lara hollered, fearful he was going to barrel straight into her.

In seconds, he was confronting her, shouting aggressively. 'What're you doing with my wife?'

Bingham wound down his car window. 'Your wife is fine, Mr Cronshaw, but your daughter has received a nasty scald from a cup of tea. We're—'

'What's she been doing now?' the man yelled, banging a fist down hard on the car roof as Lizzie sat petrified in the back, clinging to her child.

'That's enough, Ed!' Bingham shouted through the window.

But Lara could see it hadn't made a bit of difference; the man was filled with fury and by the way he slurred his speech and swayed on his feet, she knew he was also drunk.

She reached out to him, laid a gentle hand on his arm. 'You need to try and calm down, Mr Cronshaw.'

He switched round with a snarl and she caught the stink of strong liquor on his breath. 'I need to calm down? What the hell's happening here? I've been slaving away at that sawmill all day and I just get back from work to find *this* going on. And that fancy-pants doctor who's never got his hands dirty doing a day's work in his life is telling me "that's enough"?'

She noted the raw fury burning in his bloodshot eyes; he was flexing his hands and she felt sure he was about to pull open the car door and assault Dr Bingham. Without thinking, she stepped in front of the snarling man, blocking him. Instantly, he raised his fist to her face. She was eye to eye with him now, her heart hammering so fast, it was painful, but unflinchingly, she held her ground.

The moment stretched on. She drew a slow breath and when she spoke, she made sure her voice was steady. 'Please, Mr Cronshaw, you have to let Dr Bingham take your daughter to the hospital. She needs urgent treatment for her scalds.'

He leant in even closer. 'You must be that new nurse they're all talking about,' he spat. 'Just like the rest of them: think you know it all.'

She felt her temper rising now and she fought to control her voice before she spoke again, repeating, 'Your daughter needs urgent treatment for her wounds; she needs to go to the hospital.'

As if on cue, she heard the terrified wail of the child from inside the car; clearly, the little girl was distressed. In that same second, Ed grabbed her by the upper arms, his fingers digging painfully into her flesh, and she felt a spray of spittle on her face as he began to rant incoherently. She could hear Bingham shouting and desperately trying to open the car door. The man was shaking her now; she began to feel dizzy. A different shouting voice came at her then and suddenly, Ed released his grip and fell back as he was dragged away.

She stood gasping as the doctor struggled out of the car, instantly checking she was all right. 'Yes, yes,' she was saying, her only concern for the terrified mother and her child.

The man who had come to her rescue was leading Ed away and when he glanced back over his shoulder, she realised why the shouting voice had sounded familiar. It was Leo Sullivan, the vet she'd met yesterday, and even at this distance, she could see his eyes full of concern. She nodded a thank you before turning to Bingham, who was hurriedly clambering back into the driver's seat. Lizzie and Sue were crying, with Marion desperately trying to soothe both of them at the same time. Bingham fired up the engine and accelerated away with a spray of grit.

'What's been going on?' Angus called, emerging at a leisurely pace through the front door of the surgery. 'Mrs Hewitt thought she overheard a commotion.'

Lara almost laughed out loud at his lack of awareness. He'd probably been sitting chatting at the kitchen table or eating a piece of cake while all of this had been happening. She turned to face him. 'Dr Bingham was just about to set off with Sue Cronshaw and her mother to the hospital, but the child's father turned up in a very agitated state; he was drunk and quite aggressive.'

Angus looked immediately crestfallen. 'Oh, I had no idea; sorry about that. I was just in the kitchen telling Mrs H about the village cricket match I'll be playing in at the weekend.'

'Don't worry, we sorted it.'

He ran a hand through his tousled hair. 'I'm shocked, I must say. I know Ed Cronshaw from The Fleece; he works at the sawmill. He can get himself a bit worked up sometimes, usually when he's been drinking, and that's when he can turn nasty. But he's a good sort really, a decent chap. Maybe he was shocked, worried about his child.'

Still feeling the painful imprint of the man's fingers on both her upper arms, she was sceptical of Angus's assessment of the situation. However, it didn't feel appropriate to voice her concerns out here in the street, especially since she was a complete newcomer and didn't have the full picture. However, she'd dealt with enough violent male relatives of female patients in Liverpool to feel pretty sure that Lizzie's situation hung in a very precarious balance.

'It looks like our vet has the situation under control, though,' Angus added, nodding in Leo's direction. 'Handy his surgery is just down the road.'

'Mmm,' Lara replied, already turning away, ready to go back inside to finish her tasks.

Angus began to chuckle as he trotted beside her. 'You seem to have brought drama in your wake, Nurse Flynn. Who knows what other excitement lies in store for us now?'

She didn't reply; she was rapidly getting used to Angus's rhetorical flourishes.

Before she went back into the surgery, she glanced down the street to see Leo at the door of the vet's, persuading a now slump-shouldered Ed inside. Leo caught her eye and raised his hand. She thought of reciprocating the gesture but instantly changed her mind, because what she'd found annoying in the vet yesterday had now been overturned by his stepping up to help manage a difficult situation. Clearly, there was more to the man than met the eye and she had to admit, he was good-looking, in a tousled kind of way. But right now, after the disappointing turn of events with Patrick, she felt it best to steer clear of any complications. This was a fresh start for her in a brand-new setting, a chance to reclaim those weeks of pain and trauma after her accident. She couldn't afford to focus on anything other than adjusting her practice to fit a new way of working in a startlingly different environment.

8

After a broken night's sleep with nightmarish visions of shouting men and violent scuffles, Lara retrieved her bicycle from the shed at the back of the surgery and set out on her first day of unsupervised visits. When Bingham had returned from the cottage hospital last evening, he'd been quiet, uncommunicative, and she'd wondered if this was, again, just his way of being, or if there had been a deterioration in Sue Cronshaw's condition. Finding him sitting alone at the kitchen table nursing a glass of whisky, she'd tried gently to question him about Sue just to set her mind at rest. But he'd mumbled some meaningless response, then jumped up with a curt goodnight and left the room. Angus had been out again last night to The Fleece doing God knows what, but probably laughing his head off with Leo Sullivan. And Marion had been involved with what Lara would have been doing if she'd been allowed to escort her patient to the cottage hospital: she'd stayed to help settle the child, only returning after Lara had gone to bed. So she'd had no information about Sue until this morning when Marion had run into the kitchen to grab her toast and jam and she'd told her between mouthfuls that the little girl was very settled, there was no undue concern, and the nurses at Ridgetown hospital absolutely loved her.

The instant relief had been gratifying but what had also struck her was the level of engagement she already had with her new colleagues – except Dr Bingham of course, but that was a whole other story. She was still at the beginning of these relationships and maybe what she felt was nothing more than the forced acceptance of having to live together in the same house, like some strange family who also worked together. Whatever the reason, it intrigued her to feel this so soon. And even though things were still tricky with the senior doctor, she hoped she'd be able to establish a more stable footing soon.

But on this lovely summer morning, she didn't want to think about that right now and as she mounted her bicycle and headed back out to the country lanes, all she could do was smile.

It was refreshing to be in the open air and already, she caught the smell of newly mown grass. Mrs Hewitt had told her that during this dry spell of sunny weather, the farmers would begin their hay time in earnest. She imagined scenes akin to the rural idylls she'd seen portrayed in paintings on display at the Liverpool art galleries. But even from just a few days in the country, she already knew that life out here was far grittier than that.

As she freewheeled gently downhill towards the hump-backed bridge, she was struck by the beauty of the ancient sandstone cottages with their impossibly low doorways and tiny windows. Passing the steep steps on her left which led up to the village church, she noted the same warm brown and yellow stone that the whole village was built from. And when a black-robed, elderly vicar appeared at the top of the steps, she raised her hand in greeting, then felt a little disappointed when all she got in return was a frown. But as she passed the butcher's shop, Sam Collins was unloading his van and he called out a lively 'good morning'. The Old Oak pub, the village shop and post office took their turns to go by, then as she slowed to negotiate the bridge, she noted a mill with a waterwheel set back from the street on the bank of the river.

Having almost lost control of her bicycle the first time she'd tackled the bridge, she took it carefully, enjoying the sound of the brook gurgling gently over smooth stones. Then as she pedalled out of the village, she picked up speed and was soon riding between hedgerows laced with dog roses and wild honey-suckle. It made her feel warm inside and as she cycled, she felt her body begin to hum with pleasure. Meeting once more the thin, grey-haired man driving a black horse pulling a milk-cart, she moved to the side of the lane to let him pass. He slowly raised a bony hand as they rumbled by.

The first visit on her list was to Manor House Farm, a tenanted property which formed part of the Ingleside Hall estate. 'The big house where the top brass live' was how Mrs Hewitt had described the hall. And Marion, overhearing the conversation before she'd rushed out of the kitchen, had told her, with eyes round as saucers, about the Harvest Ball that Sir Charles and Lady Olivia Harrington presided over every year, and to which the staff at the surgery were always invited. She felt a little daunted by the prospect of attending such a grand event, but given Marion was already beside herself with joy, she knew that of course she would accompany her.

Still enjoying the warm sun on her face and the vibrant colours of the wildflowers, Lara felt increasingly carefree as she cycled. Then, sensing she would soon be arriving at her first call, she ran through the detail of the case in her head. James Alston was a sixty-two-year-old farmer who had been diagnosed with

Parkinson's disease just over ten years ago. The purpose of her visit was the removal of stitches from a head wound he'd sustained during a fall. His case interested her because he'd developed Parkinson's at a much younger age than any of the other patients she'd nursed previously. Diagnosed aged fifty after he'd noticed a tremor of his right hand, he'd soldiered on with his work on the farm for as long as he possibly could. But the disease had progressed rapidly and within five years, it had taken his other arm, his legs, then his whole body, with horrendous shakes and muscle rigidity. And with no effective treatment, the poor man was now completely dependent and almost permanently distressed. Parkinson's was a cruel disease and from what Marion had told her, Mr Alston was completely riven by his condition. Since the death of his wife, he was cared for by an unmarried sister, Agnes, and his thirty-year-old daughter, Grace, who had also taken over the running of the farm.

Cycling uphill, Lara pushed hard enough to sweat and her starched collar began to chafe against her neck. She smiled then as she recalled clinging to Marion on the back of the motorcycle yesterday. It thrilled her to know she'd stuck it out, but even though being on the bicycle was more laborious, she enjoyed the slower pace because she could take in her surroundings.

At the loud bleating of a sheep, she spotted the fork in the road where she needed to bear right. Marion had told her she would then see the roof and the chimneys of Ingleside Hall and straight after, there'd be a track on the right to Manor House Farm. Confident of her colleague's advice, she pushed ahead and when the high chimneys and green slate roof of the Hall came into view, she knew she was heading in the right direction.

After she'd negotiated the five-barred gate that marked the entrance to the farm, she dismounted her bicycle and wheeled it over a potholed track. As she skirted cow pats and waited politely for sheep to cross in front of her, she spotted the farm up ahead and was soon in a cobbled yard with a shippon and a range of outbuildings including a large barn. The farmhouse with its flecked red-gold stone walls and slate roof was set back a little but it was clearly a focal point. Then as she walked farther, she startled at the angry bark of a black and white farm dog that jumped up and down on its heavy chain.

Within moments, a tall woman with unruly brown hair, wearing a checked shirt and brown cord trousers cinched at the waist by a broad leather belt, strode out from the barn, called out a greeting and waved enthusiastically. Lara raised a hand in return, propped her bicycle against the yard wall, then grabbed her medical bag out of the basket and walked briskly across to meet the woman who now stood with her hands on her hips.

'You must be Nurse Flynn, I've been hearing *all* about you. I believe you're a dab hand at delivering a calf.' The woman laughed.

'News travels fast,' Lara replied, reaching out to receive a firm handshake. 'And you must be Miss Grace Alston?'

'Yes, that's me. And I'm also a dab hand at delivering a calf. But we have no cows calving today… so it looks like you will have to be satisfied with removing the stitches from my dad's head.'

As they walked together towards the farmhouse, Lara was barely able to keep up with Grace's long stride. Then at the open door, the woman kicked off her mucky boots and gestured for her to enter the large, low-ceilinged kitchen. Two stray hens were pecking on the stone-flagged floor and as Lara stood just in through the door clutching her medical bag, Grace shooshed them out; they were flapping their wings and clucking loudly. A single brown feather floated down to land on the kitchen table and Grace swept it off, laughing.

'They're always coming in here, those chuckies; I just wish they'd learn to do the washing up.'

Lara giggled, probably a nervous reaction; she'd been a little afraid of the hens with their sharp beaks and claws. Then, as if coming to her aid, a black cat with a white-tipped tail sauntered through from another room and brushed against her legs. She leant down to give it a stroke and instantly, it purred.

'Shoo, shoo, puss cat, the nurse hasn't come to see you; she's got work to do,' Grace said, gently moving the cat aside with her stockinged foot. And then in the next breath, 'Can I get you a cup of tea before you start?'

'No, thank you,' she replied, knowing on this, her first proper day, she needed to get the measure of things and make sure she got back to the surgery in a timely fashion. She opened her mouth to ask where the patient was, but in that moment, a heavy rattling and shouting came from the direction the cat had emerged from.

Grace raised her eyebrows. 'Well, as you've probably guessed, that's your patient in there. And I'm thinking you might be needing a cup of tea or something much stronger when you've finished with him.'

Unsettled by the violence of the noise, Lara fought not to show it as she gave a nod, then strode with apparent confidence towards the clatter of furniture and what had now become vigorous swearing.

Tapping on the partly open door, she spoke firmly but politely. 'Hello, Mr Alston. I'm Nurse Flynn, the new district nurse.'

'Not now! Not now!' was what came back with a growl.

She glanced back to Grace, who offered a resigned smile. 'Sorry, Nurse Flynn, my father used to be a gently spoken, patient man but this is what he's like every morning now. I'd go in there ahead of you, but it would probably agitate him even more.'

Something crashed to the floor with a loud splintering noise; it sounded like breaking china.

'I keep telling Aunt Agnes to use the tin cups for Dad, but she says he only deserves the best... which is correct. But we're going through pottery at a rate of knots.'

Lara offered a sympathetic glance then tapped at the door again. All she had in return was the shaking and rattling of furniture. 'I'm sorry, Mr Alston, I'm going to have to come in. I need to sort out those stitches for you.'

He roared in response, but she pushed open the door anyway and entered the room. Immediately, she was shocked to see her patient writhing violently in a high-backed armchair at the side of his bed. The poor man was completely unable to control his body, and he was gripping the arms of his chair so tightly that his knuckles were white. Gasping, trying to communicate, he dissolved into tears, huge sobs racking his body. 'I can't do this,' he croaked. 'I can't do this any more. I just want to die.'

A sliver of pain went through her; she'd never seen a Parkinson's case like this before. Those she'd encountered previously had been elderly people with much milder shakes. She felt so moved by his plight, she was stuck for words, then seeing a white cup broken into two pieces on the red-tiled floor, she bent down to pick it up and placed it neatly on a side table. The simple act allowed her to gather herself and she was ready now to engage with her patient.

'I'm so sorry to disturb you, Mr Alston,' she offered, placing her medical bag on the bottom of his bed, 'but Dr Bingham has asked me to remove the stitches from your head.'

Closer now, she spotted four black silk sutures on his thinning hairline. His face was drenched with sweat and the wound looked red and angry, but from what she could see, it appeared to have healed.

'Not today, leave me alone!' he shouted desperately, lunging forward in his seat as he fought with an alarmingly jerky, full-body tremor.

Afraid that he was about to lurch out of his chair, she grabbed his arms to physically support him. His strong, convulsive tremor repeatedly pushed her away but she clung on. 'You will feel more comfortable when the stitches are removed; they must be pulling by now.'

His head was shaking violently. 'You won't be able to get near them, not with me in this state,' he wailed; then he began to cry again.

Her heart twisted with sympathy for him but there didn't seem to be anything else she could do right now other than complete the task she'd been assigned. But his tremor was so strong, she felt as if she were fighting with him. 'What if I come back tomorrow, see if I can catch you at a quieter time?'

With tears streaming down his cheeks, he laughed savagely. 'You'll be lucky. It doesn't get much better than this.'

'I see,' she said, still holding onto him, shaking with his tremor.

Grace was at the door now. 'If I grab him and pin his arms a bit, you might be able to dodge between the worst of the shakes and get the stitches out bit by bit. After all, that's how Dr Bingham put them in. Having said that, Dad had just had a nasty blow to the head, so he was a bit knocked out.'

As Lara took in the terrible state the man was in, she made a rapid assessment of the situation. If his shakes wouldn't be any better tomorrow, then there was no point leaving it. 'Yes, all right, let's have a go,' she said firmly, stepping back for Grace to come alongside.

Then placing a hand on the man's shoulder, she spoke gently. 'Are you all right for me to take the stitches out, Mr Alston?'

'I don't care. Do what you want,' he replied mournfully. 'I'm sorry I'm so useless. There's nothing I can do to help you.'

She felt her throat tighten at the man's predicament, but it made her more determined than ever to get the stitches out, to do whatever she could to help her patient.

The suture scissors and forceps had already been sterilised at the surgery and wrapped in one of the surgical cloths Mrs Hewitt prepared daily in the hot oven of the Aga. Lara unravelled the cloth on the bed and laid them out. Given her patient was moving so erratically, she decided to use her fingers to grasp the sutures. So, getting as close as she could and wedging her body against the chair, she caught hold of the first suture, moving her hand with the rhythm of his head. Once she had a feel for it and knew there were in-between moments of stillness, she took her first snip with the suture scissors. She hit the mark but accidentally cut the whole of the suture knot off, leaving very little thread to grasp and pull through. Swearing silently to herself, she maintained an outward calm, knowing she could still use the forceps to draw it through. Stretching her arm, she grasped them off the sterile cloth and held them firmly in her right hand. She would need to gauge the timing to a split second, and it was far from easy. And after two failed attempts, she felt the heat of Grace's sceptical glance and the hairs at the back of her neck began to prickle. This was probably one of the most challenging first visits she had ever been given and for her own sense of competency, she had to get it right. And she knew that if she failed here, the news would spread like wildfire through the local community. Her clinical practice would be scrutinised, judged, and not just by Dr Bingham.

Breathe, just breathe, she heard in her head. And with the next try, there was no mistake; she grasped the stump of the suture and pulled it cleanly through the skin.

She had the rhythm of the task now and the remaining three stitches were expertly removed.

'All done, Mr Alston, and the wound looks fine. I'll just swab the area with some iodine solution. It might sting a bit, but it'll keep it clean.'

'Thank you, Nurse,' he murmured quietly, his strong tremors now beginning to ease a little, enabling a calmer atmosphere in the room.

Grace straightened up, pushed back her unruly strands of brown hair and smiled broadly. 'That was a bit of a tussle, Dad. But you've got a good nurse here, you have for sure. Even Nurse Beecham would have struggled with that one.'

Mr Alston was clearly exhausted, but he managed a lopsided smile. 'Are you the nurse who delivered that calf for Tom Douglas?' he asked slurrily.

'Yes, I am.' Lara laughed. 'And I don't think I'll ever be able to live it down.'

'I'm making you a brew of tea whether you like it or not,' Grace announced when they were back in the kitchen, leaving Mr Alston nodding off to sleep in his chair. She pointed to a wooden ladder-back chair at the broad kitchen table. 'Sit yourself down, Nurse Flynn.'

She had no choice but to comply but while the tea was brewing, she took out her pen and notebook and wrote up her notes. Glancing at Grace as she stood at the stove waiting for the kettle to reach full boil, she observed the tense set of her shoulders.

And when she turned with the teapot, there was a sheen of unshed tears in her eyes.

'It must be hard, seeing your father go through agony every single day,' she offered gently.

Grace heaved a sigh. 'It's like torture,' she said, placing the teapot on the table, before swiping at her eyes. 'But what else can we do? There's no choice but to take it as it comes every single day.'

'It's quite something though, what you're doing. I've never seen a Parkinson's patient with such a violent tremor.'

Grace shrugged, offered a resigned smile. 'That's exactly what Dr Bingham said. It seems that my dad holds the record... When he gets fully out of control, the doc comes to give him a morphine injection, and sometimes the liquid stuff – laudanum – can help in between, but it's just temporary respite. If only they could find a cure or something that would keep the tremors at bay.'

'I'm sorry there isn't any effective treatment. If I do hear of anything that might help, I'll let you know.'

Grace sighed as she poured the tea. 'I know you will, and Doc Bingham has said the same thing. But in the meantime, all we can do is keep going.'

'That sums it up, at least for now,' Lara said gently as she pushed her notes into her leather bag so she could give full attention.

But instead of continuing with talk of her dad's condition, Grace raised her teacup and said, 'Cheers, Nurse Flynn. And here's to keeping going.'

'Cheers,' Lara echoed, raising her own teacup.

Then came a complete change of subject. 'Do you like dancing?' Grace asked as she leant across the table.

Taken aback, Lara replied, 'Yes, as a matter of fact, I do,' instantly catching her breath when she remembered the last time she'd danced had been with Patrick in the Adelphi Hotel. It made her feel a bit queasy just thinking about it.

'It's just that, on Saturday night, there's a dance at the village hall. The farmers never want to join in and most of the other men are either too drunk or just clumsy, so mostly the women dance with one another. Are you up for it, Nurse Flynn?'

Grace's amber eyes crinkled at the corners as she smiled. Despite all her troubles, the woman had a flame burning brightly inside of her and Lara caught the warmth of it.

'Yes, I'm up for it.' She grinned. 'Of course I'll come to the dance.'

'Fabulous.' Grace smiled, raising her teacup in another cheers before swigging the remains.

As Lara placed her cup down on the table, an older woman with bright eyes and unruly hair just like Grace's bustled in through the door with a large wicker basket over one arm.

'Oh, Aunt Agnes, this is our new district nurse, the one who's replaced Nurse Beecham. She's done an outstanding job removing Dad's stitches.'

'Well, blow me down with a feather,' Agnes said. 'I didn't think anybody would be able to get those blighters out.' The woman was shaking her head and smiling as she placed her basket squarely on the table. 'We've all been wondering who we'd get after Nancy Beecham retired; some of the oldies have been really worrying about it. But now I can tell them we seem to have found ourselves a good one.'

Lara felt her cheeks flush pink and hoped she could live up to Aunt Agnes's strong recommendation.

The woman was now busily removing the blue and white tea-cloth which covered the basket and pulling out two large tins. 'I've made you some more scones, a large Dundee cake and plenty of those thick shortbread biscuits the men like. We can't ever have too many baked goods when it's hay time.'

'Very true,' Grace said, pushing back her chair, rising from the table. 'Speaking of which, I need to go up to the top meadow. The men will be arriving soon to cut the grass, and I need to sharpen my scythe and get up there to help.'

Lara rose to her feet, already saying her goodbye to Agnes before she walked out into the warm sunlight beside Grace.

'Don't forget the dance next weekend,' she called as she pushed her feet into her mucky work boots, then pretended to waltz.

'I won't.' Lara laughed, raising a hand in farewell as she headed towards her bicycle.

It gave her a warm glow; she'd never met anyone with such a lightness of being as Grace. She already knew they were going to be friends.

Still smiling, she wheeled her bicycle past the farm dog barking and rattling its chain, then headed back down the rough track.

About halfway along, two young men with bronzed faces and scythes over their shoulders were walking towards her; each of them touched their caps in greeting as they passed by and the taller one, a handsome fella, offered a warm smile, but neither of them said a word. A few strides further on, she heard them laughing, the sound of it rising to the clear blue sky. Maybe they were making fun of her, the new nurse fresh from the city... But right now, it didn't matter, because the sound of their laughter, mingled with the afterglow of spending time with Grace, made her even more joyful amid a glorious summer morning.

9

_____

'Nurse Flynn!' Bingham roared the next morning, slamming the telephone receiver down so hard, it rocked the small hallway table.

'Yes, Doctor?' she replied, trying but failing to keep the shock from her voice as she stepped out of the kitchen she'd just entered.

His face was bright red, he could barely speak, he was so agitated. 'It was you, wasn't it, who took those stitches out for James Alston yesterday?'

'Yes, it was,' she replied, keeping her voice even, trying not to flinch as she stepped towards him along the corridor. Aware of the silence that had fallen in the kitchen behind her, it gave her some comfort knowing that Mrs Hewitt would be listening and could intervene if necessary.

'What the blazes did you do? His sister just rang. She couldn't tell me the proper story, she was so upset, but the poor man's bleeding all over the show.'

Her stomach clenched with anxiety, her mind instantly flitting back over the procedure she'd performed yesterday. Was it possible she'd missed something, or taken the stitches out too early?

She made her voice firm as she replied. 'The wound was well healed; it was a bit tricky working around his Parkinson's symptoms, but I removed all of the stitches... There's nothing else to report.'

Bingham almost growled. 'You must have taken them out too soon. There's no other explanation. What the heck else did they *not* teach you at the Liverpool Royal Infirmary?'

She was about to falter but then she sensed Mrs Hewitt emerging from the kitchen behind her. 'There must be some other explanation, Dr Bingham, surely there must,' the housekeeper soothed.

'No time for that,' Bingham called, grabbing his medical bag from the floor and his checked trilby from a hook on the wall. 'I want you outside and ready to go in thirty seconds, Nurse Flynn.'

She raced upstairs to collect her hat and her district nurse's bag and, with a sympathetic nod from Mrs Hewitt, she was out through the back door before Bingham could fully reverse the Rover out of its garage. Sliding deftly into the passenger seat, she forced a strictly professional demeanour. Whatever the cause, their patient needed urgent attention so what mattered most was that he receive timely intervention.

Seeing the set of Bingham's jaw and the still bright-red spots of anger on his cheeks, she knew it was best to remain silent. Even the sound of his mildly stertorous breathing set her teeth on edge as he revved the engine and raced away from the surgery at some speed. Narrowly missing Sam Collins as he stepped out of his butcher's shop, Bingham swore under his breath and when they swerved down the hill towards the hump-backed bridge, her stomach flipped as the car bounced over it. As she clung to the leather seat with both hands, he accelerated out of the village and as the hedges and drystone walls whistled by, she was grateful she hadn't had time to consume any solid food at breakfast.

Bounding and bumping over the farm track she'd walked over with her bicycle so carefully yesterday, she saw sheep leaping out of the way and more than a dozen brown hens almost lost their lives.

'This is a medical emergency,' he growled, almost under his breath. 'The local livestock come second.'

In a spray of grit, they came to a halt. Lara felt a little dizzy, but she leapt out of the car to the sound of the grizzled farm dog in the yard barking fiercely. Running now towards the house, she could see Aunt Agnes at the door gesturing her in as Bingham huffed and puffed behind.

Alarmed, she noted Agnes's tear-stained face, and her white apron spattered with bright-red blood. 'I can't stand it when he's struggling like this,' she sobbed as Lara ran towards Mr Alston's room.

'Try not to worry – a bit of blood goes a long way,' she offered over her shoulder, hoping she was right to be optimistic. The sound of Grace's voice, soothing and gentle, helped her to collect herself.

'Hello, Mr Alston,' she called from the doorway, sucking in a breath, slowing right down before she fully entered the room. The farmer was thrashing in his chair, groaning, blood on his face, on his pyjama top, and on the floor. Grace was clinging to him and pressing a white handkerchief to his head as he shook and swayed. Her eyes were wide. She gasped a greeting. 'This has happened because he won't do as he's told. I keep telling him he needs to wait for help,' she said forcefully.

Before Lara could ask any questions, Bingham stepped around her, wanting to be the first to examine. 'Let me inspect the wound please, Grace,' he said authoritatively.

In the moment he placed his medical bag down on the bed, Lara clicked that Grace was pressing the blood-soaked handkerchief to the opposite side of where she'd removed the stitches from yesterday.

A bubble of relief blossomed in her chest.

'Now, let's see what we've got here,' Bingham was saying, his voice kindly, professional.

She saw the doctor tip his head to one side. 'It looks like all of the stitches have—'

'No, Dr Bingham, it's not the old wound that's the problem,' Grace said. 'He's only gone and tumbled again, caught the other side this time.'

Lara saw Bingham's shoulders drop; she couldn't help but feel a moment of triumph.

'Oh, I see,' she heard him say, then clearing his throat, 'So he's split his head open yet again... And from what I can see, it's more of a skin flap than an incision. So it looks as if we might get away without any stitches this time.'

'I told you,' Mr Alston groaned, Grace still clinging to him, trying to hold him steady. 'I said it was only a scratch.'

'It's more than a scratch, Jim,' Bingham said firmly. 'Agnes was right to call us.'

'Aye, but you could have sent that lovely young nurse who came yesterday. She's not a doctor but she knows what she's doing,' he groaned.

'Oh, Nurse Flynn is here also.' Bingham glanced back over

his shoulder but didn't meet her eye. 'And do you know what, Jim? I'll let her sort you out with a dressing for this laceration. A bit of pressure on there and it should all be fine.'

'Tell him, will you, Doctor, tell him to use his bell and call for help when he needs to get up from his chair,' Grace urged.

'I think you know that, don't you, Jim?' Bingham said, his voice low, a rounded, understanding tone that Lara hadn't heard him use before.

Mr Alston growled an unintelligible response and then he was shaking even more violently. She couldn't help but feel for him and instantly, the concern for her patient displaced any sense of injustice or ill-feeling towards her boss. Bingham was stepping back now and pulling his bag from the bed, lured towards the kitchen and Aunt Agnes's voice promising a cup of tea and a slice of toast.

She felt freer once he'd retreated and after placing her own medical bag on the bed, she had some swabs and a clean dressing ready in moments. 'If you can hold onto him, Grace, I'll see what I can do.' Then to Mr Alston, 'I'm going to clean with some iodine solution first, so it'll sting. Then I need to apply a dressing and a firm bandage to keep it in place.'

'Do what you need to do,' he groaned miserably.

With Grace's support, the procedure was performed in between Mr Alston's strong tremors and wild lunges, and he was made as comfortable as possible. As soon as she was done, she left Grace settling him with a few drops of laudanum and walked back to the kitchen to find Bingham rising from his chair, 'Thank you for the tea and the bite to eat, Agnes. I have a full surgery this morning so we need to get back right away.'

Lara supressed a groan and offered a resigned smile; the smell of buttered toast was so tantalising, it made her empty stomach growl with hunger. She fought against the notion that

Bingham was making sure she didn't get any breakfast, and he was still somehow punishing her. But she knew she could grab a quick bite to eat when she got back to the surgery and of course, what he'd claimed about the clinic rang true – their patients did always come first.

However, as he strode ahead, she knew by the square set of his shoulders that there was still an adversarial air about him. Clearly, he didn't cope well with being proved wrong. She didn't know what she was expecting from him now, not an apology; given her previous experience with senior doctors, she'd never expect that. But there wasn't even a nod or a glance; he just marched off in front. She prickled with indignation. *For goodness' sake, acknowledge you jumped to the wrong conclusion.* The snapping and barking of the yard dog set her even more on edge, but the moment felt rescued when she witnessed Bingham unwittingly catch his shoe in a fresh cow pat.

She held back a smile as she slipped into the seat next to him, clicking the door shut and placing her medical bag on her lap. He cleared his throat and for a moment, she thought he was going to speak but instead, he turned the key and revved the Rover into life. They sped out of the yard with hens flapping and clucking and even the farm dog falling momentarily silent. Their progress down the farm track and along the narrow lanes was only marginally slower than their emergency dash, so she found herself clinging to the leather seat once more. Bingham leant over the steering wheel, all his attention focused on cornering or veering to prevent the brush of the hedgerow on his precious black car. She was beginning to feel a little queasy, then she was thrown violently forward as he swore loudly and rammed on the brakes to let a stray sheep cross the road.

In the moments they were waiting, she could almost hear his mind ticking over and she half wondered if he was trying to form some kind of apology. But when he spoke, his voice sounded loud, confident, within the confines of the car. 'I was supposed to be making a visit to the cottage of an elderly patient this morning. But I haven't got time now, not with all these shenanigans.' And she knew he had no understanding whatsoever of how unjust his treatment of her had been.

He glanced at her then.

Could *he* be expecting an apology from *her*?

She felt her jaw clench and she gripped her medical bag tightly. She would not be intimidated by this man. But she also knew from past experience with other senior doctors that he would perceive her as the wrongdoer if her voice came across as anything other than professional. 'Do you want me to see the patient for you?' she offered calmly, her tone of voice impeccable.

He didn't reply at once.

She kept her cool, feeling the tension ricocheting between them, enhanced by the confines of the car.

He cleared his throat as he slipped the car into gear and moved off at a much steadier pace. 'Yes, that's an idea. The patient just needs his pulse and blood pressure taken... I assume you can manage that.'

She drew a slow breath, determined not to rise to the barbed comment.

'Yes, that's well within my field of competence,' she replied, her voice clear-cut. 'You will, however, need to lend me your sphygmomanometer. We nurses don't tend to have our own; they are quite an expense.'

He grunted an affirmative response.

'Could you give me some detail of the case?' she asked, using her most professional voice.

'Mr Daniel Makepeace is an eighty-eight-year-old gentleman

who is cared for by his niece, Esther, a farmer's wife who lives just outside the village. He has advanced heart failure which has recently deteriorated, requiring an increase of his daily dose of digitalis. He needs regular pulse and blood pressure checks.' His voice softened then, and she gave him credit for that. 'The poor man lost his wife suddenly, five years ago... He's still grieving for her and rarely gets out of his bed.'

She felt for the elderly man instantly.

'No doubt he'll tell you all about it; he's very accepting of all and sundry.'

'Even outsiders like me?' she offered with a wry smile.

'Yes, even you,' he huffed, bringing the car to an abrupt halt at the edge of the village. 'This is the house,' he said, pointing to a single-storey cottage with a steeply angled, corrugated iron roof. 'The sphyg is on the back seat. Be careful with it; it's brand new, and as you've already pointed out, these pieces of equipment are damned expensive. Just knock on the door and go straight in. Then, when you're done, you'll have to walk back up to the surgery but it's a short distance.'

'Righto,' she called, already out of the car and opening the rear door to retrieve the shiny, leather case that contained the blood pressure monitor.

As Bingham drove away, she walked to the door of the cottage with her medical bag in her hand and the blood pressure monitor tucked under her arm. The whitewashed walls were patchy and fading in places but the low building, with its sharply pitched roof and pink roses growing along the wall, was very picturesque. Walking briskly up the stone-flagged path, she caught a delicious waft of scent from the roses. After knocking and entering as instructed, she announced her presence and found herself in a dark, low-beamed sitting room with an empty, soot-blackened fireplace.

'Mr Makepeace?' she called, adjusting the sphyg under her arm.

'In here,' a gentle voice croaked from an adjoining room with a boarded wooden door propped open.

'Hello, I'm the new nurse, Lara Flynn,' she announced, stepping through to see an ancient-looking man with a thick head of snow-white hair. He was so thin, he appeared almost lost amid a wood-framed double bed which was set beside an open window with a view of the fields and the trees. Even as she stood, a cheeky robin with a bright-red breast came to perch on the sill.

'He's looking for some breakfast crumbs,' the man smiled, turning his head to reveal a single tooth.

'Oh, so that's his game, is it?' She laughed.

The bird, disturbed, instantly took flight.

'I seem to have scared him off, sorry about that.'

'Don't you worry, Nurse... he'll be back as soon as you're gone.' Mr Makepeace was still smiling, his dark eyes twinkling with good humour.

'I need to apologise on behalf of Dr Bingham. We had an emergency call first thing and he had to head straight back to the surgery... so you've got me instead,' she offered, scrutinising his lined face to judge his reaction.

His smile broadened, making the single tooth even more of a feature. 'Don't you be worrying about that, lass. I've been hoping to meet the new nurse sooner rather than later.' He stretched out a bony arm to shake her hand and she returned his smile unreservedly.

'I see you've got the contraption,' he sighed as she carefully laid the sphygmomanometer on the bed. 'They always have problems reading mine... They say I've hardly got a pulse.' He laughed hoarsely, setting off a coughing fit.

'Let's see what we can do,' she replied once his cough had settled. 'If there is a pulse, don't you worry, I will find it.'

His shoulders twitched in a gesture of a laugh.

As she stood holding his left wrist to feel for the radial pulse, she breathed in the warm morning air from the open window. In fact, there was no glass, and it wasn't so much a window as a set of wooden shutters that had been opened inwards.

As the tips of her fingers located the delicate, irregular thread of his pulse, she waited to have it secure before she timed it. Mr Makepeace was lying back against his pillows with his head turned to look out to the meadow. And as she followed his line of gaze, a large, brown and white cow ambled slowly into view, lazily swishing its tail. The creature dropped its head and started to crop the grass.

She gently grasped her fob watch and angled her head to measure his pulse for a full minute. The sound of the cow steadily munching the grass, the low drone of summer bees out through the window and Mr Makepeace's slightly wheezy breath were an unexpected yet soothing backdrop to the silent counting of her patient's heartbeat. The pulse wasn't slow, coming in at seventy beats per minute, so there was no problem with him continuing to take the digitalis for his heart failure. But it was so thready, it felt like the heartbeat of a tiny bird, and she wondered how he still managed to cling to life.

'That's fine,' she said with a reassuring smile. 'Now I just need to take your blood pre— Oh!' she gasped, shocked to see that the brown and white cow had come right up to the window and was now staring straight in, its glassy eyes and sharp horns right there at the other side of the bed.

'Don't you worry, Nurse,' Mr Makepeace said. 'This one won't do you any harm... It's the bulls you have to worry about.'

As if in response, the creature lowed quietly and as if sensing her disapproval, it turned and plodded away.

'Do you not mind them coming to the window like that?' she asked, still feeling a little nervous in case the sharp-horned creature returned.

He gave a low chuckle, fixed her with his bright eyes. 'I moved here when me and my Martha were first married. I've lived over sixty years in this cottage and livestock were in the field well before that. And what's more, they'll still be there after I'm gone. We're the ones who should be asking whether they mind *us* being here.'

'I see what you mean,' she murmured, instantly drawn back through time to an impression of the life that he'd lived. It felt as if she'd already fallen under the spell of this quiet-spoken, gentle man.

'We moved in here as newlyweds in the summer of 1873 after the tenant – another farm labourer – had just moved out. I carried my Martha over the threshold, she was the bonniest young woman in the village, and she was laughing and giggling. We were so happy...'

She gulped, swallowed hard to hold back tears.

'You don't appreciate it when you're young, such happiness as that. It's only when you're old and you've not got many years left on this earth that you've got time to lie in bed and think about it... but those early years here together...'

His voice broke then, and he raised a bony hand to wipe tears from his cheeks.

He cleared his throat, gave a ragged chuckle, but his voice was still thick with emotion. 'One morning, we woke up and there'd been a high wind during the night. The shutters had blown wide open and one of the farm horses that were in that field at that time, it had shoved its head right through over the bed. My Martha, she screamed out loud when she saw it, but the horse just snorted and nodded its head.'

She could picture the scene; she was completely caught up in his story and she was laughing with him now.

'And in winter, we sometimes used to wake up with the bottom of the bed covered in snow...' His voice had drifted quieter now, his eyes far away. 'But we never felt the cold back then; we just laughed and gathered it up in our hands and threw it out to the meadow. Nothing troubled us... All I needed was the land beneath my feet, the sky above, and my darling wife beside me.'

She felt her throat tighten and to steady herself, she reached out to lay a gentle hand on his arm. 'What happened to your Martha?'

His eyes grew shiny with tears again and for a moment, she wished she hadn't asked the question. But then he spoke again. 'She passed five years ago, in her sleep... I woke to find her lying there, still beautiful even though her hair was silver and her face was lined with wrinkles. She was always a young lass in my eyes. But she'd left me that night while I'd slept on. Doc Bingham... he told me after that she'd had a stroke, a big one, and she wouldn't have felt a thing. I thanked the lord that she didn't suffer... but I still miss her every single day.' He heaved a sigh, sounding wrung out.

Lara swallowed hard, drew a slow breath to steady herself. 'Thank you for telling me these things, Mr Makepeace; it's good to hear your story. You and Martha must have been so happy together.'

The corners of his eyes wrinkled upwards as he smiled. 'Aye, we were lucky... and I'll be luckier still when I'm able to leave this world and be with her in heaven.'

She gave his arm a pat.

'Well, before that day comes, Mr Makepeace, I've been instructed to measure your blood pressure.'

He groaned gently. 'Go on then, I don't want you getting into trouble with Dr Bingham. He's a good doctor but he can be a right bad-tempered so-and-so.'

She bit her lip to stop herself from laughing at his very apt description of the senior doctor. Then she opened the leather case that contained the blood pressure cuff, applied it gently but firmly around his upper arm and inflated it. As she listened through her stethoscope to the tenuous, irregular bump of his pulse, she couldn't help but imagine his broken heart struggling to keep going.

Even as she completed her reading, Mr Makepeace was already dozing off to sleep, so after removing the cuff and slipping it back into the leather case, she straightened his bed sheet, checked he looked comfortable, then quietly said goodbye. With one final glance to the sunny meadow beyond the wooden-shuttered window, she picked up her bag, tucked the sphygmomanometer under her arm and made her way back out to the street.

Closing the cottage door gently behind her, she stood for a few moments on the worn stone step to breathe the scent of the pink roses. And she imagined Daniel all those years ago with his young bride in his arms as he carried her over the threshold. She felt a shiver run through her and uncanny as it was, she was certain she could hear the tinkle of their laughter. It made her feel the sadness of loss but also appreciate how lucky Daniel and Martha had been to live so happily together for all those years. Maybe one day, she would be able to find love like that for herself but right now, she couldn't even think that far ahead.

Leaving the cottage behind, she made her way up the ancient, cobbled street towards the surgery with her medical bag in one hand and Bingham's sphyg clutched in the other. And as she walked by the low doorways of the stone cottages with their window boxes crammed with pink and red geraniums, she heard the clatter of pots and lively chatter from within.

Halfway up as she passed the red pillar box, the bell on the post-office door tinkled and a customer stepped out. It was Lizzie Cronshaw, about to post a letter.

'How are you doing, and how is Sue?' Lara asked, pausing to listen to news of the little girl's progress, and it was so good to hear the burns were healing nicely.

As they continued to walk together, they chatted some more, and it felt reassuring to note that Lizzie was managing well while Sue was in hospital. But when she asked after Ed, she saw an instant guarded look in Lizzie's eyes and straight away, Lizzie made her excuses and walked over the road towards the butcher's shop. It brought back the same stab of concern Lara had had on her first day, when she'd met the young mother in the waiting room.

She was almost back at the surgery now and she tried to regain the calm she'd felt during her visit to Daniel Makepeace. But just as she began to relax, she almost walked straight into a white-haired woman heading briskly towards her.

'Sorry,' she muttered, offering an apologetic smile, feeling a jolt when she recognised the elderly patient who'd been leaving the surgery on the day she'd arrived. Instantly, the woman glanced her up and down and stepped by without a word.

Can't win 'em all, she mused as she increased her pace, eager to leave behind the sound of the elderly woman warmly greeting another villager who replied, 'Oh hello, Miss Frobisher. Yes, I'm very well thank you... Nice to see you out and about in the village.'

At least she had the woman's name now so if she had the

option, she knew who to avoid if she was given a choice of patients. But then again, maybe it was best to take the bull by the horns.

At the sound of a commotion further up the street and the rough shout of a man's voice, to her horror, a whole herd of sheep turned the corner at the top of the hill and headed straight down towards her. She glanced behind to see Miss Frobisher entering the Post Office and firmly closing the door, and her brain clicked over whether she had time to run back. In the seconds she lost thinking about it, it was too late. All she could do was flatten her body against the stone wall of a house. She stood frozen, gripping her medical bag with both hands as the bleating, woolly creatures approached. They were moving so fast, they were almost upon her already. Desperately, she wondered if she should just close her eyes and let it happen. Then the house door behind her clicked open and a strong arm dragged her up onto the step, knocking the sphygmomanometer from her grasp and sending it flying into the street. She screamed in horror at the sight of Bingham's expensive piece of equipment about to be trampled by a herd of sheep, and she was ready to jump down and grab it, but the sheep were already there doing irreparable damage to the pristine leather case. Almost as bad, when she turned to thank the person who had rescued her, she found the young vet, Leo Sullivan. He seemed very amused and began to chuckle as he joked about city girls let loose in the countryside. Then when he realised she'd dropped the sphyg and it was Dr Bingham's, he laughed even louder.

She felt her cheeks flush with fury. 'This is no laughing matter!' she shouted as the sheep continued to trot by, bleating and jostling.

'Doc Bingham will understand,' he called in her ear above

the noise of the sheep, as the young, red-faced farmer driving them shouted a cheery hello and raised his stick in Leo's direction.

'Hello, Martin,' Leo called jovially, still grinning.

Lara envied his light-hearted approach to the world, she truly did. But it frustrated her that he never seemed to take anything seriously. Fair enough, this was a minor issue compared to most things they were both used to dealing with. But there was something about Leo Sullivan she couldn't quite put her finger on, and he'd sowed the seeds of that when he'd turned up late to deliver that calf on her first day. To his credit though, once the sheep had all trotted by, he seemed to sense her genuine anguish, and he stepped down into the street to retrieve the scratched and dinted leather case. Dusting it off and wiping away traces of sheep muck with his shirt sleeve, he handed it back to her. 'It's in a sturdy case, so it'll all be fine in there,' he said, offering a tentative smile. 'Just a bit of cosmetic damage, that's all.'

She felt a twist of despair; already she knew how particular Bingham was about his medical equipment and general cleanliness, and they'd already got off on the wrong foot. She groaned as she turned the leather case over in her hand to make her own assessment of the damage. If she gave it a proper clean, maybe it would look better. But given how sharp-eyed and irascible Bingham was, she knew he'd spot the damage, and she'd end up in even more trouble.

Feeling Leo's eyes still on her, she looked up at him and felt surprised by the concerned scrunch of his brow. It helped cut through her anxiety and when he smiled, the slight twist of his mouth intrigued her.

'Thank you for helping me... but I need to get back to the

surgery,' she breathed, feeling jangled as she stepped across the cobbled street with a studied air of independence.

When he called out to say she was very welcome, she glanced over her shoulder to meet his wide-eyed gaze and it sent a prickle of sensation right through her. And as she raised her hand then turned away, her semblance of composure was completely undermined by a flush of blood that made her cheeks burn.

10

'Where the heck have you been?' Mrs Hewitt met her head-on as soon as she walked in through the front door. 'His lordship's been having conniptions... Good job he was called out to a case at Ridgetown hospital.'

She felt a jolt, as if she were waking from a dream; she must have looked unsettled because immediately, Mrs Hewitt softened her tone. 'Don't fret, Nurse Flynn. I'm on your side and I know how busy you've been.'

Instantly, she felt relieved, but she'd been ready to defend herself because the reason she'd spent longer with Daniel Makepeace was because it had been as important to listen to his story as it was to record his pulse and blood pressure. These were the things that mattered for a patient's and a nurse's well-being. And of course there was nothing she could do about being caught in the mass movement of sheep through the village. But it niggled her knowing Bingham was still on the warpath.

'I heard the baaing and the bleating; it must have been the woolly backs that delayed you,' the housekeeper offered over her shoulder as she walked ahead. 'But you'd best get yourself out quick before the doctor comes back.'

As soon as they were in the kitchen, Mrs H handed her the list of visits then pointed to a bacon butty on the table. 'Take that with you. No young nurse should go without her breakfast... Now, shoo! Vamoose!'

'Just one thing,' Lara said, dropping her head for a second then holding out the damaged blood pressure monitor. 'Dr Bingham lent me this brand-new sphyg to use on Mr Makepeace. I accidentally dropped it in the street when the sheep were coming, and they trampled it... I think it's spoiled.' Her voice sounded forlorn even to her own ears.

The housekeeper grasped the leather case, turned it over in her hands to inspect both sides. She furrowed her brow and spoke gently. 'Leave it with me, Nurse Flynn. I'll give it a bit of spit and polish and it'll look like new.'

Lara doubted it would, and she was still anxious. But she felt better when Mrs Hewitt told her the piece of equipment was only Bingham's third best, the most highly prized being those in their shiny wooden boxes in his clinic room.

'Now, go, go, before he comes back,' she urged. 'Today is already chaos and we haven't even got to lunchtime yet. Marion's only just got off on her visits after helping in clinic. Angus is running behind, so no change there. In fact, I'll be having words with that young man; he was far too late back from The Fleece again last night.'

Mrs Hewitt's rant helped to ground her; she was ready to tackle her visits now and scanning down the list when the telephone jangled loudly. She waited, just in case, and when the housekeeper's body tightened and she raised a delaying hand, she knew instantly this was an urgent call and she needed to wait for further instruction.

'So, you've found her on the floor. Is she breathing?'

Lara strained her ears to catch the tinny response: 'I think so... but she's not a good colour.'

She sucked in a breath, spoke firmly. 'Who is it? I need to go *right* now.'

Mrs Hewitt gasped. 'It's Miss Dunderdale: the vicar's found her on the floor and she's struggling to breathe. You go, go right now. I'll call for the ambulance.'

Already running, Lara grabbed her leather bag, exited through the back door and leapt on her bicycle. With her heart hammering in her chest, she sped down the hill, almost taking off over the humpbacked bridge. Pedalling furiously on the gritty lane, her legs burned with pain, but she was consumed by the urgent call and pushed on.

As soon as she reached Brook House, she rapidly dismounted the bicycle and let it fall to the ground. Grabbing her medical bag from the basket, she ran in through the wide-open door and pelted down the hallway. An elderly man wearing a dog collar dodged out of the kitchen, his face ashen and his breath coming quick. He seemed unable to speak but he beckoned to her urgently with his hand, so she pushed straight past and in through the door.

Miss Dunderdale's face was deep blue.

Lara threw herself to her knees, pressed two fingers to the side of her neck to check for a carotid pulse, all the while scanning for signs of breathing.

No pulse.

Her own heart skipped a beat, then she palpated again. Still no pulse.

As her brain clutched at next steps, Miss Dunderdale sucked in a single shallow breath. It could have been her last gasp for all Lara knew, but she took it as a positive sign. Instantly, she tipped back her patient's head, gave her mouth a quick sweep with a finger to check if she was choking. All clear, so she began the kiss of life, and with every breath, she watched for the rise and fall of her patient's chest. Still no signs of her regaining consciousness, but Lara just kept going, repeating the breaths again and again. Just when she thought all was lost, Miss Dunderdale's body twitched and she made a gurgling sound. It sent an arrow shot of hope through her. And when her patient coughed, then sucked in a shallow breath, Lara groaned with relief as she rolled her over onto her side.

Pressing two fingers to her neck, she felt the first thready bound of a carotid pulse and it filled her with pure joy.

'Is she going to live?' the vicar asked.

She glanced up to see his pale eyes brimming with tears.

'I can't say for sure, but she's making a good effort to do so.'

He pressed his palms together, gazed up to the ceiling and offered a silent prayer.

Miss Dunderdale was blinking her eyes open now, starting to moan. It was a good sign.

'Please, can you find a cushion or a pillow for her head, and a blanket?'

The vicar nodded, turned and exited the room as quickly as he could, given he was stiff-legged and slow-moving.

She spoke softly to her patient. 'You're going to be fine, just fine.'

Miss Dunderdale groaned, then with a whisper of breath, she said, 'I want Dr Bingham, not...'

'Of course you do,' she murmured, unable to hold back a smile. It was a good sign her patient still had her fighting spirit.

When the vicar returned with a moth-eaten velvet cushion and a dusty blanket, it struck her once more how dilapidated this way of living was for Miss Dunderdale. It still intrigued her to know how a seemingly well-born woman had ended up like this. And she knew it was probably too much of a stretch because rarely did people climb out of the ruts they made for themselves, but she truly hoped her patient would take what had happened here today as a sign that she needed to change how she lived. Because despite the difficulties she was still having with some of the villagers, she sensed good humour and deep generosity at the heart of the community, and it troubled her that Miss Dunderdale wasn't currently benefitting from any of that. In fact, the vicar and Dr Bingham were probably the only visitors she ever got here at the house. And it felt sad.

As if grasping the drift of her thoughts, Miss Dunderdale's weakened, thready voice called out, 'Are you still there, Reverend Hartley?'

He leant down to her then. 'Yes, Celia, I'm staying right here until the ambulance arrives.'

'That's good,' she sighed, then closed her eyes.

On her knees beside her patient, Lara checked her pulse and breathing every few minutes and took note of skin colour – her lips, earlobes and fingertips were still blue, but her face was pinking up a bit now.

Her patient groaned as if in pain and rather alarmingly, the vicar began to lower himself to his thin knees on the hard kitchen floor.

'Thank you,' Miss Dunderdale breathed as the Reverend took her slim hand. Given his level of concern, it seemed he'd known her for a very long time. Moments later though, he was wheezing and needing to shift his position, so Lara assisted him up from the floor with a loud creak of his arthritic knees.

'Stay with me, Edwin,' Miss Dunderdale gasped.

Lara noted his slight fluster, maybe at her using his Christian name, but instantly, he bent at the waist and reached down to give her hand a squeeze. 'Bless you, Celia. Of course I will stay with you until the ambulance comes.'

It was time to check Miss Dunderdale's vital signs again and it made her own heart skip a beat when she realised her patient's already thready pulse was more erratic and her lips had developed a deeper bluish tinge. Clearly, her patient was holding a very fine balance between life and death after what had probably been a heart attack. Where was that ambulance? How long did it take to drive from Ridgetown?

She was palpating her patient's pulse almost continually until she heard the clang of the ambulance bell. And as soon as she glanced up to Reverend Hartley and murmured, 'The ambulance is coming,' he volunteered to stand outside so there'd be no mistake as to which house it was. Left alone with her patient, she gently grasped her hand, told her help would be here soon. Half expecting her, even in her collapsed state, to object, she felt a lump in her throat when Miss Dunderdale squeezed her hand and murmured a ragged, almost inaudible, 'Thank you, Nurse.'

'It's all part of the service,' she replied gently, wishing she'd been able to say something more meaningful. Then, with a wry smile, she wondered if Miss Dunderdale thought it was Nurse Beecham who was holding her hand. Though of course, as long as her patient felt secure, none of that mattered right now.

At the sound of rapid footsteps in the hallway, she prepared herself to hand over to the ambulance crew. And it threw her when the first person through the door was Dr Bingham, followed by two elderly ambulance men in navy-blue peaked caps.

'Oh, so it is you,' Bingham offered.

'Yes,' she said, then immediately, she was in full flow, giving an account of the incident and detailing pulse and respiration rates.

As he listened, Bingham went down to his knees to assess Miss Dunderdale's condition. His hair was dishevelled, and he sounded slightly out of breath, but there was no fluster about him. He was calm and fully present, and she felt that same buzz she'd had when they'd worked together on little Sue Cronshaw. It struck her then that he was absolutely in his element with these emergency cases, and it reminded her of those senior doctors at the Royal who'd served during the Great War and of course, that could be it; he might well have been an army surgeon.

She must have been smiling to herself because she caught his puzzled glance.

'You've done well here today, Nurse Flynn. But don't let it go to your head,' he said crisply. 'You need to buckle down and get on with your other visits.'

She heard his words, but they didn't unsettle her... Of course she wouldn't let it go to her head. As an experienced nurse, she was used to moving on to the next patient, whatever was thrown at her. And right now, given she was still buzzing with adrenaline from the urgent call and the knowledge she'd probably helped to save someone's life, she was almost completely immune to anything Bingham had to offer.

After Miss Dunderdale had been transferred to a stretcher and loaded into the back of the ambulance with Dr Bingham in attendance, the vehicle bumped slowly away. She then helped Reverend Hartley to lock up with the large, iron key they'd found on a hook behind the door. As he said his goodbyes and wobbled away on his heavy, ancient-looking iron bicycle, she pulled her own bike up from the ground and retrieved the list of visits from her pocket. She was running behind time now, so she'd be on catch-up for the rest of the morning. But as she pedalled briskly away with the warm breeze on her face, it

refreshed her and lifted her spirits so high – on top of the boost
of adrenaline she'd had from attending an emergency – that she
felt ready to float up to the blue sky.

Thankfully, the rest of her morning visits were routine and
they went well, but she was late back to the surgery for lunch
and that put her even further behind with the afternoon list.

Returning at the end of the day, she expected to hear the
chatter of voices around the kitchen table, but all was quiet.
When she walked in, Mrs Hewitt got up and offered the
semblance of a smile and said a little bit too brightly, 'I should
have told you at lunch, Nurse Flynn, but you were in and out so
fast. You did very well with Miss Dunderdale this morning.'

'Yes, good work,' Marion offered, jumping up and scraping
her chair so loudly, Tiddles the cat yowled with shock and shot
out through the door.

'Thank you.' Lara smiled as Marion gave her a hug.

But the mood still felt flat and when she looked over to
Bingham at the head of the table, he offered the merest twitch of
a nod – he was stony-faced and preoccupied. Angus sat ramrod
straight in his chair, eating silently; he looked exhausted and the
edgy way he avoided Mrs Hewitt's gaze was enough to tell her
that she had probably had the chat she'd been threatening
about spending too much time in The Fleece. However, there
was still something unexplained about the frisson in the room
and as Mrs Hewitt placed a sizeable helping of chicken pie in
front of her, she felt her stomach constrict even though she was
very hungry. Sneaking a peak back at Bingham, she noted once
again his hostile expression and remembered the damaged
blood pressure monitor.

As if picking up on her thought, Mrs Hewitt mouthed across
the table, 'It's nothing to do with you.'

Bingham lifted his head as if he'd caught a whisper of something, but with the steely glare he shot in Angus's direction, she was sure that what the housekeeper was telling her was the truth.

Marion, sensing her disquiet, opened her eyes wide, nodded almost imperceptibly in Angus's direction, then swiftly drew a finger across her throat.

Oh dear, Lara thought, knowing what it was like to be on the wrong side of the senior physician.

She felt sorry for Angus then and it made her consider him in a different light. Not so much the carefree, young doctor who was given plenty of leeway by his supervisor but a young man who was also struggling to keep on the best side of Bingham in just the same way that she was.

When Marion winked at her and snuck a cheeky smile across the table, it made her relax a little, but still the kitchen was uncomfortably quiet. She wished she could think of something to say to break the ice, but nothing would come. Instead, she studiously worked her way through the chicken pie. Every now and then, she glanced up to catch Marion's eyes twinkling back at her, but she still felt sorry that Angus was so miserable. Then again, maybe Bingham had just cause to be angry with him because if that weren't the case, surely Mrs Hewitt would have intervened on the young doctor's behalf.

There was no way to work out what was going on, so she kept her head down as she ate. Once she'd finished and placed her knife and fork neatly together on her plate, Mrs Hewitt rose from the table and announced the arrival of one of her special rice puddings. Lara felt the whole table draw a slower breath and instantly, the tension began to ease. And as Marion smiled and leant forward to rest her elbows on the table, it felt as if the pieces of a puzzle had clicked back into place.

11

Waking abruptly to the brisk, tinny sound of her alarm clock, Lara felt annoyed as she always did when the device had woken her because her eyes hadn't automatically pinged open by half past six. Lightly cursing and still a little bleary-eyed, she hopped out of bed and pulled her paisley-patterned robe around her shoulders so she could make her visit to the bathroom opposite. *Damn*, somebody was already in there and she daren't venture downstairs to the cloakroom because that was Bingham's domain. He occupied a large, ground-floor room that no one entered apart from Mrs Hewitt. Angus was also down there in accommodation that Marion had described as poky, smelly and not much more than a box room.

Slipping back into her room just as the bathroom door clicked open, her sharp ears caught the unmistakeable edge of a sob. It had to be Mrs H or Marion, and she didn't think it was the housekeeper. So, as soon as she heard footsteps retreating down the corridor, she quietly opened her door again and peeped out. It was Marion in blue and white striped pyjamas, her shoulders slumped and her body heaving as she fought to muffle her sobs.

It threw Lara; she hadn't even thought there might be another side beyond Marion's bright eyes and ready smile. But given the level of her colleague's anguish, she was sure there had to be some deep, difficult issue she was dealing with. Instantly, she knew it wouldn't be right to go down there and ask her outright; it was way too soon in their relationship to intrude. But she'd remain vigilant regarding her colleague and maybe in the fullness of time, it would come out and she would be able to offer some support, or at the very least a shoulder to cry on.

Down at breakfast, as Marion crunched through her buttered toast and jam, there was no trace of her previous distress, and she appeared to be her usual chatty, smiley self. It didn't fool Lara though because she knew that what she'd witnessed earlier had been genuine.

There was still no sign of Angus at the breakfast table, and she could tell by the set of Mrs Hewitt's shoulders that the older woman was annoyed. Clearly, whatever words had been exchanged yesterday with the young doctor had not made a jot of difference to his behaviour and he'd probably been out late again in the pub.

The housekeeper sighed, then pasted a bright smile. 'Right, Nurses, I've just collected your schedules from Dr Bingham... Marion, you're on house calls and emergencies and Lara... we need you in surgery with Dr Fitzwilliam this morning, then you're going out with him to Ridgetown hospital in the afternoon.'

Lara was about to open her mouth to say she hadn't been shown the ropes at the cottage hospital yet when Mrs H spoke again. 'It's an observation visit with Angus. An opportunity for you to meet the nursing staff and see how we work alongside them. It's usually just the doctors who provide cover there because the hospital has its own nurses. In fact, you'll probably meet the matron, Miss Sharples. She's a local girl made good and she's not far short of a battleship in full sail, so you'll need to mind your Ps and Qs.'

'I'm used to the type.' Lara grinned. 'They've got plenty like that at the Liverpool Royal.'

'Good, that's good. So you know to take your armour.'

Lara giggled and as she got up to leave the table with Marion, a dishevelled-looking Angus stumbled through the door. He had dark shadows beneath his eyes, his hair was all over the place and he had a dried crust of drool on his left cheek.

'Whoa,' Marion murmured under her breath as she passed him. 'You need to navigate very troubled waters with Mrs H this morning. Hope you've got your life jacket.'

Angus grunted quietly by way of reply.

It made Lara feel worried to see him in such a bad state. Despite him being outspoken and clearly in cahoots with Leo and all the others who boozed too much at the pub, she liked Angus's sense of humour and there was something brotherly and a little lost about him that made her feel protective.

'I hope he's going to be all right,' she whispered to Marion.

'Yeah, he'll be fine. He's always getting into trouble with Mrs H but she loves him like a son really.'

She hoped that was true because conflicts like this hadn't been part of how she'd expected things to be out here in what she'd imagined would be a rural idyll. Drunken young doctors, strained relationships, and Marion's deeply buried secrets hadn't factored into the picture she'd painted of country nursing. Telling herself she'd get used to the intensity of it all, she remembered she'd be spending the morning in clinic with Dr Fitzwilliam and her throat tightened at the prospect. If only she'd been given a list of house calls, she'd be feeling bright and breezy right now at the prospect of cycling the country lanes.

Halfway through the morning clinic, working alongside an almost silent Angus and regularly receiving narrow-eyed glances from patients still mourning the loss of Nurse Beecham, the appointments stretched on. The cases were straightforward enough: chronic chests, a leg ulcer, a child with scabies, an elderly man with a nosebleed. But when she'd dealt with the elderly man, she'd used the medical term 'epistaxis' instead of 'nosebleed'. She'd followed it instantly with an explanation, but it had been too late to prevent the patient's wife from muttering to her husband not quite far enough under her breath, 'She's up 'erself, that one. They should have got someone from round 'ere.'

The clinic had also been made much harder because she was shoring up Angus. It was a good job she'd already been impressed by his breadth of medical knowledge from conversations around the kitchen table, because he was slow-moving, disorderly, and clearly exhausted. And she was so glad she'd been there with him to quietly advise that aspirin – given it had the tendency to thin the blood – was not a good choice to treat the headache of the poor man who'd already suffered a torrential nosebleed.

It was a relief when the clinic had ended and after a light lunch of roast ham and crusty home-baked bread, they were off to the cottage hospital in the little blue Austin. She'd been looking forward to seeing Ridgetown but as a silent Angus huffed at the wheel and grumbled loudly when a couple of lambs strayed onto the road and impeded their progress, she began to feel desolate. By the time they hit the wider road closer to Ridgetown, she was nearing the end of her patience. And when they met a herd of cattle head-on, causing him to curse and swear and ram on the brakes so violently it made her shoot forward in her seat, she snapped.

'What the heck is the matter with you?'

He looked straight at her and blinked, as if he'd only just realised she was there.

'Well?' she asked firmly.

To her horror, he slumped his shoulders, dropped his head and began to cry.

'Oh my God, I'm so sorry,' she called, reaching out instinctively to put an arm around him.

He sobbed, swiped at his eyes, then sobbed again.

The cows were upon them now. They were streaming past, lowing and jostling. One of them brushed its brown, furry flank caked with dried manure against the side of the car, making it rock from side to side.

Still, he sobbed.

Still, she kept her arm around him.

'You have to tell me, Angus. I promise I won't say a word to anyone.'

'It's Ada,' he gasped, sitting back in his seat.

'Ada?'

He looked at her then. 'Ada Lightfoot, the barmaid at The Fleece. I fell in love with her the first night I walked into the pub.'

'Oh, I see.'

Instantly, she felt out of her depth. Having been educated at a girls' boarding school and then living and working mostly with women, she had never encountered the affairs of the heart related to men.

She cleared her throat. 'Well, have you tried talking to her?'

'Yes. She says she doesn't like me.'

'Well, how about if you ease off your attentions a little, give her some space.'

He looked at her, scrunched his brow. 'Do you think that might work?'

'I don't know, but women don't like to feel hemmed in by men. We need to have our freedom. So if you're not having any luck with what you're already doing, it might be worth a try.'

He was nodding now, then he straightened up in his seat. 'It's so hard for me to talk to women I think about in that way. Immediately, I'm tongue-tied, and they must think I'm odd. I suppose it doesn't help not having sisters and attending an all-boys boarding school. And in my cohort at medical school, there were only men.'

'I see your difficulty,' she offered gently. 'But that doesn't mean to say it's unsurmountable.'

In her heart, she knew he would struggle to make any progress with Ada the barmaid. If there hadn't been a spark by now, he didn't stand much of a chance. But he was so emotional, she knew she couldn't lay out the stark facts, so she repeated her advice about giving Ada some space, waiting to see if that made any difference.

He sighed heavily, turned to her. 'Thank you for listening, Nurse Flynn; I feel a bit better now. And please, don't tell Marion or Mrs H about this.'

'Your secret is safe with me.' She smiled. 'But you need to manage your expectations. And if giving Ada some space doesn't make any difference, then maybe you should back off completely. Wait a while for the right one to come along.'

He nodded, pulled a spotlessly clean white handkerchief from his pocket and wiped his eyes, then began to pump the accelerator. The Austin backfired then lurched forward and she grabbed at her seat to steady herself. As they took off at speed, his mood seemed to be revving with the engine, and they were soon on the outskirts of Ridgetown. And as they raced into the small market town, Lara noted cotton mills, rows of terraced houses, shops, pubs and a large co-operative grocery store. At the top of the main street, he jammed on the brakes alarmingly, then rolled back a little as they waited for a slow-moving bus to pass by. Visibly impatient, he pumped the accelerator to turn sharply right and as they zoomed by a row of quaint stone cottages, she noted a small picture house with a film poster for *Trouble in Paradise* which she'd seen in Liverpool but would love to watch again. She craned her neck to check the details, but the cinema was left so quickly behind, she had no chance.

Screeching to a halt outside the cottage hospital, she felt a little breathless and was still gripping her seat as Angus hopped out, then stood clenching his fists impatiently. She clambered out and followed him as he strode towards the single-storey stone building. At the solid front door, he pulled a pack of cigarettes from his pocket and lit up with a flourish.

'It always feels a bit like going into battle with Matron Sharples in charge,' he quipped before grasping the iron door handle, pushing open the door and striding through.

The strong carbolic hospital smell hit her and took her straight back to working at the Infirmary. It surprised her to feel a twist of emotion given she'd been desperate to get away from Liverpool after the accident. But even as she walked along the green-tiled corridor, she realised how special the Infirmary had been during her training and those early years as a qualified nurse. The work had been challenging, exhausting, but that's where she'd become the self-reliant woman she now was.

She followed Angus as he strode ahead smoking his cigarette; he seemed to develop a confident swagger as he nodded a greeting here and there to the nurses in their starched white caps and aprons. But she knew now just how vulnerable he was, and it made her feel even more protective of him.

'Ah, Dr Fitzwilliam,' a crisp voice rang out through an open office door close to the entrance to the two wards. Male to the left, female to the right.

She noted the twitch of Angus's body and the stiff set of his shoulders as he turned with a pasted-on smile. 'Ah, Matron Sharples, I do hope we find you well this sunny morning?'

'Perfectly well,' she replied, as she leant slightly forward at her desk to catch Lara with a narrow, piercing gaze.

'Ah, yes... let me introduce you,' he stumbled. 'This is the new member of our Ingleside team—'

'Nurse Flynn,' Matron cut in.

As the sharp-eyed, steel-grey-haired woman openly scrutinised her, Lara stepped forward and reached out to shake hands, but a reciprocal greeting was not forthcoming. Instead, Matron peered at her as if she were a specimen. 'So, you trained at the Liverpool Royal...'

'Yes, I—'

Matron cut her off. 'I have a friend who works there. She moved down from Preston Royal Infirmary where we both trained. She told me Liverpool isn't a patch on PRI. It's far too big and certainly nowhere near as clean.'

She felt a familiar prickle of discomfort at the woman's rudeness. It didn't shock her; she'd heard many similar outspoken comments from senior staff in Liverpool and she knew it was their way of testing the nurses, seeing if they had the 'mettle'. It was still rude though, whatever the root cause, and she'd vowed many times that when she became senior, she'd adopt a style that chimed with the gentler ward sisters and matrons, the ones who took time to get to know their nurses and understood their difficulties.

As Matron Sharples slipped from behind her desk, Lara's heart sank. She'd hoped Angus or one of the nurses she'd seen offering a smile or a friendly nod would be supervising her visit. But it looked like she was going to be stuck with Matron Sharples. But then the large black telephone on the desk began to ring loudly and Lara raised her eyes to heaven to pray for a reprieve.

As Matron picked up the receiver and identified herself in what sounded like her most well-spoken of voices, Angus took the opportunity to stub his cigarette in the cut-glass ashtray on her desk. The moment she shooed them away with her hand, mee-mawing to Angus that it was a call from a consultant at Preston Royal Infirmary, Lara sensed his relief, and it matched her own. And as he grabbed her arm and briskly led her away, that shared sense of a narrow escape made her feel like his co-conspirator. She almost giggled as he steered her through the door to the male ward.

Gazing down the spotlessly clean, shiny-floored ward with neat iron beds and lockers down either side, she felt instantly familiar with the environment. And knowing she was a new nurse, some of the patients as they lay against their white, starched pillows offered a smile or raised a hand in greeting. In the corner of the ward, one very poorly, bed-bound man with sunken cheeks lay on his side, his breathing shallow. And the meticulous way his few strands of grey hair had been brushed and one arm positioned carefully outside of the counterpane indicated the time the nurses had taken to make him comfortable and give him dignity. She felt an instant stab of recognition... This was the standard of practice she had been schooled in and took pride in maintaining.

'Everything seems to be in order,' Angus said as he spoke to the young staff nurse who was in charge before turning to Lara.

'Nurse Flynn, this is Nurse Greenwood. She is an absolute marvel and without doubt a pillar of strength here on the male ward.'

'And you must be the new member of staff at Ingleside Surgery.' The dark-eyed woman with short-cropped, red-brown hair smiled, then reached out to shake her hand.

'Yes, that's me,' Lara offered, instantly noting the two pink spots of colour on the nurse's cheeks and the way her eyes shone when she glanced at Angus, which might indicate she was sweet on him. He, of course, appeared completely oblivious to her charms. But maybe if he stopped entertaining hopes of a liaison with Ada the barmaid, this young woman would be a very good match for him.

As Angus made to walk with Nurse Greenwood to the ward office to discuss the patients who needed to be seen, knowing she wanted to catch up with Miss Dunderdale and little Sue Cronshaw, she murmured, 'I'll go over to the female ward, wait for you there.'

As she entered the ward, she easily spotted Sue's bandaged head as she stood by a bed occupied by another patient. She was so fixated on the little girl at first that she didn't realise the bed Sue was standing beside was Miss Dunderdale's. Judging the older woman might not be someone who enjoyed the company of small children, she walked briskly over but as she approached, she realised that Miss Dunderdale was holding a knitted teddy and she was jiggling it up and down, making it dance, and Sue was giggling.

'Hello, Sue,' Lara called gently, noting the reddened, flaking skin at the edge of the bandage around her head. The little girl offered a brief, shy smile, then dipped her head.

Miss Dunderdale spoke up instantly. 'It's all right, Suzy, this is our friend, the nurse who helped you when you had your accident, and she came to my rescue when I got poorly.'

Miss Dunderdale handed the knitted teddy to the little girl who stood twisting it in her hands for a few moments before trotting back across the ward to a nurse who was beckoning to her.

Lara felt instantly delighted by the huge shift in Miss Dunderdale's demeanour. Still pale from her collapse and slightly out of breath, the warmth of her gaze and the gentleness of her voice denoted a drastic change. Still not entirely sure the transformation was secure, Lara asked tentatively, 'How are you doing?'

'As well as I possibly can be... but it was touch-and-go when I got here. They've told me I've had a heart attack and they're giving me some pills. I don't think they're helping all that much, but I'll do as I'm told because I want to get back home as soon as possible.'

'You'll need lots of rest. I can see you're doing well but you were very poorly.'

'That's what the nurses keep telling me and they're fussing around me all the time. I'd be better off at home, I'm sure I would.'

'What are the tablets you're taking?'

'Digitalis.'

'Oh, well, that makes sense. You need to stay in hospital because they have to titrate the dose, make sure it doesn't slow your heart too much.'

She heaved a sigh. 'Humph, that's what they're saying. And I suppose I'll have to comply.' She offered a mischievous grin then. 'But as you already know, I'm not good at doing that.'

'Yes, I do know that.' Lara smiled, reaching out to give the woman's hand a gentle squeeze.

They chatted for a while longer, then as she made to walk away, Miss Dunderdale called after her. 'Thank you, Nurse Flynn, for all that you did for me. They're saying I wouldn't have survived without your intervention.'

'Oh no, really... it's all part of the service,' she said, never comfortable, like many of her nurse colleagues, at being in the limelight. Work like theirs was often a team effort and the trick of it was to have all the parts clicking together.

'I'll be coming to see you when you're back home,' she called over her shoulder, just as Angus appeared and beckoned urgently for her to follow.

He looked on edge as he whispered, 'There was just that one male patient Nurse Greenwood asked me to review and there's no one for me to see on the female ward. So let's run, quick, before Matron finishes her telephone calls.'

She nodded, grinned.

Then they scampered to the car like two naughty children.

As they drove back to the village, Angus was quiet, but she felt much more at ease with him now. Not that she wasn't still clutching her seat as he screeched around corners and put his foot down on the flat. And after a particularly sharp corner when he narrowly missed a stray sheep, she screamed out loud.

'Oops!' he shouted. 'We don't want to be making any more work for the vets, do we now.'

What was it with these doctors and their driving? Yes, the roads were very quiet, but what about stray livestock and the comfort of passengers? It made her vow that one day, she would get behind the wheel and show these male doctors how it was done.

As they arrived on the outskirts of Ingleside, skimming by a high stone wall that enclosed the village school, she began to relax a little when she knew they were on the home stretch. And as they passed a row of stone cottages then swung left at The Fleece, she groaned with relief as at last Angus eased his foot off the accelerator.

'Ta da,' he called triumphantly as he skidded onto the cobbles at the side of the surgery and parked up skew-whiff as always.

'Thank you, Angus... at least we got back in one piece,' she muttered as she flung open the door and scrambled out. Raising her eyes to the sky to whatever spirit on high had protected her on the journey, she then walked in through the back door. And as the calm of the surgery and the familiar clinical smell met her, and then mingled with something freshly baked from the kitchen, she felt for the first time as if she were coming home.

12

It was already Saturday, the day of the village dance, and Lara felt perplexed because when Grace Alston had asked her to accompany her, they hadn't arranged a time or a place to meet. She'd toyed with the idea of picking up the phone and calling the Alstons' farm, but knowing Mrs Hewitt and Dr Bingham wholeheartedly disapproved of anything other than work calls on the precious telephone, she'd already ruled that out. Also, the arrangement had been made so lightly that day, and she hardly knew Grace, so her new friend might have forgotten. In the end, she decided that given she now lived in Ingleside where there was only one village hall and one dance, then if Grace was there at some stage, nothing more was required.

At breakfast, Marion was already chattering excitedly about what she might wear and who might be there. But Angus was sitting quietly in his place at the table denying any thoughts of attending. 'I'll be in The Fleece,' he said with a manly jut of his chin, 'and I'll see what Leo and the lads want to do.'

'All right, Mister "Man About Town",' Marion teased as they

sat eating Mrs Hewitt's sugar-sprinkled porridge with a swirl of fresh cream that Lara now relished every morning.

The young doctor waggled his head and muttered under his breath something about women always having a go at the men.

'Oi, stop that,' Mrs Hewitt quipped, pointing a wooden spoon at him. 'Who says we're always having a go? Every right-minded woman knows that if men weren't kept in order, then the world would fall to wrack and ruin.'

Angus rolled his eyes, sighed good-naturedly. 'I'm not even going to waste my time responding to that, Mrs H, given I'm massively outnumbered at this kitchen table every single morning.'

'Except, whether you like it or not, you have just responded,' Marion shot back at him.

'You can't win; you'll never win,' Mrs Hewitt crooned, then clearly feeling a little sorry for the young man, she walked over to put an arm around his shoulders.

Lara saw his smile; she could tell he was enjoying the house-keeper's gesture of affection. Clearly Mrs Hewitt cared for the young doctor and as she gave out the daily lists of visits compiled by Dr Bingham, she stayed by him, her hand lightly resting on his shoulder.

'So, as we all know, it's Saturday, so there are only essential visits this morning and our usual weekend clinic for emergencies. Then we have an early finish before the village dance tonight.'

'Whoopee!' Marion called, as Angus pretended not to give a damn, and all Lara had was that lingering anxiety about the informal arrangement she'd made with Grace.

Almost on cue, the telephone rang, and it startled her. When Mrs Hewitt shouted through to say it was Grace Alston for Lara asking if she was still up for the village dance tonight, she felt a blossom of relief and jumped up from the table to speak to her. When she returned, Marion looked sheepish and her voice was husky when she enquired whether Lara still wanted to go to The Fleece with her first before she met up with Grace. Her colleague seemed a little crestfallen because she'd already made plans.

'Of course I'll come with you.' She smiled. 'Grace said there was no set time for the village hall; she'll see me when she sees me.'

'Excellent,' Marion said, her eyes brightening.

Then Lara was the one to have doubts because she'd never been to anything resembling a village dance ever before.

'Don't look so worried, Nurse Flynn,' Mrs Hewitt called. 'From what I remember, the dances are absolute chaos. It doesn't matter who you go with or who you end up with; the whole thing happens in its own sweet way.'

'Amen to that,' said Marion, then moved swiftly to discussing with Mrs H what she was thinking of wearing and what she wished she could wear but didn't have. As the light-hearted chatter continued, Lara felt as if she were set apart from it. But then realised that she would also need 'something to wear'. Instantly, she discounted the turquoise, silk gown she'd worn to the Adelphi because it felt too soon to reclaim it, and it was far too dressy for a village dance. But she had those two summer dresses fitted to the waist with gently flared skirts. They weren't flashy but they were smart enough to wear to a local dance, and she felt reasonably confident that with her heeled black shoes, the yellow patterned one would more than suffice.

Seeing a faraway look in Marion's eyes and a twist to her mouth as she lay down her porridge spoon, she assumed she was still mulling over her choice of dance frocks. And feeling the need to fill the silent space with a comment, she offered something along the lines of not wanting to spend too much time worrying about what to wear.

Marion glanced up, stared blankly for a few seconds and seemed not to grasp what she'd just said. Instantly, Lara sensed the disquiet in her new friend and it triggered thoughts of the morning she'd seen her emerge from the bathroom sobbing. She knew now, for sure, there was some secret Marion was keeping deeply buried. Trying to lift the heaviness, she smiled across the table, spoke again about clothes for the dance. 'I think culottes and a blouse are a very good choice for what I assume will be a lively dance floor.'

In that moment, Marion seemed to force herself back to her usual bright mood. 'Yes,' she said, throwing a sharp but good-humoured glance in Angus's direction. 'It is lively, isn't it Angus... especially if some of the young men turn up drunk and start fighting.'

'Look, that last time, it wasn't my fault. Ed was very drunk; I was just trying to restrain him but then... well...'

'He was so drunk, he hit you in the face and bust your nose.'

'Something like that. I don't really remember much about it.'

'Of course not, you had to be led home by Dr Bingham.'

Angus emitted the low rumble of a laugh, then spoke in a hushed tone. 'Yes, I did. And that wasn't the worst of it. The next day, when I had the lousiest hangover of my whole life, Bingham was there at my door on a Sunday morning saying he was checking on me. And then insisting I get up and come down-stairs for tea and toast.'

Mrs Hewitt began to chuckle, then she said, 'You looked like you were about to expire. And if I hadn't grabbed you when you lurched sideways, I think you would have cracked your skull open on the corner of the kitchen table and ended up with a head injury alongside your busted nose.'

Angus rubbed a hand around his face. 'I know,' he groaned, 'and you'd think I should have learned from that.'

'But you haven't, have you, and I'm thinking you might be a lost cause,' Marion chuckled.

'No, Nurse Marion, don't desert me in my hour of need,' he groaned theatrically, reaching an arm across the table.

Marion pretended to turn away and he groaned even louder until Mrs Hewitt raised her wooden spoon and said, 'Right, you two, settle down. If Dr Bingham walks past that door, he's going to think I've lost a grip on you lot.'

Angus and Marion began to laugh, and Lara couldn't help but join in.

Seemingly desperate to maintain control, the housekeeper shouted, 'Anyone for toast and jam?' and that did the trick.

'Sorry, Nurse Flynn,' Mrs Hewitt called to her. 'You must be wondering what the heck you've let yourself in for coming to work here with these two daft beggars. Then on top of that agreeing to attend the village dance.'

'Oh, that's all right. I'm enjoying it, all of it.'

Marion grinned. 'You'll be fine at the dance. I'll be there with you, and we've got Grace for backup. She's a tough cookie and I've seen her get the better of many an unruly young man.'

Angus jumped up from his seat with a piece of toast in his hand. 'Well, I'll be off to my visits and then I'll call by the cottage hospital. Get it all done so I'll be ready to be out early doors.'

'Are we meeting up in The Fleece?' Marion called after him.

'Well, like I said, I'll be with the lads, but we'll be in there, yeah.'

'Just so you know,' Mrs Hewitt called as Lara and Marion also got up from the table, 'Dr Bingham is on call this evening so he will see to any emergencies. He'll stay fully sober. Not that he ever goes to the dances anyway, but he does like a few single malt whiskeys on a Saturday night. Young Rose Ryan has gone over her due date so she could go into labour at any time and her baby is lying in a breech position.'

Lara instantly understood the added level of complexity a breech birth could bring, especially with a first baby. Having witnessed an infant delivered feet first but then become wedged in the birth canal, she felt a dull twist of pain at the memory of her first infant death. The mother had suffered a post-partum haemorrhage and had been left barely clinging to life. After a blood transfusion, her condition had stabilised but that terrible, gut-wrenching wail from the mother when she'd been told her baby had not survived was something that would stay with her forever. Even at the thought of it now, she felt a shiver go through her.

'You OK?' Marion asked as they left the kitchen.

'Yes... just thinking about Rose Ryan, that's all. I hope everything will go to plan for her.'

'Me too... and just so you know, I do the midwifery when I need to, but it's never felt like my specialty. So if a time ever comes that we can choose... I think you should be number one to attend the deliveries, just like Nurse Beecham used to.'

'Yes, of course. That suits me down to the ground. I've always enjoyed catching the babies.'

Thankfully, the morning clinic was quiet, so she had a chance to relax a little as she caught up with the cleaning rota and mentally took note of the contents of all the cupboards with their lotions, potions and surgical instruments. As Bingham sat quietly at his desk writing up notes, it felt like a companionable silence until she accidentally knocked into the table holding the wooden anatomical model and all the body parts crashed to the floor.

Instantly, she was on her knees gathering the pieces and

fitting them back in the right order as Bingham offered a loud tut. 'You would never have struck me as a clumsy person at first meeting, Nurse Flynn. So you are either deliberately trying to sabotage a quiet Saturday morning surgery, or you are an absolute idiot.'

'I think the answer to that is neither,' she stated boldly.

'Humph,' he replied with a shrug of his shoulders, then settled back to his note-writing.

With the extra stress of fitting the anatomical model back together, she was feeling ruffled and in the cooped-up heat of the surgery, she began to sweat so much, her starched collar chafed at her neck. So when Mrs Hewitt came through the door with tall glasses of home-made lemonade, it was very welcome.

'You have two patients in the waiting room now, Dr Bingham: a young boy with abdominal pain and Miss Frobisher reporting a headache which she thinks is almost certainly a brain tumour.'

Instantly, Lara recognised the name of the female patient as the hostile elderly woman she'd met at the surgery door on her first day, but she wouldn't let that affect her treatment of the patient.

Bingham huffed, then said, 'Diagnoses – constipation for the boy, hypochondriasis for the retired schoolteacher.'

His scathing tone was offset by a twinkle in his eye, so she forgave him his cynicism. But maybe this is what happened in a close-knit community where the pool of patients was small and very well known. She made a note to herself not to get to a place in her own practice where she was pre-judging and therefore failing to look closely enough. But to be fair, once the patients had had their observations done and were checked over by Dr Bingham, he did a very thorough job, and the diagnoses did turn out to be those he'd predicted. And he spoke kindly to both patients and used his firm but gentle voice to offer advice and reassurance.

Still hot and beginning to feel increasingly confined within the thick stone walls of the surgery, she wished now she'd been assigned to the home visits instead of Marion. But then it would have taken her ages to cycle all the way up to Fell Farm to see little Lucy Taylor; it was so much quicker for Marion on her beloved motorcycle.

'Is it all right if I nip down to check on Daniel Makepeace?' she asked, after she'd finished the tidying and the sterilising of the instruments.

Bingham barely looked up from his desk. 'Yes, do that. I was going to call in anyway and it'll save me a job.'

As she made to leave the room, he called, 'Oh, and Nurse Flynn... I know you will be checking his pulse, but please can you record his blood pressure again for me?'

She stopped in her tracks, aware of what might come next.

He left her hanging for a few moments, then without glancing up from his notes, he said, 'You can take that new sphyg, the one with the scuffed case that you borrowed previously; it's on the shelf above the sink.'

Noting the square set of his shoulders, she wasn't sure whether he was holding back a laugh or was annoyed. She didn't stay to find out; she grabbed the blood pressure monitor, called a goodbye and exited the room as quickly as she could.

* * *

'Are you off to the dance tonight, Nurse Flynn?' Daniel asked as she prepared to check his pulse and blood pressure, but instead found herself gazing out through the open shutters to the green field beyond.

'Yes, I think so,' she murmured dreamily, soothed by the brown cows munching their grass and swishing their tails as they wandered lazily to the shade of a large oak tree. The warm air with its hint of hay time was becoming very familiar. And here, with Daniel, she felt that calm, that instinct to take things slowly that had struck her right away on her first visit.

Once she'd finished making her recordings, he drew a slow breath. 'Those dances have been going on since before I was born. And that's a heck of a long time ago.'

'Well, it'll be my first. So can you give me any advice?'

'Not really,' he chuckled, 'except to stay away from the drunken men... I shouldn't be saying that really because I'd always had too much when I went there; all the lads had. I'm amazed my Martha even gave me a chance after seeing me in that state.'

'She did though, didn't she... so there must have been something special,' she replied, straightening his bedsheet then carefully pushing the sphyg back into its damaged case.

He was gazing out of the window now, a faraway look in his eyes. Then he sighed, shook his head. 'It was my Martha who was special.'

'Well, she must have thought the same about you,' she said gently.

'I suppose you're right,' he replied with a slow smile. 'After all, you women are usually right on most things.'

'Maybe,' she offered quietly, her gaze following his back out to the field. Then drawing a breath, she said, 'I felt a bit scared of those cows at first, but I think I'm getting used to them now.'

'Aye, I can tell you are, lass... and this place will hook you in; it'll get under your skin if you let it.'

He smiled at her then as she stepped away from the bed and

raised a hand in farewell. 'I'll be seeing you again soon, Mr Makepeace. Now you take care.'

'Have a good time tonight, Nurse Flynn... and if any of those ruffians give you any trouble, report them back to me.'

'I will,' she called as she exited the room, leaving him resting against his pillows, gazing out to the cows in the field.

As she walked back up towards the surgery, she prayed there wouldn't be a flock of sheep descending on her today. Thankfully, all was quiet, just the tinkle of the post office bell as an elderly woman emerged. She barely noticed her but when a voice called from behind, she instantly clicked it was Miss Frobisher.

'Hello again, Nurse. I didn't get a chance to chat to you earlier when I was up at the surgery seeing Dr Bingham, but I was just wondering how you're settling in?'

She turned, surprised at the woman's gentle tone; quite rightly, she'd maintained a fully professional distance when she'd seen her in clinic and now meeting her again, Lara felt happy to stand and wait as she advanced, the metal tip of her walking stick marking every step as it tapped on the stone-flagged pavement.

'Oh, everything seems to be going all right,' she said once the woman was standing in front of her.

Miss Frobisher's eyes narrowed then. 'I heard about what happened to Celia Dunderdale. And I've been told you were the one to find her and some say you might have saved her life.'

'Yes, I did find her, but—'

'So what happened to her? Is it her heart, a stroke, or did she have a seizure?'

'I'm sorry, I can't reveal any detail of Miss Dunderdale's case.'

The woman scowled. 'But that's ridiculous; you are *our* nurse.'

'Yes, I'm aware of that. But it would be a breach of confidentiality to reveal the diagnosis of any patient to anyone other than their next of kin.'

'What?' The older woman hissed, clearly outraged. 'I've known Celia since we both moved to Ingleside many years ago.'

'Yes, I understand, but that doesn't make you next of kin.'

The woman huffed, then turned to walk away, spitting out, 'And you call yourself a nurse!'

Even though she was very sure of her grounds for maintaining patient confidentiality, the woman's rude response needled her.

'They all like to know everybody's business round here,' a man's voice called from behind. 'Especially Miss Frobisher... She used to be the village school mistress.'

It was Leo Sullivan, and him arriving to make a direct comment on top of the altercation she'd just had made her feel even more suffocated by the intensity of village life.

She sucked in a breath. 'Oh that's all right, I'm used to that kind of thing.'

'It must be far more diluted though in a big city like Liverpool.'

She felt as if she had no words; she just wanted to get back to the surgery.

He furrowed his brow. 'Are you all right?' he asked, genuine concern in his voice.

She cleared her throat. 'Yes, yes. I'm absolutely fine.'

She was already walking away as he shouted after her, 'Maybe I'll see you later, at the dance.'

'Maybe,' she called over her shoulder. Then a split-second later, a rosy-cheeked village woman with a basket over her arm met her head-on and offered a knowing smile.

'Looks like there might be a bit of romance in the air tonight, Nurse Flynn.'

She gasped; she couldn't form a response. It felt exasperating to be on view like this and it was all compounded by Leo fussing over whether she was going to the dance or not. She tightened her grip on her medical bag, picked up her pace and darted across to the surgery. In through the door, the thick stone walls muffled the sounds of the street and instantly, she felt easier. And hearing the now familiar sound of Mrs Hewitt humming a nondescript tune as she went about her kitchen duties, she began to calm down.

As she entered the kitchen, the housekeeper turned with a smile. 'There you are, Lara. I've just pulled a batch of scones out of the oven, and I was hoping they'd still be warm for you coming back in.'

'That's so kind, thank you, Mrs H,' she sighed, already slipping onto the smooth worn chair in her place at the table. And as she sipped her tea and ate the scone with butter and homemade strawberry jam, she wished now she hadn't agreed to go to the village dance this evening. It would perhaps have been better to stay in with Mrs H and Tiddles the cat and listen to the radiogram in the sitting room. But she'd made a firm commitment with Grace to meet in the village hall and even though she felt a little daunted by her first visit to The 'Dorchester', she certainly wasn't going to let Marion down, especially after the upset she'd sensed in her this morning.

13

_____

As Lara slipped into the yellow summer dress she'd settled on wearing for the village dance, she felt a jolt, a knee-jerk reminder that she'd worn it that first time she'd gone back with Patrick to his lodgings. She hadn't even remembered until now and straight away, she knew she wasn't going to swap the dress for something else, in fact, she wanted to wear it even more so she could reclaim it. As she smoothed the skirt with the flat of her hand, she lifted her chin and gazed at her reflection in the wardrobe mirror – the dress fitted perfectly; she loved it. And as she stood to apply her face powder, eyeliner, and the exact same red lipstick she'd worn for her birthday celebration at the Adelphi, she began to feel even more powerful.

She was barely ready when she heard Marion shout for help from her room down the corridor. As she pushed her feet into her heeled black shoes and trotted down to her friend's room, she heard her raging and bumping around. And when she tapped on the door, Marion shouted theatrically, 'Come in! Please come in and save me!'

The room was slightly smaller than hers, but it had the same red patterned square of carpet and an iron bedstead that was now piled high with clothing, mostly dresses.

'I can't find a thing to wear,' Marion roared, pulling at the pile, tossing the skirts and tops and dresses into an even more chaotic mess.

'You're too agitated; you need to calm down,' Lara offered firmly. 'You have lots of options here. There shouldn't be any problem whatsoever.'

Marion shot her a fiery glance, but Lara was not daunted. She'd spent years dealing with Maeve who had a similar temperament and once threw a pair of shoes out of the window when she was struggling to decide what to wear. So she used the tactics she'd learned with Maeve – first, she got her to calm down, then she advised her to just pick something she was comfortable in.

After Marion had spent a while holding one dress after another in front of her, glancing into the full-length wardrobe mirror before casting them aside, Lara knew they were going to be late at The Fleece. Not being on time troubled her but according to Marion, there was never a proper set time for anything in the village when it came to social events. It was often a question of 'I'll see you when I see you', and given the village was so small, everyone knew what everybody else was doing. It niggled her; she really wasn't sure whether she'd ever get used to the lack of privacy.

Marion was still holding up dresses then throwing them aside but as soon as she picked up a pair of navy culottes and matched them with a bright-pink blouse, Lara knew they were going to be the ones. Once the choice was made, Marion was soon ready and with her halo of black, wavy hair such a dramatic contrast to her pink blouse, she looked stunning. And when her red lipstick and black eyeliner were applied,

Lara had no hesitation in telling her she looked like a movie star.

'Ha!' Marion cried. 'Movie stars don't ride motorcycles through cow muck, which was what I was doing this morning on my visits.'

But Lara could tell she was pleased by the compliment and as they linked arms to walk downstairs, she felt close to Marion in a way that was surprising given they'd only just got to know each other.

'You both look smashing,' Mrs Hewitt called as they dodged into the kitchen to 'give her a twirl'. 'You two lasses have a lovely time. Dr Bingham has it covered, so you enjoy yourselves.'

As they exited the surgery, Lara felt an instant buzz at the raucous noise emanating from The Fleece. Her tummy flipped with expectation, and she didn't know if it was anxiety or excitement, but it committed her fully to whatever came at her on this first night out.

The Fleece was packed and full of cigarette smoke as Marion pulled her in through the door, then turned with a grin and said, 'Welcome to The Dorchester.' Almost instantly, faced with the clamour of bodies and the noise, Lara knew it wasn't much different from the nights out she'd had in Liverpool.

Except there was Angus at the bar and right next to him, laughing raucously and patting the young doctor on the back, was Leo.

'Thick as thieves, those two,' Marion shouted in her ear. Then, 'What do you want to drink?'

'Port and lemon,' she shouted back as Marion nodded, then pushed through the press of bodies to get to the bar.

As a space opened against the wall, she neatly slotted herself into a position where Marion could see her. Looking over towards the bar, she saw Leo glance in her direction and raise a hand in greeting. She waved in return and would have liked to have gone over there to say hello, but that bat squeak of something from when he'd helped rescue her from the sheep held her back. It felt annoying but she knew how tuned in Marion was, and she didn't want to risk opening herself up to being questioned over something and nothing. So she held back.

Seeing Marion squashed up against Angus at the bar and the way their heads were together, deep in some shouted conversation, she felt a little excluded by the jokey friendship they shared. But then she'd been the one he'd confided in on the way to the hospital. And she felt sure Marion would already have mentioned Angus's issue with Ada the barmaid if he had also told her. So his tearful confession was hers, and hers alone.

In moments, Marion was returning with two glasses held high. 'Here's your port and lemon, and I'm starting with a whisky and soda,' she called as she squeezed by two young men in work overalls with strands of hay stuck to their hair. One of them looked familiar and as she tried to work it out, he glanced in her direction and offered a smile. That was it: he was one of the young men, the taller, handsome one who'd been walking up the track to Grace's farm with a scythe over his shoulder.

Swept up in the next second as Marion thrust a glass into her hand, she took a sip of her drink. It tasted strong, a bit too strong. So she would take it slow. Whereas Marion knocked hers straight back and then went off to the bar for another. More space opened as the farmhand she'd recognised offered a warm smile, then pushed his way out of the pub with his friend.

Then as more revellers headed out through the door and more space opened, Marion beckoned for her to join them at the bar. As soon as she got close, she could see Angus was already swaying on his feet and although Leo was steady, his speech sounded slurry and it was loud, so loud. Marion grabbed hold of her arm and pulled her towards the bar, tucking her in next to Angus. She knew instantly that the good-looking young woman with red-blonde hair who was ably serving pint after pint had to be the Ada Lightfoot that Angus had told her about. She felt for the young doctor as soon as she picked up on the way he kept glancing in her direction.

The barmaid caught Lara's eye and offered a beaming smile. 'You must be Lara Flynn, the new nurse.'

'Yes, that's me.' She smiled in return. 'However did you guess?'

Ada shrugged her shoulders, then jokingly offered, 'I know, it's a miracle, isn't it? Given there's absolutely no gossip in this village and nobody ever knows what anybody else is doing.'

'True, so true,' she laughed, knowing she already liked Ada.

Angus turned to her then, his eyes glassy. 'Cheers,' he slurred, sloshing his tankard of ale as he raised it in a toast. And she felt slightly awkward and out of step with the others as she offered a fully sober cheers and took a chaste sip of her drink.

'No thank you, I have enough here,' she urged when Marion tried to persuade her to have another port and lemon.

'It's worth getting more here, because they only have bottles of beer and some lemonade at the village hall.'

'That's OK.' She smiled. 'I'm happy with lemonade.'

It hadn't always been the case; previously, she'd enjoyed more than a few drinks with her friends. But after that night she'd drunk champagne with Patrick at the Adelphi, she'd hardly been out at all.

Marion soon had a third, then a fourth whisky lined up, and she was ordering doubles now. Lara had seen Maeve tuck drinks away, but never anything on this scale. It made her feel concerned for her new friend, but everyone else in the pub seemed to be drinking heavily. However, once they'd left Leo

and Angus in the pub and headed out into the fresh air, she had
to grab hold of Marion when she staggered.

'Thish way,' Marion slurred, pointing unsteadily beyond the
surgery towards the village hall.

Lara put an arm around her, pulled her close. She felt extra
concern because she was picking up again that melancholy
she'd first observed the morning she'd seen her coming out of
the bathroom. Again, she sensed Marion's vulnerability, and it
came at her now with even more force. It was possible that she'd
got it wrong, this could all be down to the drink, but she felt
increasingly aware that beneath her friend's bright exterior,
there might be something else going on.

Catching the sound of lively voices and a band playing
inside the village hall, she drew a slow breath and began to feel
a little lighter. And when Marion turned to her with a lopsided
grin and said, 'I think I might have drunk too much to dansh,' it
made her chuckle.

'Yes, that might be so. But don't worry, I'll look after you.'

'Thanksh,' her friend slurred. 'I like you, Lara, I really like
you... and one day, I'm going to teach you to ride my
motorshycle.'

'Thank you,' Lara said, guiding her friend towards the door
of the village hall.

Once they were inside, she headed straight for the nearest
table at the edge of the dance floor. The hall was only half full,
but the floor was packed with women dancing together to a
lively barn dance played by three grey-haired musicians on a
small, rickety-looking stage. The few men who had already
arrived were slouched against the wall or lounging at tables
close to the bar, gazing towards the dance floor with bottles of
beer in their hands.

'Shorry,' Marion groaned as Lara guided her onto a wooden

chair. Then she began to giggle. 'I always get like thish on a dance night... and the harder I tell myself I'm not going to drink too much ever again, the more I do it.'

'That's life,' Lara murmured as she made sure her friend was securely positioned on the chair.

'Hello there, Lara,' a bright voice called from across the dance floor. 'I'll see you for a dance soon.'

It was Grace, partnered with a smiling young woman she was sure she'd seen behind the counter in the butcher's shop.

Lara smiled, raised a hand, then headed straight to the bar to buy two bottles of lemonade. As she walked, a couple of young men nudged each other and looked her up and down. But she went straight past them to the steel-haired woman behind the bar. She knew she'd seen her somewhere before and then it clicked: she was Miss Shaw the postmistress. Two bottles of lemonade complete with straws were passed to her efficiently. Money taken, change given, without so much as a flicker of the woman's stern expression.

'Next,' the postmistress called to whomever had just arrived and was waiting in line behind her.

When she turned, she saw it was Angus. He was swaying from side to side and grinning ridiculously.

'Did you shee Ada in the pub, did you shee her?'

'Yes, I did. Now shh,' she offered, pressing a finger to her lips as she clutched the necks of the lemonade bottles in one hand.

As she stepped by, she noted Leo at a table in the corner. He looked tipsy but nothing like the same level as Angus. She already knew the young doctor would be facing a terrible hang-over in the morning and it was likely that he might also have to deal with the wrath of Dr Bingham.

'Drink this, all of it,' she urged Marion who sat slumped on her rickety, wooden village-hall chair.

Marion grasped the bottle, then slurred, 'Cheers... and I'm shorry, Lara; I wanted to be the one looking after you at your first dansh.'

She gave her friend's arm a gentle squeeze. 'That's all right, and I'm perfectly capable of looking after myself.'

'I know you are. You are sho fine, sho good, sho capable.'

Marion seemed on the verge of tears now, so Lara offered another cheers with her bottle of lemonade, put an arm around her shoulders and encouraged her to drink.

When another barn dance finished, Grace beckoned to her. 'It's a waltz up next; do you want to dance?'

'Yes, but I'm not sure what to do with Marion.'

'It's OK, everybody knows her, and we all look out for one another.'

The response was reassuring so she quickly told Marion she was going to dance, and then urged her to drink the rest of her lemonade.

Marion offered a wobbly salute as Lara jumped up from her seat and joined Grace on the dance floor.

'It's so good to see you, Lara,' her new friend beamed, her eyes flashing with warmth.

Grace looked so different in her cornflower-blue fitted dress with a flared skirt, her wavy, brown hair tidied up. But then again, so did she, out of her uniform for once and wearing make-up for the first time since the Adelphi Hotel.

'It's still a bit quiet; the dance will get into full swing in an hour or so when more folk leave the pubs.'

Lara nodded. She didn't mind; she liked it quieter.

As soon as the band struck up a waltz, she felt as if she might have forgotten the steps. But Grace was a very able partner, more accomplished than any of her previous male or female partners, and her confidence was key to Lara managing the dance much better than she expected.

As they glided around the floor, she blotted out all else apart from the dance steps and the music and it made her feel calm. Given the newness of their friendship, she was surprised at how relaxed she already felt with Grace. The slight creak of the dance floor, the smell of polish mingled with beer, the lively voices of the villagers at the tables, all added to an experience that was much more enjoyable than she'd anticipated. Stepping and twirling, she enjoyed the dance and the more turns of the floor she accomplished, the more at peace she became.

At the end of the dance, she stepped back a little, thanked her partner.

'Do you fancy another?' Grace asked.

As soon as she opened her mouth to reply, a high-pitched voice screamed out across the hall.

'Nurse Flynn, I need Nurse Flynn right now!'

She felt the urgency of the voice like a knife, then seeing the terrified face of the tousle haired young lad who had delivered the message, she ran straight over to him.

'Nurse Flynn?' he shouted, his eyes round like saucers.

'Yes, that's me, what is it?'

He gulped in air, then spat, 'It's my aunty, Rose Ryan. Her baby's coming and Dr Bingham's there, but things aren't right. So he told me to run like the wind, tell you to come now. Right away.'

Her heart jumped a beat.

She yelled over her shoulder to Grace, 'I need to go *right now* to an emergency. Look after Marion for me.'

As she grabbed the boy's arm and ran with him towards the door, she heard Grace shout reassurance. Then heading out of the village hall, she raced over the cobbles in her high-heeled shoes, slipping once or twice but managing to stay upright. Her heart felt full as it pounded in her chest and already her brain was clicking over Rose Ryan's antenatal details – this was her first baby, a suspected breech position, but nothing else untoward. Rose was a redhead though, so she would probably be a bleeder. With that thought, she pushed herself even harder. Determined to do all she could to save the life of the sweet, first-time mother and her unborn child.

14

Straight in through the door of Rose Ryan's stone terraced cottage, still gasping for air, Lara called out to Bingham as she ran towards the narrow stairs. 'It's Nurse Flynn. What do you want me to do?'

'I need urgent assistance. It's a footling breech and currently, the mother is not progressing in labour.' Already, she could hear the desperation in his voice; it sounded like he'd gone way beyond the level at which he could manage.

She gulped in air; she was an experienced midwife but she had nowhere near as many years under her belt as her predecessor Nurse Beecham. Her heart lurched when Bingham turned with an extremely harried expression, blood up his arms and soaked through his surgical apron and a large bright bloodstain on the bed.

Rose was groaning in agony, trying her best to push with the contractions but she was white-faced and exhausted, her red hair plastered to her head with sweat. When she gazed beseechingly in her direction, Lara felt her breath catch sharp in her chest. That's when she clenched her jaw, made sure her face didn't give any clue to her level of anxiety. However, she knew at first sight that this was one of those deliveries where mother and baby could both be lost. 'Have you sent for the ambulance?' she murmured to Bingham.

'Yes, I sent the husband to the surgery to tell Mrs H to make the request.'

'Good, that's good,' she said, turning her full attention to her patient. 'I'm here to help you, Rose. I've managed many deliveries like this, and I need you to listen carefully and do as I say. Do you understand?'

Rose gasped, nodded.

Bingham had stepped back from the bed now, his hands balled into fists, his voice tight with anguish as he hissed in her ear, 'The baby is wedged in the birth canal. I can feel one foot... but it isn't budging an inch.'

She heard him suck in a ragged breath as he stood in his bloodied shirtsleeves.

'I need to examine her,' she said, already pulling a pair of surgical gloves from his open medical bag. Glancing down at her yellow cotton frock, she asked, 'Do you have a spare apron?'

He shook his head, stepped aside as she boldly took her place beside the bed.

As another contraction hit, she spoke gently to Rose as she gasped and grunted her way through. 'I'm just having a feel inside, see how you're doing.'

Rose emitted a deep, other-worldly groan.

The doctor had been exact with his assessment: this was a footling breech but thankfully, no sign of a prolapsed umbilical cord. At least not yet. And the cervix seemed fully dilated... She checked again just to make sure; even the slightest of obstructions to the passage of the baby's head could have catastrophic consequences. And out here in a cottage in a remote country village... the mother and baby wouldn't stand a chance.

When she withdrew her hand, blood gushed freely onto the sheet.

Bingham spoke quietly over her shoulder, his voice tight. 'I think we need to move swiftly to a forceps delivery.'

She switched round, kept her voice low but firm. 'Not yet. Let's try for a normal delivery. In my experience, a surgical intervention can do more harm than good.'

To his credit, he didn't try to argue the case; he simply offered a nod.

Quickly, she grabbed the foetal stethoscope from the bottom of the bed and pressed it against the curve of Rose's abdomen, moved it once, twice. Then finally, she caught the rapid thready thump of the baby's heart.

'Still going strong,' she murmured, 'but time is of the essence.' She leant over the bed to speak to her patient. 'Baby's holding its own, but we need to deliver as soon as possible. It might help if you roll onto your left side. Is that all right? Can you manage?'

Her patient nodded, gasped, as Lara and Bingham helped her over.

In a split second as she settled Rose on her side, she saw Bingham shake his head. She ignored it. Told herself to follow the instincts she'd honed by delivering babies every week of her district nursing career.

With the next contraction, she grabbed Rose's hand. 'Now, tuck in your chin and push as hard as you can... That's it, keep going. You're doing so well.'

Rose let out a slow, blood-curdling noise from the back of her throat.

'Try not to shout out too much,' she urged. 'Use the energy to get this baby moving.'

'Yes,' the woman groaned, and her face contorted with effort, but she was paler now, rapidly weakening.

Lara reached for a square of surgical cloth, dipped it in a bowl of water at the side of the bed. Gently, she sponged her patient's face, all the while whispering words of encouragement. 'You're doing so well, Rose. Just keep going.'

With her hand resting gently at the top of Rose's swollen belly, she felt the next contraction building. 'Here it comes,' she called, aware of her patient's breathing, keeping the link with her. 'That's it, Rose, tuck in your chin, keep going. Push. Push as hard as you can.'

Deep in her core, she felt a strong, intuitive link with her patient and as Rose squeezed her hand, she knew she felt it too. The sheer effort she was putting in now was incredible given her weakened state. And when Lara examined again, with a gasp of relief, she found two tiny feet now ready to descend.

'We're on, she's ready to deliver,' she told Bingham.

Instantly, he reached for his forceps.

'No,' she said firmly. 'A metal instrument can be brutal; we're doing this the midwife's way. I just need some gloves and the episiotomy scissors.'

To his credit, he instantly passed her the equipment.

'One more big push, Rose, then we'll have your baby almost out.'

Rose offered a strangled sob, then her face contorted as a huge contraction began to build. Lara had already donned a clean pair of surgical gloves and without hesitation, she gathered the scissors and performed an episiotomy. Then, reaching to grasp the infant's legs, she pulled steadily to assist Rose's efforts. Once the body had been delivered to the level of the shoulder blades, she called for Rose to push as hard as she could. Bingham was there with the patient now, holding her hand, urging her on. Then, gasping with the effort of the intricate manoeuvre, she rotated the baby's body to deliver one shoulder, then the other. Still on a razor's edge, she didn't allow herself any satisfaction at getting this far. The job was almost done but the head came next and that was the scary one... if it got stuck, things would turn bad very quickly. She gulped in air, clenched her jaw, told herself that nothing on this earth was going to stop her pulling this baby out. In the moment she felt more movement, she deftly twisted the child's body full circle. For a second the baby felt stuck, and her heart almost stopped. Then, with a rush of blood and amniotic fluid, the head came, and she gave a cry of relief as the baby was delivered.

'It's a girl, Rose. You have a daughter.'

Her patient groaned but weakened as she was, she couldn't form any words. Then she whispered, 'Thank you, Nurse Flynn.'

But the baby girl lay lifeless on the bed with no sign of breathing. Bingham was already there assessing the newborn, and he shot her a grim glance as she quickly tied off then cut the cord. Instantly, he was working on the baby: rubbing her tiny body with a towel, turning her upside down to drain the fluid from her airways. Still no response, so he grabbed a rubber suction bulb from his bag to clear the child's mouth and nostrils.

Still the infant lay lifeless, her skin dark blue.

'Is the baby all right?' Rose croaked, her voice on the edge of breaking.

Lara replied gently, 'She just needs a bit more time, that's all. It sometimes takes a while for them to cry.'

Rose appeared satisfied with that; she closed her eyes and seemed to drift off to sleep.

As Bingham continued rubbing the child's body, then

tipping her upside down again to clear her airways, he muttered constantly, almost praying. His face was red with exertion, his eyes bloodshot with exhaustion but no doctor could have done more as he fought to save the baby's life.

With a painful lump in her throat, Lara closely observed her patient as she waited to deliver the afterbirth, glancing every few seconds to Bingham and the still lifeless baby.

As the placenta began to emerge, she gently called to her patient. 'Push as hard as you can now, Rose.'

Her patient tried to reply but then made a gurgling noise in the back of her throat.

'Jesus!' Lara gasped, as she shook Rose's arm then called her name. But her patient barely roused. 'The mother is struggling,' she called urgently to Bingham, who was still working on the baby.

In the split-second she feared they might lose both the baby and the mother, the infant made a noise, coughed, then emitted a weak cry.

'Thank the lord,' Bingham hollered as he raised his eyes to the ceiling, then instantly, he was rubbing the baby's tiny body again, again clearing her nose and mouth with the suction bulb.

In that instant of relief for the baby girl, Lara saw a strong gush of bright-red blood onto the bed.

'She's bleeding out,' she shouted and instantly, Bingham placed the newborn in the crib at the side of the bed.

Straight away, Lara was massaging Rose's abdomen in a desperate bid to make the womb contract.

Her patient was barely conscious but Lara shook her awake. 'You need to push Rose, push as hard as you can.'

Bravely, the white-faced young woman, clinging to life by not much more than a thread, bore down with the dregs of her strength.

With gritted teeth, Lara waited, then with a stab of relief, she sensed movement, and the placenta was delivered. Her patient was still bleeding profusely but now the afterbirth was out, she could massage the uterus to make it contract.

Her gloved hands were slick with blood but she rubbed and massaged, determined to stem the bleeding. She wouldn't lose the young mother now, not after how hard she'd fought to deliver her baby girl. Holding her breath, still putting every bit of energy into the procedure, she felt the first tightening of the uterus.

Rose was still bleeding out though, even though it had slowed.

As her mind scrabbled for anything else she could do, there was a shout from downstairs. 'Ambulance!'

'Thank Christ!' Bingham spat, as Lara raised her eyes to the whitewashed ceiling to give thanks.

As the ambulance men waited quietly at the door, Bingham gave the exact details of the case while Lara continued to massage Rose's abdomen. The bleeding had slowed some more, so that was encouraging, but she didn't want to risk changing tack too soon, not with how long it would take the ambulance to reach the Infirmary in Preston where Rose would receive an urgent blood transfusion. Once Lara was satisfied the uterus was firmly contracted, she applied plenty of padding, wiped away the worst of the blood-staining and gently told her patient about the hospital admission.

Rose was barely conscious, but she nodded her head and seemed to understand. Then with moments to go before the ambulance men took her on the stretcher, Lara gathered the baby girl from the crib, wrapped her in a shawl and lay her right there beside her mother. 'This is your daughter, Rose, and she is very beautiful.'

The young mother's eyes flickered open and she nuzzled the child, then with a bleary smile, she slipped back into a drowsy state. But there was no doubt Rose had sensed her baby next to her and Lara knew it had been an important moment.

As the ambulance men moved close to the bed, Lara gathered the baby girl and held her snuffling in her arms while they gently transferred Rose to the stretcher. Following as they descended the stairs, she saw a white-faced, stricken young man leaning on the back of an armchair. He held back a sob as the ambulance men passed, then shot an agonised glance in her direction. It was obvious this was Danny Ryan, the baby's father.

'Rose has lost a lot of blood, but they'll transfuse her at the hospital,' she told him as soon as she was beside him with a gentle hand on his arm. He emitted an agonising groan and his eyes filled with tears when he saw the extent of blood spatter on her yellow frock. She put her free arm around his shoulders, stayed with him until he'd come round enough to show interest in his baby daughter.

As he reached to stroke the snuffling baby's tiny face, she heard him croak, 'She's got red hair, just like her mother.'

'Yes, she has... and I can tell you now, she's a little fighter.'

He gulped, straightened up then. 'Can I hold her, nurse?'

'Yes, of course you can.' She smiled, handing the child over, impressed by how competently he handled his firstborn.

He glanced up then with an exhausted smile. 'I'm the youngest of a big family and my sisters and brothers have plenty of kids. But this little one... she's mine and Rose's...'

He gulped, swiped at his eyes with the back of his hand but then he was rocking his daughter back and forth.

Once the ambulance had set off with a clanging of its bell, Bingham came back inside the cottage. 'You come with me in the car, Danny. You can hold your baby girl in the back... She was a bit slow to start breathing so she'll need to be checked over at the hospital too.'

'Righto,' the young man said, swallowing hard and already following Bingham out through the door.

When the two men had gone, the silence of the house closed in around Lara as she stood alone in the tiny front room. In the dim light, she glanced down at her yellow-patterned dance frock and saw dark patches of blood all down the front and spattered over her high-heeled shoes. She'd lost track of time, and it felt disorientating when she recalled she'd started this dramatic evening in The Fleece.

Ah well, there'll be other village dances, she thought, suddenly feeling a hit of fatigue. But she needed to rally; there was a clean-up operation to undertake and no nurse worth her hospital badge would leave any trace of a mess.

Just as she was about to look for cloths and a mop and bucket, the door clicked open and two older women bustled in.

'Hello there, Nurse Flynn,' the shorter, stockier one called. 'You look like you could do with a cup of tea.'

'Or something stronger.' Her companion laughed. 'It looks like you've been through the mill with that delivery.'

Tired as she was, for a few moments, she couldn't work out who these women were and what they were doing here.

'I'll draw some hot water from the boiler. Then you can get yourself in that kitchen and clean up a bit,' the stockier one instructed.

'I'll need to go back upstairs, sort things out up there first... It's a heck of a mess.'

'Don't you be worrying about that, Nurse Flynn; we've come to put it right. This here is Danny Ryan's aunt and I'm her best friend – we went to school together and we work at Hargreaves Mill in Ridgetown, so we're used to mopping up after accidents.

We've even delivered one or two babies as well and one lass gave birth right next to her loom.'

Lara tried to offer a response, but her head began to feel fuzzy with exhaustion. So as the women shepherded her into the kitchen and instructed her to wash, that's exactly what she did. Once she'd got the worst of the blood off her arms and her shoes, she went upstairs to gather Bingham's medical instruments and cleaned them in the bowl of hot water duly provided by the women. Once the instruments were wrapped securely in a clean pillowcase taken from the drying rack above the stove and she was preparing to leave, Danny Ryan's aunt called to her, 'I know you're not from round here, Nurse Flynn. But for what it's worth, I don't think what some folk are saying about you having a lot to learn because you're a city girl is worth listening to. You're doing all right, Nurse Flynn, I'm damned sure you are.'

'Thank you.' She smiled as she made to go out of the door, and even though it wasn't an outright compliment, it was something she could work with.

When she'd followed the young lad from the village hall to deal with the emergency, she hadn't taken much note of her surroundings. But now she saw that Rose's cottage was set in a row of six that formed part of a large group of houses that provided accommodation for the mill workers. They were newer and bigger than the tiny cottages she'd become used to in the centre of the village and with lights twinkling in their windows, they appeared picturesque. For a moment, she felt disorientated and unsure of which direction to take to get back to the surgery, but then she caught the sound of voices, probably the tail end of the revellers at the village hall, and headed that way. As she walked, she felt the cool night air on her face and she glanced up to the sky crammed with bright stars and hoped Rose and the baby were safe. 'What an evening,' she sighed into the darkness. And when a lone owl hooted as if in agreement, it made her smile.

As the solid shape of the surgery loomed, she noted a light on in the downstairs front window where Mrs Hewitt had her sitting room. As soon as she opened the front door, the house-keeper appeared and clicked on the hall light. 'My goodness, Nurse Flynn, when Dr Bingham nipped in to call the hospital before he went off with Danny and the baby, he said you'd fought hard to save that mother and baby, but you look like you've been in a war zone.'

Glancing down at her dance dress, she felt shocked by the extent of the bloodstaining now stark in the glare of the electric light.

'Get that frock and those stockings and shoes off right away,' Mrs H ordered. 'Leave them with me; I'll get them sorted.'

'Are you sure?' She gasped.

''Course I'm sure; sorting out clothing that's used in the line of duty is part of my job. And anyway, Marion and Angus came back in a bad state from the dance, so I've already been mopping up tonight.'

'I'm sorry, Mrs H.'

'It's not your fault, lass,' the housekeeper replied. 'Now slip that frock off and get straight to bed. At least it's Sunday tomorrow and unless there's another emergency, we can all have a bit of a lie-in.'

15

_____

'How did you get on at the dance?' Daniel Makepeace asked first thing Monday morning as Lara pulled the blood pressure monitor in its scuffed case from her medical bag. Just as she straightened up, one of the brown cows in the field lifted its head and gazed directly at her.

'Oh, well... I didn't stay long because I was called to attend a patient.'

She glanced back at the cow, but it had lowered its head now and was munching the grass.

'I did hear about that emergency you attended. And I've been told Rose Ryan's in the Infirmary and she's had a blood transfusion but she's doing very well, as is the little one.'

'You know as much as me.' She smiled, increasingly aware of how news spread fast in the village. 'All fine with your blood pressure, Mr Makepeace. But your pulse is slower than usual, so I'll call by to check it again later.'

He sighed. 'There's no need for that, Nurse Flynn. I'm doing all right and whatever happens now, it's like to be.'

'I'm aware of that, Mr Makepeace,' she offered gently, 'but I have a duty to monitor your condition and make sure you're as well as you possibly can be.'

He shrugged good-naturedly. 'As always, I'm at your mercy, Nurse Flynn... and it'll be nice to see you coming back in through that door.'

'It's a deal then,' she said, clicking shut her medical bag. 'I'll see you later.'

It gave her a boost to start her day with such a cheerful patient and it put a spring in her step as she made her way outside. Pulling her bicycle from the wall, she glanced up the street to see Mr Collins unloading his butcher's van and farther down, Miss Shaw was unlocking the door to the post office. It was still early days for her here in Ingleside but after delivering Rose Ryan's baby, she had begun to feel more comfortable within this tight community.

It niggled her though that she hadn't seen Marion this morning at breakfast or the whole of yesterday. After sensing that edge of melancholy to her at the village dance on top of the morning she'd seen her crying as she'd left the bathroom, Lara knew her friend's carefree appearance wasn't the full picture. Mrs Hewitt had told her Marion was 'resting up' as she often did after she'd been out to the pub. But in the careful way the house-keeper had spoken, it made her think that she also had concerns. She'd toyed with the idea of going down to Marion's room and tapping on her door, but at this early stage of what she hoped would be a worthwhile relationship, it still felt too soon to intrude.

Almost as if she'd willed it, she heard the thrum of a motor-cycle engine from the top of the street and in moments, Marion sailed by with a wave and a smile. Probably on her way to see Lucy Taylor at Fell Farm. Seeing her so cheerful, Lara felt relieved as she mounted her bicycle and pedalled towards the bridge. And as she passed over the brook, she caught the murmur of water rippling over smooth, brown stones and her thoughts moved on.

Her visits were straightforward, dressing changes and a routine check on a farmer's daughter recently discharged from the fever hospital in Preston after a nasty case of mumps. As she cycled from one farm to another, she realised how much more settled she felt, and she'd even got used to the potholed farm tracks and the noisy yard dogs that rattled their chains.

When all her cases had been dealt with satisfactorily, she pedalled back towards Ingleside, content with her morning's work. The purr of a motorcycle up ahead indicated that Marion was also making her way back to the village. That was good; at least she'd be able to catch up with her over lunch.

Then seeing a hedgehog run across the road right in front of her, she was so surprised, she momentarily lost attention and wobbled on her bicycle. Tutting to herself, she focused back on an upcoming sharp corner. Then a violent screech of metal and an ear-splitting bang came at her so hard, she felt a heavy clutch of fear in her chest.

With a horrible jolt, she knew it had to be Marion's motorcycle. She felt light-headed, as if she might be sick, but she stood up on her pedals and pushed hard with her legs. Sucking in air as she hurtled around the next corner, she pedalled frantically, moving as fast as she could. Then rounding the next bend, she saw dust in the air and the back end of a smashed motorcycle, and her chest tightened in a vice-like grip.

Skidding to a halt, she jumped from her bicycle, letting it fall to the ground. Then she ran. She wanted to shout and scream for help, but her breath felt stuck.

The front end of the motorcycle had slammed hard against the trunk of a huge tree; it was twisted wreckage. But there was no sign of Marion. Frantically, she tugged and pulled at the wreck, scraped it back over the stony ground just in case she was lying underneath, but still there was nothing.

Gasping for breath, she pushed aside tall grass, scanning furiously for any clue. As the cows lowed in the field and the birds twittered above, she strained her ears, desperate for any sound of an injured human.

She screamed, 'Marion, where are you?'

Her heart was hammering so hard, it was painful and for a moment, she couldn't think what else to do. Then it crossed her mind that maybe Marion had staggered up from the wreckage and limped away. But no, there wouldn't have been time and the damage to the motorcycle undercut that theory in a single second. She shuddered; there was a bitter taste in her mouth at the possibility that her friend might not have survived.

She widened her search, knowing if the motorcycle had been going at a fair whack, Marion could have been thrown. Seeing a dip in a bank of long grass, she plunged in.

'Marion!' she shouted 'Marion, where are you?'

Horror clutched her heart when she saw a booted leg protruding from the grass, and when she pushed through, she saw a bloodied mass of dark, curly hair.

She choked on her breath; the shock of finding her colleague overwhelmed her for a split-second. Then her training kicked in.

'Marion!' she shouted, throwing herself to the ground beside her.

She squeezed her arm. No response.

She cleared the grass and earth around her nose and mouth. Was she breathing? She couldn't tell.

An urgent voice screamed in her head. *Look again. Is she breathing?*

Immediately, she saw the rise and fall of her chest.

Airway. I need to protect her airway. And she might have frac-tured vertebrae so she can't be moved.

She crouched closer, horrified to see a significant head injury. Also, Marion's left wrist was bent out of shape. Broken, it was broken. She must have hit the tree hard, then been thrown into the grass. It twisted her heart right then to see her vibrant colleague brought so low. But even as her brain struggled to take it in, her medical training kicked in and she was monitoring her vital signs and recognising the need to call for an ambulance. But how the hell was she going to do that, out here on a deserted country lane?

She gulped in air, her heart still hammering, pounding in her ears. She had to calm down but being here with an injured colleague was a far different scenario than anything she'd ever dealt with. Yes, she could rely on her enhanced knowledge to do the right things, but all the worst-case scenarios were also swirling through her head.

She ground her teeth in frustration. She had to get a grip on herself; she was always so good at forming a plan. Then, right when she needed it, a voice inside her head began screaming information at her.

Check, she needed to check her vital signs again – her breathing was shallow and when she felt for the carotid pulse, she was sure it was weakening. Her hands were shaking, and as panic tightened her chest, she fought back tears. She balled her fists, dug her nails into the palms of both hands. She had to get a grip because right now, there was no one else.

Come on, she growled to herself, sucking in air, forcing herself to steady up.

That's when she knew her only chance was to alert a passer-by because there was no way she could leave Marion unconscious at the side of the road to call for help.

'It's just me and you for now, Marion,' she said, jutting her chin. 'But don't you worry, I'm going to find someone. I'm going to stop someone, and I'll get this sorted.'

She strained her ears for any sound of a motorcar or a tractor.

Nothing. There was nothing.

She'd just have to hold fast, keep listening. Someone had to come along eventually.

Jumping up, she ran to her bicycle, grabbed her medical bag.

Throwing herself back down beside her friend, she pulled out a dressing and carefully, ever so carefully, applied it to the head wound. It was impossible to see the full extent of the injury due to Marion's mass of wavy hair, but at least the dressing would stem further blood loss and keep the area clean.

Suddenly, Marion's breath gurgled in her throat and became even shallower. Shock swept Lara in a fresh tide, but she fought hard for composure and clutched her friend's hand, gasping then murmuring words of encouragement; she told her everything was going to be all right. It seemed to work; her breathing strengthened a little. But she knew there was a limit to how long she could wait like this.

More time ticked by. A black and white cow came to the fence to snort and peer over, flicking its ears backwards and forwards.

'I'm doing all I can,' she said. 'Just waiting for assistance.'

Even as she spoke the words, she heard horse's hooves.

She jumped up, dashed into the lane.

As a horse-drawn vehicle rounded the bend, she saw it was the milk-cart with the skinny black horse that she'd seen in the village. Stepping boldly out in front, she held up a hand. 'Stop!'

she yelled. 'There's been an accident. My nurse colleague, Marion, has been badly injured. I need you to go as fast as you can to the village surgery, tell Mrs Hewitt to call an ambulance.'

The thin, elderly driver pulled up, pressed a hand to his chest and sat gaping as she relayed the essential detail.

Feeling the urgency, needing him to set off at speed, she felt spiralling despair as he still sat staring open-mouthed in her direction.

'Did you get all that?' she shouted. 'You need to go now! As fast as you can.'

'I've got it,' he said, then he straightened in his seat, vigorously shook the reins and called urgently to his horse. The cart shot off at a fair whack with milk churns rattling at the back.

She was already back with Marion, monitoring her breathing, making regular checks of her pulse. 'Help is on its way. You're going to be fine,' she breathed, comforting herself more than anything.

Angus was the first to arrive from the surgery. He leapt out of the blue Austin and was by her side in moments.

'She's breathing. I haven't moved her in case there's a spinal injury.'

'Good thinking,' he grunted, swiping at his eyes, then beginning his own checks of pulse and breathing.

'I can't believe this has happened,' he almost sobbed. 'She's such a good motorbike rider.'

'Accidents happen, I suppose. And I'm thinking she must have lost control on the bend,' her voice tailing off as it fell way short of her usual confident tone.

He cleared his throat, reached to feel for the carotid pulse. When he spoke again, his voice was thick with emotion. 'Herbert told us you were following close behind her. It doesn't bear thinking about but sometimes, this road can be deserted for hours. And her lying here... in the grass, even if the motorbike had been found, it doesn't mean to say—'

She gripped his arm. 'All of that is what could have happened. It was fortunate that I did find her.'

He bowed his head then, sucked in a ragged breath.

As time ticked on and still there was no sign of an ambulance, Angus became even more restless, and he began to pace back and forth between Marion and the road. 'I think we should try to get her in the back of the car. Or maybe I could drive up to one of the farms, organise a cart to move her.'

She was so tempted to agree with him but without a stretcher to hold Marion steady, the act of moving her any other way would be extremely risky. 'They can't be much longer; we need to wait.'

At the first sound of an ambulance bell, Angus leapt up, ready to flag the vehicle down. She remained steadfast at Marion's side, checking her vital signs yet again. 'The ambulance is coming,' she told her friend, 'and we're going to get you straight to hospital.'

Even as the ambulance men were climbing out of the vehicle, Angus was relaying all the information. The men listened as they pulled out their stretcher then walked to where Marion lay. With utmost care, they moved her, keeping her spine straight and at Lara's insistence, they applied a neck collar. Only when the stretcher had been slipped into the back of the ambulance and Angus had insisted on escorting her because of all that Lara had already done, did she begin to feel easier.

As the ambulance assistant made to close the back doors, Angus called out, 'As soon as she's settled at the Infirmary, I'll ring Stan Smith from the garage, get him to come with his truck to collect the motorcycle.'

'All right,' she called back, not giving a damn about the

tangled wreck of the bike but wanting it gone as soon as possible. She couldn't even look at it without feeling that same violent swoop of her heart she'd had when she'd heard the crash. She hoped the infernal machine never got to run on a road ever again.

Angus had given her the key to the Austin and as she listened to the ambulance bell receding down the lane, she clutched it so tightly that she felt the metal dig into her palm. Her throat tightened then, and she felt tears streaming down her cheeks. She let them come; she needed to cry. And as she swiped them away with the back of her hand, she began to feel steadier.

Walking slowly, feeling a little light-headed, she slipped into the driver's seat of the blue Austin. She hadn't driven for ages, not since she'd borrowed a car to take Fiona and Maeve on a day out. It felt odd at first to be behind the wheel and she made the vehicle jump and backfire until she got the measure of it.

Driving carefully, excruciatingly aware of every single corner, she made her way back to Ingleside and parked up skew-whiff down the side of the building in the exact same style as Angus. Her legs felt weak as she clambered out and made her way to the back of the surgery. As soon as she had the door open, Mrs Hewitt was there pulling her into an embrace.

The housekeeper tried to speak but her voice broke in a sob, then she gulped, 'I've always worried about her on that motorbike.'

'She's all right, she's going to be all right,' Lara said, trying to reassure herself. Then slowly, Mrs Hewitt led her through to the kitchen.

'Cup of tea, we both need a cup of tea.' The housekeeper's voice broke again for a second.

Lara sat quietly in her place at the table, staring into space, images of Marion lying at the side of the road and the twisted metal of her motorcycle flashing in and out of her head.

When a mug of tea was placed in front of her, she took a sip of the hot liquid and it grounded her a little.

'Is there anything I need to do here? Are there any patients to be seen?'

'No, lass. We cancelled the afternoon clinic and Dr Bingham will be back soon from Ridgetown hospital. It's typical, isn't it, that there was quite a list for him to see today.'

'That's good,' she breathed, struggling to grasp the edge of the words.

When the kitchen door burst open and Bingham appeared wide-eyed and red-faced, it was clear he'd already heard about Marion's accident.

As she conveyed the detail, he listened intently, asking a question here and there but satisfied with how the case had been handled.

'So she was still unconscious when they put her in the ambulance.'

'Yes, she was. But her pulse and breathing were steady.'

'Good, that's good,' he muttered, jumping up from his seat then and pacing up and down before abruptly leaving the room.

'He'll be going to his clinic room,' Mrs Hewitt said. 'That's where he deals with things.'

Lara felt exhausted but restless all at the same time. An uncomfortable state, but one which was best remedied by applying herself to her work. Rising from the table, she straightened her uniform. 'Right, so, I said I'd call back in to recheck Mr Makepeace's pulse because it was slower than usual this morning. Are there any other visits that need to be made?'

'Not that I know of,' Mrs Hewitt replied. 'But don't you think you should rest up? It must have been a heck of a shock to find Marion like that.'

'Yes, it was... but in times of trouble, I'm best if I keep busy.'

Mrs Hewitt offered a ragged laugh. 'I understand completely, I'm the same... but, apart from what you've just said about Mr Makepeace, I can't think of anything else you need to be doing right now.'

She nodded. 'Well I won't be long, just in case anything else does come in. And once I've seen him, I'll come back to check with you and if there isn't anything else, I'll walk up the lane to collect my bicycle.'

'Sounds like a good plan.'

Before she left the surgery, she wasn't sure why, but she climbed the stairs and took a moment to gaze down the corridor towards Marion's room. It was probably too soon, and Mrs Hewitt would take charge of it anyway but in due course, her colleague would need some personal items for her hospital locker. She remembered from her own time spent in bed after her accident, the smell of her favourite soap and a photograph of her group of nurse trainees had been important for her. Especially given that her thoughts had been so jumbled after she'd regained consciousness. It had been a frightening time and when her memory did click back in, it had come with the dull thud of metal on metal and the blood-curdling scream of a passer-by. She shuddered now and inevitably, the scar began to throb, and she pressed a hand there to soothe it. But even as she tried to settle her thoughts, a nagging voice in her head was telling her that maybe Marion had had a similar accident because she'd brought the bad luck with her from Liverpool. It was Maeve's voice that came to her then: *Jeez... don't be thinking that. Accidents do happen, you know.*

16

———

As she walked down to Daniel's cottage, she felt relieved that the street was quiet. Just a sharp glance from the postmistress as she stood at the open door of her shop, and a raised hand from a sturdy woman farther down the street that turned out not to be for her, but the person walking behind her. She moved briskly, not wanting to have to field any questions regarding Marion's accident because undoubtedly, many of the villagers would already know. As she tapped on Daniel's door and walked through, she felt as if she were escaping prying eyes. He lay sleeping peacefully, his snow-white hair blending with the spotless pillow. A breath of air through the open shutter felt refreshing and as she stood clutching her leather bag, she drew solace from the slow amble of the cows in the field. And when a tiny bird, a wren, came to perch on the window ledge, it felt like a sign of hope.

'I heard what happened; it must have been a shock,' Daniel said softly, rousing so quietly as he hovered between sleeping and wakening that it didn't even startle her.

'Yes, it was,' she replied. 'But of course, it could have been a lot worse.'

'Herbert Threlfall told me he was the one to raise the alarm and tell Mrs Hewitt to call the ambulance.'

'If he's the man with the milk churns and the black horse, then yes, that's true.'

'Aye, that's Herbert all right... He's a sleepy sort, usually away in a daydream. But sounds like he managed to pull out all the stops today.'

'He did indeed,' she breathed, 'and you have no idea how relieved I was to hear the sound of his cart coming down that lane.'

'Somebody must have been watching over you, Nurse Flynn.'

'Mmm,' she replied, thinking if that had been the case, then why had they waited so long to send Herbert?

As she reached for Daniel's wrist to check his pulse, he lay quietly gazing up at the whitewashed ceiling. And when he spoke again, the sharp line between his brows deepened. 'She's a lovely lass, Nurse Wright. I remember her from when she was on the district before she went off up to Scotland... But when she came back, she seemed changed somehow.'

'In what way?' she asked, feeling something chime with her own recent thoughts.

'It's hard to say, but I could sense she was carrying a weight that she'd never had before. Shadows in her eyes, something was different. You know me, I speak my mind, so I asked her about it. She brushed it off, said it was just getting used to being back, but her voice didn't sound right.'

'Probably just the busyness of the job. The responsibility of coming back from Scotland to work at a more senior level,' she told him, hearing the worry in his voice and needing to allay his concern.

'Aye, it could have been... but the last time she came to visit me here, she was almost in tears when I told her the story of how my Martha had lost a newborn babe all those years ago. I don't know how we got onto the subject; must've been something to do with one of the new babies born in the village. But it hit her hard, I could see it did.'

She felt there was some weight to what he was saying but any story involving the loss of a helpless little baby was always emotive, even for a trained nurse. She'd bear it in mind though for when her colleague came home. A wave of anxiety washed over her then and her chest felt tight. She knew it was shock from the accident but as she drew a slow breath, she recognised there was perhaps more to it than that.

'Sorry, Nurse Flynn, I didn't mean to worry you. I can sometimes be a wistful old fella.'

She placed her fingers gently on his wrist to recheck his pulse. 'No need to apologise; there's nothing wrong with speaking your mind. It would be helpful for my job if more patients did so... and what's more, Mr Makepeace, I am very pleased to report that your pulse is now satisfactory.'

'Thank you very much.' He smiled, displaying his single tooth.

'So, I'll leave you to it, and if you're on my list for tomorrow, I'll see you then.'

Just as she reached down to pick up her bag, a head poked through the open shutter and a voice called so abruptly that she shot up with a start.

'Hello there, Nurse Flynn – and of course, Mr Makepeace.'

It was Leo and right then, she felt agitated because he'd given her such a shock.

'Sorry if I gave you a start.' He grinned. 'I rent this field from Mr Makepeace here and I was just checking on my cows.'

'Nurse Flynn isn't at her best today, Leo,' Daniel said quietly. 'Have you not heard about the accident?'

'What accident? I've been out at the farms all day. What's been going on?'

'It's young Nurse Wright: she crashed her motorcycle, and she's in a bad way. Nurse Flynn was first on the scene, so she's had a lot to deal with.'

'God, I'm so sorry, Lara... I mean Nurse Flynn. I had no clue.'

She felt unexpectedly moved by his concern and gulped back tears.

'Is there anything I can do? Do you need any help?'

The vet appeared so worked up, she thought for a moment he was going to clamber through the open window, and the ridiculousness of it lifted her spirits a little.

'No, that's all right, thank you,' she said. 'And there's no more news from the hospital at present. So we need to hold tight and assume she's doing okay.'

He blew out a breath, shook his head. 'But she's such a good motorcyclist.'

She shrugged her shoulders. 'It's just one of those things, I suppose. It was on a corner; maybe the road was slippy.'

'But everything's bone dry at present. All the farmers are complaining the grass isn't growing.'

Suddenly weary and not up to going over the accident again, she stooped to pick up her bag and raised a hand in farewell. 'I need to get on; I'm going to retrieve my bicycle from the lane. I'll be seeing you again, Mr Makepeace. And no doubt you too, Mr Sullivan.'

'Wait up!' the vet shouted, and without any warning, he leapt up and vaulted in through the open shutters.

'Wish I could still do that,' Daniel laughed.

She stood, shocked; whatever did this man think he was doing?

He looked her straight in the eye. 'I'll go with you to collect your bicycle. You're bound to be shaken up by what happened.'

'No, honestly, I'm perfectly fine,' she trilled.

He took no notice whatsoever and strode past her to wait at the door. Then after she'd called another goodbye to Daniel, he walked beside her.

'Really, there's no need. And I'm sure you're busy with your work.'

'You're in luck; I'm all finished for the day.'

She didn't have any choice but to accept his company and as she explained her need to check back in with Mrs Hewitt in case there were any new calls, he told her he'd wait for her by the bridge.

After she'd collected him, they walked in silence and at first, it felt awkward, but then, once she'd become distracted by the wildflowers and the luscious green of the hedges, she realised that Leo was also taking in the detail of the country lane. At one point, when an orange-tipped butterfly fluttered onto a tall stem of cow parsley, she stood entranced with him quietly beside her until it flew away.

She made no comment, but it intrigued her to recognise the other side to this man who was more often seen as a mocking presence, or drunk in the pub with Angus.

'It's not far now,' she said.

'Must be at chestnut corner. I thought it might be; it's caught many another out, usually in cars, though. She must have been going at a fair whack.'

'You know Marion; she tends to move fast.'

He grunted an acknowledgement.

Once they reached the corner and she saw the twisted metal of the motorbike, a deep shudder ran through her body.

Leo stood shaking his head. 'It sends shivers down my spine,' he said. 'So many times I've whizzed around this corner in my van, almost on two wheels.'

She sighed, moved towards her bicycle. As hard as she tried not to glance towards the place where she'd found Marion, she felt her eyes drawn to the spot with its flattened grass and still bright bloodstain.

She felt a cold wash of unease rise through her and she knew she needed to be away from here as quickly as possible. 'I'll just get my bicycle,' she croaked.

That's when her hands and her whole body began to shake.

She fought to keep it contained but in seconds, it had taken a grip on her.

He grabbed hold to try and steady her. 'It's shock, just shock... You need to let it out.'

Her teeth were chattering so hard, she couldn't form a reply. So she let him hold onto her and when he pulled her close against his chest, she felt the warmth of his body and it was oddly comforting. She'd not been held by a man like this since Patrick, and that thought triggered a whole new wave of the jitters.

'I'm sorry, I'm so sorry,' she groaned, still shaking, still feeling the warmth of his body.

He soothed her with a mix of gentle words as if he were calming a skittish horse. She knew he was acting instinctively, and he was good at what he did.

She had no choice but to let the shakes work their way through and as they began to settle, she drew some slow breaths.

'I'm fine, perfectly fine,' she said quietly, as soon as her body began to calm.

As she placed her medical bag in the bicycle basket, then began to wheel it away, he reacted instantly. 'No, definitely not. You're not anywhere near ready to ride that thing.'

'I was just going to wheel it. I'll leave the riding till tomorrow.'

'I suppose that's all right.' He smiled.

Then firmly, he grasped the handlebars and took the bicycle from her, and she had no choice but to let him assist. And as they walked quietly away together, she made her peace with it because it was a friendly gesture on his part and the right thing to do.

Once they were at the outskirts of the village, she took charge of the bike again and he walked beside her as far as the vet's surgery where they said their goodbyes. When she glanced back over her shoulder, he was still gazing after her and he offered a warm smile.

After securing the bicycle in the shed behind the surgery, she was starting to feel much calmer as she walked back in through the door. But even before she got to the kitchen, she sensed a charged atmosphere. Angus was in his usual seat with Bingham at the head of the table, but Mrs Hewitt was standing by her chair crying and swiping at her eyes with a lace-trimmed handkerchief.

'What is it?' she gasped, 'is there news about Marion?'

'Yes,' the housekeeper hiccupped.

Her heart tightened with horror. 'Has she deteriorated?'

'No, no,' Mrs Hewitt croaked. 'In fact, she's come round a bit now.'

Instantly, her body slumped with relief and she grabbed onto her own chair.

'I'm sorry, Lara, to give you a shock. It's just that I've been keeping it all locked down inside. Hoping for the best, preparing for the worst.'

'That's all right, Mrs H. It's been a very stressful day,' she breathed.

Angus spoke up then. 'She's going to be all right; she *has* to be all right.'

Bingham was staring straight ahead, his eyes red as if he'd been crying. 'I've just got off the telephone from speaking to her consultant. She's had an X-ray and a fractured skull has been confirmed, but it's not a depressed fracture and her vital signs are stable. They've sutured her scalp, set her broken wrist, but there's no way of knowing yet if she'll make a full recovery.'

Lara felt her heart twist; what Bingham had said about the outcome being uncertain was true. And seeing Marion's empty chair opposite, she felt tears sting her eyes.

'There, there, lass,' Mrs Hewitt called, still dabbing at her eyes, but she was instantly by her side and had an arm around her shoulders. 'You know our Marion; she's a fighter... Of course she's going to get better.'

Mrs Hewitt had a cup of tea laced with brandy in front of her in due course, encouraging her to drink it down. 'It must have been the biggest shock ever for you, Lara, finding her like that. But thank goodness you did.'

'Every credit,' Bingham called, raising his teacup.

'Any one of us would have done the same, we all know that. It's just I happened to be the one.'

Bingham leant forward in his seat. 'Nevertheless, you did all the right things, and you held your nerve. If you'd tried to move her or left her alone to call for help, then the outcome could have been very different.'

'Hear, hear, to that,' Angus added. Then he scraped back his chair, coughed, and when he spoke, she could hear the raw emotion he was barely keeping at bay. 'I'm off to The Dorchester to raise a glass to Marion's recovery. Anyone want to join me?'

They all shook their heads and Mrs Hewitt added, 'Go easy, Dr Fitzwilliam. We're a member of staff down tomorrow. So it'll be all hands to the wheel.'

'Roger that, Mrs H,' he replied as he walked slowly to the door.

Once the young doctor had gone, the kitchen felt even emptier, and Lara had to fight to keep back the tears she'd managed to contain. The quiet was broken only by the clink of cutlery and the spit of fire in the Aga. But when she gazed across to see Tiddles, the tabby cat, oblivious to all as he lay stretched in the warmth with his four white paws pointing towards the fire, it gave her some solace. She would have liked to go over there and give him a stroke, but he never liked to be disturbed by anyone other than Mrs Hewitt.

Once Bingham had bidden them a good evening, Mrs H opened a cupboard and pulled out the sherry bottle. When she lifted it in her direction, Lara murmured, 'Go on then. Just a small one.'

'Might as well because we'll be busier than ever tomorrow,' Mrs H sighed as she walked back to the table with two small glasses filled to the brim. The housekeeper's voice was husky with emotion as she raised her glass. 'Here's to Marion: may she make a good recovery and be back with us soon.'

'To Marion,' Lara called as she clinked her glass.

And as Mrs H settled back in her chair and they sat quietly together for a while longer, it was on the tip of her tongue to tell her about her own accident in Liverpool. But she didn't want to send ripples through the moment of unity they had right now.

And of course, the telling of a traumatic experience always brought it back in some part, and she knew she wasn't ready for that, not yet.

17

The plan Mrs Hewitt had devised to provide cover during Marion's absence involved Lara taking the Austin so she could make the visits to the outlying farms. It would take too long to bicycle there if they were to keep any semblance of her fellow nurse's daily round. She would go first to Lucy Taylor at Fell Farm, not to be confused with Fell Foot Farm which would be number two on her list to see George Seed, a farmer who'd just been discharged from the Infirmary following an accident with a trailer that resulted in a broken left leg. Then after calling by Mrs Ashworth to redress her diabetic leg ulcer, she would bring the car back to the surgery by lunchtime. Angus was to cover the clinic single-handedly this morning while Dr Bingham went out to Ridgetown hospital.

'And there's good news,' Mrs Hewitt announced. 'Dr Bingham called the Infirmary first thing, and our Marion is rallying nicely.'

'Hurrah,' Angus cheered groggily; Lara could see he was trying to hide his exhaustion because despite Mrs Hewitt's plea, she'd heard him come in very late again last night.

'Also, we've had a call from the cottage hospital and at Dr Bingham's request, it has been confirmed that Nurse Sally Greenwood, a staff nurse on the male ward, will be helping out in clinic three afternoons per week until Marion's return.'

Instantly, Lara recognised the name of the friendly nurse whom she'd met briefly on her visit to the hospital. The one who'd had such a glint in her dark eyes when she'd been speaking to Angus.

'That's good news; she's an excellent nurse,' Angus called between munches of toast and jam. Beyond that, his expression remained blank. He was, of course, completely oblivious to Nurse Greenwood's charms. She shook her head, frustrated by the young doctor and his obsession with Ada the barmaid when he would be so much better suited to Sally. She smiled to herself then, aware she sounded like some older woman who saw herself as a matchmaker. Fleetingly, she wondered if it was a response to her own reticence following what had happened with Patrick in Liverpool.

Knowing the blue Austin was awaiting, she took her list of visits and the hand-drawn map Mrs Hewitt had provided, picked up her medical bag and exited the back door. The sky was a pale blue with only one or two scudding clouds, so at least she shouldn't have to deal with the flooded ditches and dodgy crossings of gushing streams that, according to Angus, appeared from nowhere on the fells in wet weather. He had revelled in the telling of his own story of being up to the axle in water with the engine cutting out. She was almost sure he'd been exaggerating but she'd keep an eye on the weather all the same. She shook her head as she recalled her first day when she'd got drenched to the bone. Already, even in the short time she'd been here, she was now much better prepared. And even though today seemed clear, she had a macintosh and a pair of wellington boots in the back of the car.

The Austin fired up straight away with no need for the starting handle and even though she hadn't driven any distance for a while, she knew the short run she'd done yesterday had pepped up her skills. But when she reached the narrower lanes that led up to the fells, it felt disconcerting to be so close to the drystone walls. On her bicycle, she could easily pull over if she met a horse-drawn cart or another vehicle. But in the car, she'd have to squeeze into a passing place or reverse down the lane. She could do it, she knew she could. But she was very aware that her proficiency as a driver would be judged by whichever local she encountered.

As she drove up a steep hill, the Austin slowed right down and almost stalled. The trusty little car responded nicely when she pumped the accelerator, but she'd be aware of that quirk in future. It made her think back to being on the motorcycle with Marion and her stomach twisted again at the shock of what had happened yesterday. She tried desperately to let those thoughts fly out to the open fields but still they lodged inside of her. She knew work would help but as she pulled over briefly to check Mrs Hewitt's hand-drawn map, she still felt very wound up.

Her first visit was to the Taylors' place and as she rattled over the cattle grid and onto the rough farm track, she felt the car bounce in and out of potholes and needed to slow right down. It seemed to take forever to wind her way through the close-cropped field dotted with scraggy sheep, but she was determined not to risk any damage to the car and get herself stuck and unable to proceed with the rest of her visits. At last, she spied the ramshackle barn she remembered from her visit with Marion and pulled up to park beside it.

Grabbing her medical bag off the passenger seat, she clambered out and instantly felt plunged into that blissful silence, punctuated only by the bleating of sheep and the mournful cry of a lone bird that circled overhead. She glanced towards the fells with their shades of green and russet-brown, then back down towards the valley with the cluster of houses in the distance that she knew to be Ingleside. There was something about this place, especially now she was here alone, that awed her with its beauty but also daunted her with its wide-open spaces. Then she recalled the abrupt reception she'd received from Mrs Taylor and it set off other thoughts. The farmer's wife had seemed harassed that day, and by the state of the farm and the comments Marion had made as they were leaving, it was clear that the Taylors were struggling to make ends meet. Lara had encountered many hard-pressed families in Liverpool, so this was nothing new to her. But she hadn't expected to find such poverty out here in the beautiful countryside. There was no escape from it she supposed – if you were poor, you were poor, wherever you lived.

Walking briskly towards the farmhouse, she focused on her visit to redress Lucy Taylor's leg wound. And as she made her way along the broken stone path that led to the farmhouse, her mind ticked over the procedure she'd memorised from her trip with Marion. This time, she avoided the stinging nettles, and she was prepared for the stink of manure and the raucous noise of the pigs in their shippon. And when the bristled head of a large pig shot out at her, she was far less shocked. 'Hello there,' she called to the creature. 'Yes, it's me again.'

As soon as she spotted the ramshackle farmhouse with its dark windows, she lifted her chin and increased her pace. Only a few strides from the door and a muscular, unkempt man with straggly brown hair, thinning on top, stepped out from an outbuilding and barred her way.

'So, Nursey, I saw you pulling up in your swanky blue car. You lot must be raking it in.'

Shocked for a second, she quickly realised this must be Lucy's father, Vic Taylor. Instantly, she sensed the volatility of the man, the moodiness that lurked beneath his barely contained hostility. She'd have to go carefully with this one, so she tempered her tone, kept it light. 'Oh, the car isn't mine. It belongs to Ingleside surgery,' she offered, steadily meeting his gaze.

His face was smudged with dirt; his large hands hung down by his sides. And as his eyes bored into her, she felt a warning prickle at the base of her neck.

She lifted her chin. 'I'm here to change Lucy's dressing.'

'Are you now,' he replied, his face twitching towards a smile or a grimace. In that split-second, she couldn't tell.

As she took another step towards the farmhouse door, he laughed. 'Only kidding, Nurse. As you've probably guessed, I'm the lass's father, Vic Taylor.'

He stretched out his arm to shake her hand and she had no choice but to take it. 'Pleased to meet you, Mr Taylor.'

'Well, I'll let you go about your duties; I know how busy you nurses are,' he said, turning, then walking away.

Relieved, she moved briskly to the farmhouse door. Knocked, then waited.

With the hairs at the back of her neck now truly prickling, it felt as if Mr Taylor was still watching her, and it made her uncomfortable.

When the door swung open and she was greeted by the smiling, blue-eyed lad in shorts and wellington boots she remembered from last time, she began to feel much easier.

'Hello, Robin, can I come in to see Lucy?'

The lad grinned and opened the door wide.

As she walked into the kitchen, it took a few seconds for her eyes to adjust to the dark interior but then she saw once more the low-beamed ceiling, the iron stove, and the ancient kitchen table where Alice Taylor was plunging and kneading another mass of bread dough. She called a hello and waited as the farmer's wife brushed a strand of hair from her cheek with the back of a floury hand, and then frowned. 'Is there any news on Nurse Wright? We heard about what happened to her from Herbert Threlfall on his milk round. We're all fretting over her, especially Lucy. She's almost like family to us after all the weeks she's been coming to do her dressing.'

Even though Lara was aware of the genuine concern the whole community had for Marion, she couldn't help but feel again that push-back against her. She sucked in a breath, thrust the feeling aside. 'Yes, it was a shock. But from what we've been told by the doctors at the Infirmary, Nurse Wright is making a good recovery.'

Alice heaved a sigh as she pulled the bread dough from the large earthenware dish and slapped it down onto the table. 'I've always worried about Nurse Wright on that motorcycle. I've often told her that there's no protection if she hits something.'

Lara sighed, nodded; since the accident, the same thought had crossed her mind many times. 'I suppose it's a case of never being fully aware of the risks until something happens.'

Alice glanced up. 'Not so sure about that, Nurse. I mean, any fool can work out that if you're riding a motorbike, going at speed, there's every likelihood that one day, you're going to come unstuck.'

The response was sharp, well placed, and there was little she could say in return, so she graciously withdrew from the discussion. She was here to do the dressing on the little girl's leg and that was it, really.

'Is it all right if I go up to see Lucy now?'

Alice glanced up with a frown. 'Well, I suppose there's no choice, given Nurse Wright's going to be out of action for quite some time.'

'I know it's not ideal for you to have to change nurses, but there's nothing we can do about it, I'm afraid.'

It helped her in that moment to have her own understanding of what it was like for families of chronic cases or those, like young Lucy, with slow-healing wounds. Once they'd put their faith in their nurse, it was hard to accept newcomers. Trust had to be earned. She knew that because in Liverpool, she had been that favoured, regular nurse to any number of families. And it was an anxious thing when a family member was unwell, particularly a child. All she could do here was to be supportive during this settling-down time and hope that with a consistent approach, she too could earn their trust. She knew she had a very different personality to Marion's and of course, she had a harder fight to win approval because she was an outsider. But this was the challenge she'd voluntarily taken on when she'd moved from Liverpool, so all she could do was get on with it.

After a mumbled reply from Alice, she saw young Robin waiting patiently and as soon as she made to move, he was ahead of her, climbing the narrow, creaking stairs. As she approached Lucy's trestle bed, she felt the responsibility of getting this crucial dressing just right.

'Hello, Lucy, I'm Nurse Flynn. I came to see you with Nurse Wright the other week. Do you remember?'

Lucy smiled shyly and nodded. Then Lara explained the reason for Marion's absence. She didn't give any detail of the accident, just said her colleague was unwell. But then Robin came out with, 'She crashed her motorbike into a tree and broke her head; there was blood everywhere.'

The pale girl with blonde hair the exact same colour as her brother's gasped, then frowned, tears welling in her eyes.

Instantly, Robin knew he'd upset her, and he knelt beside the bed and gave her a hug. 'Sorry, Sis,' he crooned. 'I was just repeating what Dad told me, and I thought Ma had let you know.'

She gave them a few moments to console each other as she washed her hands in the bowl of soapy water that had been left ready and waiting beside the bed. Then she opened her medical bag and began to lay out the materials and the iodine she would use for the dressing. By the time she was ready, Lucy had dried her eyes, and she offered a polite nod when Lara asked if she was ready for her to begin.

As she gently removed the bandage from the girl's leg, she deftly re-rolled it in the exact same way Marion had done. Then, carefully, she peeled back the dressing pad that was stained yellow with iodine. The raw, suppurating flesh of the wound had changed very little from when she'd visited with Marion, but perhaps there was more of the bumpy red healing tissue in evidence. It sent a shiver down her spine when she thought of the wound having been caused by one of the pigs she'd passed on her way up to the house.

Carefully, she swabbed the area with carbolic solution then liberally applied iodine directly to the wound. It was a good sign that Lucy gasped a little as she felt the sting because it meant the sensation was coming back as the tissue healed. Meticulous with the new dressing pad that had been sterilised by Mrs Hewitt in the fierce heat of the Aga, she unwrapped it from its surgical cloth and placed it carefully into position.

Lucy sucked in a sharp breath. 'It's a bit sore.'

'That's a good sign – shows that it's healing.' She smiled as she pulled a fresh bandage from her bag and began to apply it from the top of the girl's toes, all the way up to her knee.

After years of practice, she was proud of her bandaging technique and confident that the dressing would hold firm but not too tight, until she came back tomorrow to renew it. As she replaced the safety pin, she remembered the caramel toffee that Marion always gave her patient.

'I'm sorry, Lucy, but I've forgotten one of Nurse Wright's special toffees. I'll make sure to bring you two when I come back tomorrow.'

'That's all right, Nurse,' the girl replied. 'I sometimes give mine to Robin anyway.'

'So I'll bring one for your brother as well.' She smiled.

'Thank you,' Lucy called as Lara pulled the patchwork quilt back over her leg. 'I've been getting up and going down onto the settee in the parlour these last few days, so is that all right for me to do?'

'Yes, of course. So long as you keep the dressing clean and dry. It's good for you to have a change of scene.'

Once she was back downstairs, she shouted through to Alice, who was now washing up at the sink. 'The dressing's done, and the wound is looking good.'

'Right you are,' Alice called over her shoulder. 'I'll see you again tomorrow, then.'

As Lara pushed open the door, she scanned the yard for any sign of Lucy's father before emerging into bright daylight. Walking briskly to the car, she slipped into the driver's seat and reversed, then turned to drive back down the rough track and out onto the lane.

The next two visits to other farms were routine and as she headed back to the surgery, she felt satisfied with her day so far.

And knowing Daniel was on her list for the afternoon, she decided to nip in to see him now to save time.

Pulling over at the bottom of the street, she grabbed her bag and slipped out of the car. Knocking and entering as she always did, she was surprised to hear the murmur of voices in Daniel's room. She tapped on the open door, called out a greeting and hearing his response, she walked into the room.

Her patient was sitting up in bed holding court with the milkman Herbert Threlfall on a chair beside him, and a grey-haired woman across the room who was folding and packing clean clothes into the dresser drawers. Lara knew this must be his niece, Esther, the farmer's wife who came in daily to care for him.

'So, here she is. The nurse who's holding it all together at the surgery,' Daniel said with a smile.

Esther turned with a frown, but her eyes twinkled with good humour as she called across the room, 'Well, lass, you'll have your work cut out.'

'I've already realised that, and I could have done with much more experience in country practice before I took this on. But I'll just have to get on with it.'

Herbert cleared his throat. 'Well from what I saw yesterday, you're doing a very good job. It must've been terrible for you, finding poor Nurse Marion so badly injured. I had a heck of a shock; I was all over the place when you stopped me. But you were so clear with the instructions; it was a real help to Mrs Hewitt when she made that call to the ambulance.'

'Oh, I'm sure any other nurse would have done exactly the same.'

'No, lass, don't say that. You've got enough detractors around and about this village already. Don't you be running yourself down.'

'True, I suppose.' She shrugged, offering a grim smile.

Esther spoke up then. 'They'll come round in time, the local folk. But it'll probably take years. Nurse Beecham was here from being newly qualified, so she nursed more than one generation of villagers and farmers. So you can understand why folks think like they do.'

The words were meant to be reassuring, but Lara felt her heart sink because what it told her was that things could be difficult here for an indefinable length of time. She couldn't help but feel the hole that was being dug to bury her was getting deeper and deeper.

'Yes, of course I understand,' she said, forcing a smile. 'And I do realise it's going to be tough but just so you all know, I'm willing to stick it out through thick and thin.'

'Well said,' Daniel offered while Herbert nodded in agreement.

Then Esther called, 'You'll need every bit of that spirit, lass... And I'm telling you now, given what Daniel and Herbert have said about you today, I, for one, will not be getting involved with any more of that nasty gossip that's going round the village about you. And if I hear anything being said, I'll set them straight.'

It made her breath catch to have hard and fast confirmation of the level of opposition she was facing, and she was tempted to ask what the locals were saying. But she didn't want to put Esther on the spot, not now she seemed to have come over to her side. And, anyway, it didn't take much imagination to know that it'd be along the lines of her being a 'not from 'round here', jumped-up city girl who couldn't be trusted because she didn't have a clue about country folk and their ways. So she held her tongue, and gratefully took the vote of confidence she had from this group in the room.

After recording Daniel's pulse and blood pressure, she left the old friends to their chatter and drove the car back to the surgery.

Even as she pulled up, Angus was running out of the back door. 'Quick, I need the car. There's been an accident at the sawmill. Sounds like Ed Cronshaw's lost a finger while using the big, circular saw.'

'Do you need me to assist?' she called, as she grabbed her bag and jumped out of the driver's seat.

'No, the men at the mill are very capable; they're used to seeing severed fingers lying in the sawdust. And you'll only have time to have a quick bite to eat before the afternoon clinic.'

'Righto,' she called through the open car window as he sped away, leaving a cloud of dust in his wake.

Coughing as she walked into the surgery, she thought of Ed's wife, Lizzie. She was almost at term now with her second child and struggling to manage her little girl, Sue, who'd been recently discharged from the cottage hospital but was still fractious and clingy with her mother. She hoped the injury wouldn't mean Ed was out of work; like the rest of the families in the village, they needed the money coming in. With that came a stab of anger; everybody in the village knew that a big part of Ed's wage was spent in The Fleece and The Old Oak. Gallons of beer were consumed by him and Vic Taylor every working week.

Walking through now and into the kitchen, she caught the smell of freshly baked ginger cake and heard Mrs Hewitt call, 'Is that you, Nurse Flynn?'

The warmth of the housekeeper's voice made her feel cared for and she felt tears prick her eyes. Instantly, she swiped them away and she smiled when she saw a cup of tea and a slice of cake waiting at her place on the table.

'What bliss,' she sighed, her mind and body beginning to

ease as soon as she slipped onto her chair. 'I have no idea what any of us would do without you, Mrs H... You're the only reason we keep our heads above water.'

'Get away with you.' The older woman grinned, but Lara's comment was sincere, and she could see that the housekeeper appreciated it.

As Lara ate her cake and sipped her tea, Mrs H continued with her tasks, and it made Lara feel content but unsettled all at the same time. She knew exactly what was missing right now, and of course it was Marion's lively chatter. And she also knew that the two male doctors would be increasingly sombre this evening, which meant they'd be more inclined to sit and eat silently or mutter between themselves. She couldn't wait to have Marion back at the table.

18

The next few weeks went by in a flash with visits to patients in the village and out to the farms in the mornings and most afternoons. With the clinics in the surgery now being covered by Nurse Greenwood, Lara had some breathing space, but given she needed to drive the Austin, she felt the loss of her cycle rides along the country lanes. And she regularly met farm carts pulled by horses and needed to reverse each time to a passing place. Often, the men up on top offered a salute or a friendly nod and it felt good to have that acknowledgement. But all the while, as the heavy horses ambled by, she was tense at the wheel, twitching to get on with her next visit. Every day felt like one more turn of an ever-tightening screw as she strove to keep up with the workload but always fell short. At least the news from the Infirmary was positive: Marion's condition was improving daily and there was talk of her being discharged. It would still be many weeks before her injuries were healed well enough for her to come back to work, though, and that was understandable. So Lara's workload wasn't going to ease any time soon.

This morning, she was out in the Austin again, calling first to see Miss Dunderdale for a routine check following her discharge from Ridgetown hospital. The signs were promising given Dr Bingham had been very pleased with how settled she'd been each time he'd visited. And last evening, as they'd sat on at the kitchen table to discuss current cases, he'd gone so far as to say she seemed like a changed woman.

Then Mrs Hewitt had added, 'Or maybe she's realised just how lucky she was to survive and is now seeking a new life.'

Lara had been about to agree but then the conversation had been abruptly interrupted when Angus had burst in through the door with a bloodied nose.

'What the heck,' Mrs Hewitt had shouted and leapt up from the table, grabbing a tea towel along the way.

Bingham had also jumped up, his face bright red as if he were about to explode and he'd shouted, 'What the blazes have you been doing now?' as Mrs H thrust the tea towel into Angus's hand, then lifted his arm and told him to apply firm pressure to his nose.

Bingham had stood gripping the table as he'd waited to hear what Angus had to say.

The young doctor had groaned and winced, then tipped his head back as Mrs H had brought a clean flannel soaked in cold water to wipe his face.

'Well?' Bingham had said, the rising intonation of his voice signalling impatience.

Angus had gasped, then coughed and when it came, his voice had sounded ragged and very nasal. 'I was in The Fleece, minding my own business, and Vic Taylor came in with a face like thunder. He walked up to the bar, slammed his hand down hard and demanded a pint of ale. I could see Ada was startled and when he shouted at her again, I told him to quiet down a bit. That's when he plonked me right in the nose. No warning, nothing.'

There'd been a moment's silence as Bingham had considered the case put before him. 'Sounds like you were an innocent victim, doesn't it?'

'I was, of course I was.'

But Bingham had already been shaking his head.

She'd felt sorry for the young doctor, especially when she'd seen the navy-blue bruising coming out around his nose and right eye. She'd known straight away Vic Taylor must have given him a heck of a whack and she'd hoped then that she wouldn't encounter the man on her visit to dress Lucy's leg this morning.

She'd briefly seen Angus at breakfast, and he'd looked awful. His nose swollen, his eye almost closed, he appeared more like a ruffian from the streets of Liverpool than a village doctor. And given they were so short-staffed, she knew he couldn't take a day off. Bingham had told him to say he'd fallen down the stairs. But that hadn't made much sense because even though she was new to the village, she was already aware that everybody would know exactly what had happened last night in The Fleece.

Still thinking about poor Angus with his bruised nose and black eye, she pulled over to park up at Miss Dunderdale's house. Hopping confidently out of the car with her medical bag, she tapped on the door. Then realising her patient would be in the kitchen, she entered and walked through to the back.

'Hello, there.' Miss Dunderdale beamed from her seat at the table.

Instantly, Lara noted how relaxed her patient seemed and how clean and orderly the kitchen was. The transformation pleased her.

'Sit down, Nurse Flynn. Would you like a cup of tea?'

'I'd love one, Miss Dunderdale, but I'm packed out with visits today.'

'Yes, I heard about poor Nurse Wright and her accident. But I believe she's making a good recovery.'

'Yes, she is.' Lara smiled, then, 'How have you been? Any issues since you were last seen by Dr Bingham?'

Miss Dunderdale raised her eyebrows. 'No issues whatsoever apart from the fact that I'm glad to be alive.'

'Well, that in itself is very good to hear.' She smiled. 'So is it okay if I check your pulse and blood pressure?'

'Of course, go right ahead,' she said with a glint in her eye. 'You, Nurse Flynn, can do anything you want. I will be forever grateful for your intervention that day.'

Lara noted the catch in her patient's voice as she spoke. And of course, it was an emotional thing for any human to know they'd been on the brink of leaving this world forever.

'That's all right, Miss Dunderdale... I'm just glad you responded to the treatment as well as you did.'

'Well, I've had to be strong throughout my life. And in my experience, most women need to be... even in this modern world with your outrageously short skirts and all that wild dancing.'

Lara chuckled as she finished recording Miss Dunderdale's pulse.

But when she glanced back at her patient, she noted a faraway look in her eyes and then she pulled a handkerchief from her sleeve and dabbed away tears. 'I'm sorry, Nurse Flynn, I'm feeling a bit emotional today.'

'That's no problem,' she soothed. 'It's perfectly understandable given what you've been through, and it's good to express those feelings.'

When Miss Dunderdale spoke again, her voice wavered. 'It's

strange, isn't it, but when I came round after my heart had almost stopped... that's when I realised it had been broken a very long time ago and I'd never given it a chance to heal.'

Lara waited for her patient to speak again, sensing there was something very important she needed to say.

'I've never told anyone this, not even Nurse Beecham, and I knew her all those years.'

She saw Miss Dunderdale bow her head then and when she looked up, the words flowed from her. 'I'm an old woman now and things were very different when I was growing up last century with Queen Victoria on the throne. There was no question of a well-born young woman like me having a choice about who I married. And when I met a young man called Michael, a teacher at a local school in Oxford where I grew up, I was certain that there was no one else for me. But I also knew that my choice would never be approved by my parents.

'I begged them, I wept, I ranted, it made me ill. But still the answer was no. My father ordered me to end the relationship, and he sent me to my Aunt Lucretia's house in London. But how can love be snuffed out? It can't. And trying to do so just makes the desire stronger. So of course, I carried on seeing Michael in secret and that's when I became pregnant with his child. I hid it for as long as I could, but my mother had an eagle eye for such things and she sniffed it out. My father physically restrained me; he locked me in my room and called the family doctor to sedate me. I was forced into a nursing home for the duration of the pregnancy and I never saw Michael again. After I'd given birth, I was sent away on a grand European tour with my aunt. It was dreadful, I hated it, but I came home suitably demure and compliant. Then, a couple of years later when I heard Michael had married an American woman in New York, my heart was shattered into pieces again.'

Lara felt tears sting her eyes. 'What happened to your baby?' she asked gently.

'They didn't even let me see her. They told me it was a girl; at least there was that. But she was whisked away, probably for adoption to some well-to-do childless couple.'

'I'm so sorry, Miss Dunderdale. I can only imagine how devastating that must have been for you.'

'It broke me,' she said outright, 'and I still think about that little girl every single day. Sometimes, I'm sure I can hear her voice... as if she's trying to reach out to me. Does that sound mad?'

'No, of course not. You were traumatised; your mind and body are still trying to come to terms with it.'

Miss Dunderdale frowned, dabbed at her eyes. 'Do you know, Nurse Flynn, you might be young, but you are very wise. You're like a guardian angel to me and you always cut through to the truth of the matter. It's a remarkable gift.'

'I'm not sure about that,' Lara murmured as she considered what her patient had said and knew straightway that even if she had a remarkable gift, she was no angel. She was a human being striving every day to do her job to the best of her ability.

As soon as she was back in the car, she jotted her notes from the visit then revved the engine and set off in a spray of grit. It made her smile when she clicked she was now driving like Angus and Dr Bingham. She'd spent longer than she'd planned with Miss Dunderdale, but it had been worthwhile, and it had been humbling to be trusted with such a harrowing personal story. She felt awed by the woman's transformation, especially when she thought back to that first day when she'd been sent packing.

Ramming on her brakes when a hare ran out from the hedge right in front of her, she sat gasping at the wheel as the creature sat in the road, staring at her. He was a magnificent beast with a scar on his nose and a torn ear and even as she nudged the car gently forward, still he sat. She revved the engine and at last, he startled, but as he lolloped into the hedge, she felt awed that he'd paused to acknowledge her just for those few moments. Shaking her head, she drove on but she kept a more careful eye out, not knowing how she'd cope if she ran over any of the wild creatures that lived out here.

She was heading up to see Lucy Taylor at Fell Farm and then she'd work her way through the other visits as she made her way back to the surgery. It felt as if the Austin had got used to the route now and with the right amount of acceleration, the trusty little blue car tackled the uphill climb. She's spent so much time out on visits, she'd become comfortable behind the wheel and very fond of the car. And as she climbed higher, and the landscape opened out around her, she felt an ease that was becoming very familiar. Even as she parked up at the dilapidated barn and hopped out of the car, she was still euphoric. But immediately, she came back down with a bang when she saw Vic Taylor striding towards her, his hands balled into fists.

'You need to tell that fancy-pants young doctor you work with to mind his own bloody business,' he shouted, his face twisted with rage.

Instantly, she was protective of Angus, and she felt a jolt of pure anger. She forced it down, made sure not to show one shred of it as she made to walk past him.

'Not so fast, Nursey,' he growled, grabbing her arm with his work-roughened hand. She could smell the stale beer on his breath, and it made her feel a little nauseous.

As his grip tightened, a shivery feeling crept up her back and she drew a slow, steady breath to contain it, vowing she would not be cowed by this man.

'Please let go of me, Mr Taylor,' she said, meeting his gaze, fighting to maintain her composure.

'Oh, she has fire in her belly,' he leered. 'Even though she looks as if butter wouldn't melt in her mouth.'

At a flash of intensity in his eyes and the tightness of that delaying grip on her arm, she felt something click inside of her. 'That's enough now, Mr Taylor,' she growled as deftly, she twisted free.

She forced herself to take a succession of deep, steady breaths as she walked away, straining her ears for the sound of footsteps behind her. Instead, she picked up his laughter and it made her even more determined to not let him stop her from carrying out her duties.

As soon as the door was opened by Robin, she sensed tension in his pale face and wide eyes. Alice was at the table kneading bread and as she glanced up, Lara noted a bruise around her left eye.

'Is everything all right?' she asked.

The woman shrugged. 'As right as it'll ever be.'

'I can see you have a bruise there—'

'I walked into a door; I'm clumsy like that,' she offered without looking up from her bread bowl. 'Our Lucy's upstairs; she's waiting for you.'

'Right you are, but if you do want me to take a look at your eye—'

'No, I'm fine,' she called, an angry edge to her voice that Lara knew wasn't really meant for her.

Upstairs in the bedroom, Lucy was her usual quiet self but when Lara pulled back the patchwork quilt, she could see that the bandage had been disturbed and it looked grubby.

'Has there been a problem with your leg? Did the bandage come loose?' she asked gently.

Lucy slowly shook her head but wouldn't meet her eye.

'Okay then, I'll get it changed for you.'

'Thank you, Nurse Lara,' the little girl said, her voice small.

As she removed the bandage, she saw instantly that the dressing pad had been disrupted. But Lucy's head was bowed now and she was almost in tears, so Lara didn't want to upset her even more by asking questions.

The wound was perhaps a deeper pink around the edges but thankfully, there were no overt signs of infection, so she followed her meticulous routine of cleaning with carbolic solution, applying an iodine dressing and a fresh, spotlessly clean bandage. Fishing in her pocket for the caramel toffees she'd remembered to bring, she passed one to Lucy but when she looked around for Robin, he was gone.

'I'll give it to him,' Lucy said quietly. 'He was meant to be going back to school this week, but Father still needs him to help on the farm. So he's probably gone back out to the barn.'

It gave her a bad feeling, knowing the little lad was deliberately being kept back from school and had no escape. She could still feel the burn of pain on her arm where Vic Taylor had grabbed her, and she already knew she would report all this back to Dr Bingham. There was no mistake about it; she had increasingly serious concerns for welfare here.

As expected, Alice was tight-lipped over an explanation for the grubby, disturbed bandage and dismissed it as Lucy having had a restless night. But as Lara left her silently kneading the bread with her head bowed, she was very troubled by the threat she could feel hanging over the whole family. There was little else she could do right now though and with a long list of other visits, she had no choice but to continue her round. Highly alert and still on edge, she walked quickly back to the Austin without laying eyes on Vic Taylor. She did, however, note a smear of fresh manure across the bonnet of the little car and she knew it had to have been left by him. What she sensed now was an increasingly threatening situation and she only began to feel more comfortable once she'd pulled out of the farm track onto the road. But as she drove to her next visit, all that she'd witnessed at the Taylors' played in her head. She would report every detail to Dr Bingham, then see where they went from there.

As she motored along the country lanes, she kept the car window down so she could feel the breeze on her face and sense that closeness to the beauty of nature which helped calm her after such a troubling visit. Then, at the loud bleating of sheep and the now familiar tramp of hooves and a yap from a farm dog up ahead, she needed to pull over to let a flock of sheep pass by. Although it frustrated her to be held up, she enjoyed seeing the woolly, black-faced Lancashire sheep trot by. Tom Douglas, the farmer she'd helped deliver the calf on her first day, was driving them and he grinned and raised his stick in greeting. 'Don't forget, you're welcome to call by the farm any time. And if I'm needing help with another calf, I'll let you know.'

'You do that.' She laughed.

He smiled and raised his stick again and the genuine warmth of the gesture felt like balm to her soul after the tense time she'd had up at Fell Farm. And as she pulled away from the grass verge, she began to feel restored. It daunted her though, knowing she'd have to go back to the Taylors' farm in the morning, but nothing would stop her from doing her duty for a patient, especially such a sweet little girl as Lucy.

19

As she set out for her visits the next morning, she felt fortified by the detailed discussion she'd had with Dr Bingham last evening. She'd reported Vic Taylor's threatening behaviour, the bruising on his wife's face and that heightened sense of unease. Given the ongoing intensity of their schedules, he was unable to accompany her to the farm this morning, but they'd heard that Vic Taylor had been fighting in the pub again last night and the local bobby had arrested him. So, chances were, he would still be under lock and key in Ridgetown police station. She felt a flood of relief knowing she was unlikely to encounter him, and she hoped it might give Alice the opportunity to speak freely. However, she'd seen situations like this many times in Liverpool and she understood that women who suffered at the hands of their men felt so threatened, they often remained silent come what may.

As she parked the car and hopped out with her medical bag, she saw Robin walking down the path with a bucket and instantly, she sensed the lightness in him, the freedom, and she knew right away that Vic would not be troubling her today. She waited for the boy to feed the pigs then they walked together up to the house. He seemed quiet but he was smiley, and he swung the empty bucket as he walked. And once they were in through the door, he shouted to his mother, 'Nurse Flynn's here.'

Alice turned from the sink. The bruising had come out around her eye in shades of blue and green, but she offered a smile and said, 'You go straight up; Lucy's all ready and waiting for you.'

But as soon as she walked into the bedroom, she noted the little girl's ashen face with two bright-red fever spots on her cheeks, and her heart jolted with shock. Instantly, she placed the back of her hand against the girl's forehead and knew even before she checked with a thermometer that the girl was burning up. It could be a childhood fever, but it was much more likely related to the leg wound. There was a rolling, sick feeling in her stomach at the thought of a nasty infection that could lead to blood poisoning. And if that happened, there were no medicines to hold it back, so the outlook was very grim.

'How are you feeling, Lucy?' she asked, making sure her voice was steady.

'I'm a bit tired and I feel achy all over,' the girl groaned.

At least she was still alert and able to answer questions, so not delirious. But as Lara stripped back the patchwork cover and felt the heat of the girl's body rise to meet her, she knew this was a serious setback. She went straight to unravelling the bandage and when she felt the layers of cotton sticking together and noted a yellow, sweet-smelling exudate, she knew they were in deep trouble. And once she had the dressing pad removed and the full extent of the infection became clear, her heart twisted with fear for the girl.

She drew some slow breaths to calm herself. 'It's all looking a bit sticky today, Lucy. We might have to do something different to make it better again.'

Even as she heard her own measured tone, an urgent voice was screaming in her head, telling her the child would need hospitalisation. After seeing other patients deteriorate at a terrifying rate and knowing there was no treatment beyond antiseptic, dressings and painkillers, there was a loud, clanging alarm bell already going off in her head. Quickly, she cleaned the wound then poured lashings of iodine solution onto a pad and redressed it. Next step, she needed to record Lucy's observations: her temperature was very high, her pulse racing. There was no time to lose in getting her to the hospital.

'Here's your caramel toffee, Lucy,' she said gently, and the child gripped it in its gold wrapper but couldn't form the words to say thank you.

Lara ran down the stairs, saw Alice startle as she turned from the sink, her face stricken.

'Lucy has a wound infection and a high fever. I don't want to panic you, but we need to get her to hospital as soon as possible. Is there a house nearby with a telephone so I can call for assistance?'

Alice gulped, then gasped, her eyes fixed wide.

'There's no time to lose,' Lara urged.

'Hodgsons down the lane have a telephone. Turn right once you're over the cattle grid. Keep going a mile or so and it's the big farm on the right. There's a sign: Oak House.'

She was already striding to the door, calling over her shoulder, 'If you can get Lucy to drink water, it will help fight the infection.' Then quickly, she opened her medical bag, pulled out a pill bottle and dispensed one tablet. 'Here's an aspirin. If you can get it into her, it might help bring down the fever. You might have to crush it, put it in the water.'

'Right, Nurse. Yes,' Alice replied.

As she ran back through the farmyard, the pigs in their sty kicked off a cacophony of squeals and grunts. She leapt in the car, instantly fired up the engine and, reversing at speed, she lurched away as fast as she could over the rough farm track. Fully in tune with the directions Alice had given her, she put her foot down as she drove along the narrow, winding lane. Spotting Oak House farm, she skidded into the yard, ran to the house, then hammered on the door.

A startled, grey-haired woman answered, and Lara instantly fired the necessary information in her direction. 'Yes, Nurse, that's fine,' she called as she pointed to a door. 'The telephone is just through there.'

She ran through and in moments, she was dialling the surgery. Mrs Hewitt picked up instantly and listened carefully as she rapidly gave the details and emphasised the urgency of the case.

'Sorry, Lara, neither of the doctors is here right now. Dr Bingham's been called out to Grace Alston's father, James. He's fallen again and needs more stitches. And Angus is dealing with a case at Ridgetown hospital; he had to ask Sam Collins for a lift in his van because he has no car.' She heard the frustration and the anxiety in the housekeeper's voice and knew she had to make the decision.

'Right, I need to get back to Fell Farm as quickly as I can, so I want you to call an ambulance right now for Lucy Taylor. Stress how poorly she is.'

'Yes, I've got that, and I've jotted down the details of her case.'

'Righto, I'll see you later,' she said, replacing the receiver, pulling her pad and pencil from her pocket to note down the telephone number displayed on the centre of the dial just in

case she needed to contact the Hodgsons to take a message to
Fell Farm at a future time. Then striding back into the kitchen,
she called a quick thank you to the farmer's wife, who was
standing stock-still, clutching a blue and white tea towel.

'I hope the lass makes a good recovery; she's a lovely little
thing,' Mrs Hodgson called after her as Lara exited the door.

Jumping back into the Austin, she set off so fast, she felt the
wheels spin, but the trusty little car didn't waver. Once she was
heading back up the rutted farm track, she needed to reduce her
speed right down and as time stretched on, she felt her anxiety
coil like a tight spring deep inside of her. She just needed to be
back at Lucy's bedside and as soon as she parked up, she
grabbed her medical bag and ran.

Alice was beside the trestle bed sponging her daughter's face
and when she looked up, Lara saw her eyes were shiny with
tears. 'She keeps drifting in and out, Nurse Flynn. And she's not
making much sense when she tries to talk.'

'Right. Well. That's to be expected because she has a fever,
but we can do something about it,' she said firmly, making
herself rise above the tight ball of fear that lodged in her chest.
'The ambulance is on its way, but it will take a while to get up
here so let's forge ahead with trying to cool her down.'

Alice nodded and rolled up her sleeves as Lara continued to
speak gently but firmly. 'First, we need to strip off her nightdress
and all the covers so we can sponge her down. Go now, bring me
six flannels, a bowl of tepid water and some towels.'

Alice jumped up as Lara reached for the window and
opened it wide. Then she pulled the thermometer from her bag
and placed it under the little girl's arm again. The reading was
even higher. The fever was raging.

As soon as she had the bowl of cool water, she dunked the

cloths then wrung them out, placing one across the girl's fore-head, one under each arm and in both groins. The other cloth she used to sponge Lucy's face, neck, arms, torso and legs. Leaving the water to evaporate, she worked over the girl's pale body time after time, changing the cloths when they became warm and asking for cool water as often as she needed. The next time she took the temperature, it had come down a few notches, but still the fever raged. She kept going with the tepid sponging, forcing herself to focus on the task and not show one glimmer of the acute anxiety that burned like acid in her stomach.

Alice switched and changed between holding her daughter's hand and hovering at the bedside. And Robin had sobbed uncontrollably when he'd run up the stairs to find his sister so poorly. It had helped to give him a job, so Lara had told him to go down to the bottom of the farm road so he could flag down the ambulance. He'd nodded firmly, set off at a run and as she'd heard his wellington boots on every step, she'd hoped with every fibre of her being that the ambulance would arrive in time. These cases could progress rapidly, especially in children. She prayed that Lucy's skinny little body would put up a strong enough fight. If the fever could be reduced, then maybe she would stand a chance of survival. If not... she didn't want to think about if not, but she knew the reality was that Lucy's life now hung in the balance.

It seemed like forever before she heard the ambulance men at the door. Fortunately, with all her efforts at tepid sponging – and maybe the aspirin had helped as well – Lucy's temperature had come down a couple more notches, but she was only just holding her own.

The concern on the faces of the ambulance men was unmistakeable and as they moved the little girl onto the stretcher, they were gentle and careful. 'Come on then, lass, I've got a grand-daughter about your age... You're going to be just fine with us.'

Lucy opened her eyes and tried to mumble some words but nothing coherent would come.

The ambulance man at the head of the stretcher nodded to the other and they were straight away down the stairs. 'We're going all the way to the children's ward at Preston Royal Infirmary with this little one; they're not as equipped in Ridgetown for these cases.'

Lara saw Alice gasp, then gulp back tears.

'I'll call the hospital from the surgery as soon as I get back and if I'm not able to come back up to you with any news, I'll ring your neighbour, Mrs Hodgson, and send a message via her.'

'I normally don't like to trouble the neighbours...' Alice's voice tailed off then, and Lara was quick to reassure her that she would only do so if required.

Following along behind the ambulance as it bumped over the rutted farm track, Lara drew slow, steady breaths. Dealing with the emergency had been all-consuming but she now had to focus on her remaining visits. It was never easy to click back to routine cases after the heightened state that raged behind the professional façade required to manage an acute case. In fact, sometimes, at the end of a very difficult day, it could leave her feeling wrung out and exhausted. But if her patients received the best care, if her efforts helped to ease or to heal, then all of that was worthwhile.

Thankfully, the rest of her morning visits were routine, and she managed to make up time between each one, so she wasn't drastically late back.

As soon as she pulled up at the surgery, she bustled straight in to see if there was any news of Lucy. And finding Bingham at the kitchen table eating his usual lunchtime sandwich, she was eager to offload the details of the case.

He glanced up as she placed her medical bag down, removed her nurse's hat then slipped into her chair. 'Sounds like you've had a very busy morning, Nurse Flynn.'

She blew out a breath, 'Yes, you could say that... Have there been any calls from the Infirmary?'

'Yes, and the little girl is holding her own – they're doing everything they can to save her. All the usual things – the tepid sponging and lashings of iodine on the wound that you instigated – and they've put up a saline drip. The surgeon said they'll give her a whiff of chloroform tomorrow, get right in there and debride that nasty wound.'

'Sounds like a good plan,' she said. 'I'll need to go back up to the farm later or ring the neighbour, to let the girl's mother know.'

Bingham looked a little guarded. 'There's no need for that. The girl's father has been released from the police station now and he's somehow found out about Lucy. He came here just after I'd taken the call from the hospital, so I gave him the information and he said he was going straight home, and he'd give Alice the news.'

'Oh, that's good... I wouldn't have minded going back—' Seeing the deep furrow between his brows and the intensity of his gaze, she stopped what she was saying. 'Is there something else?'

He nodded.

When he spoke again, his tone was clipped, 'There's something I need to tell you, Nurse Flynn... After Vic Taylor had gone from here, we had a call from Miss Shaw, the postmistress. She'd heard Vic shouting out to anyone who'd listen that his little girl had been taken to the Infirmary with a bad infection and it was touch-and-go, all that kind of thing. Then, I'm sorry to report, but he was blaming you, Nurse Flynn, for what had happened to her.'

'What?' she gasped.

'He didn't say a word to me when he was here. But clearly, once he was off down the street, he was saying you were the one who'd been changing the dressings, so you were responsible for the infection.'

'But that's ridiculous. I did everything by the book, kept up with the treatment plan just as Marion had set it up.'

'I know that. Mrs Hewitt knows that. But there is the possibility that some of the villagers might be swayed by Vic's version of events.'

Instantly, Lara felt a flush of blood to her face. She felt devastated, unable to speak for a few seconds.

'So, what should I do?'

'The only thing you can do. Keep your chin up, go about your visits as usual and let the whole thing blow over.'

She swallowed hard.

'I'm sorry, Nurse Flynn, but until other gossip comes along to give those in the village inclined to believe such nonsense something else to talk about, things are not going to be easy for you.'

She gulped. 'Yes, I hear what you're saying.'

'You've got us to support you, Nurse Flynn,' Mrs Hewitt piped up from beside the Aga. 'You just need to weather it.'

She blew out a breath. She'd once had an issue with a patient's husband in Liverpool when she'd first been on the district. He'd spread rumours that she was incompetent, but it had all blown over when her patient had made a full recovery. But that case had been in a city, where there were many people, many streets, and the actions of the district nurses were far less intensely scrutinised. Ingleside Village was miniscule, and it felt like a boiling cauldron by comparison. It angered her to be accused even by someone as unreliable as Vic Taylor and clearly, it was false. But Dr Bingham and Mrs Hewitt were right; there was nothing she could do but weather it.

20

By breakfast the next morning, she'd begun to put the issue with Vic Taylor out of her head. She'd tossed and turned with it last night and hadn't slept at all well, but waking to the glimmer of morning sun through her curtains, she'd set herself up for a fresh start. And who knows, maybe the whole thing would soon blow over.

Surprisingly, Angus was already down when she arrived at the breakfast table. But as he turned to say good morning and she saw the full extent of the bruising and swelling from his busted nose and black eye, she grimaced.

'Ouch, that looks sore.'

'Oh, it's not too bad really. At least it hasn't closed my eye... And from what I heard in The Fleece last night, you are also on the receiving end of Mr Taylor's bad humour.'

It stung to have this broached so abruptly, but she had no choice except to confirm the rumour. 'Yes, indeed,' she replied, forcing a determined tone of voice.

'So, what happened with the dressings? Did you follow the exact protocol?'

She gasped out loud; she couldn't believe he'd even asked that question. 'Yes, of course I did! Whatever else do you think I might have done?'

Angus shrugged his shoulders. 'I'm not implying there was neglect or anything like that. I'm just aware that we're short-staffed right now and we're all rushing around like headless chickens.'

Still affronted by what he'd just said, she had to work hard to temper the edge to her voice before she spoke again. 'In my book, the busier it is, the more careful your practice should be.'

'Yes, yes, of course, I agree,' he huffed, then with a much gentler tone, 'I'm sorry if I ruffled your feathers.'

'That's all right,' she offered, but inside, she felt furious at even a hint of his lack of support.

'Morning,' Mrs Hewitt called brightly as she bustled through with the mail. 'Is everything okay? You're both very quiet this morning.'

'All fine, Mrs H,' Angus called, and Lara felt him sneak a glance in her direction.

'Ah, Nurse Flynn, there's a letter here for you... Liverpool postmark.'

'Thank you,' she said, making herself smile as Mrs H propped the envelope against her cup.

The familiar handwriting on the envelope told her it was from Fiona and right at this moment, it felt like a friendly hand reaching out to her.

After she'd eaten her breakfast, when Angus had mumbled a farewell and left the kitchen, she used her table knife to slit open the envelope. It was good to see the familiar curve of her friend's handwriting, read the chat about this and that and be told that she was sorely missed. By the time she'd got to the bottom of the letter, she was smiling. Then came a long postscript and as the words settled on her, she folded the paper and pushed it straight back in the envelope. Fiona had told her Patrick had been to the hospital and he'd been asking for her new address, saying he wanted to check how she was doing. She hadn't given him any information, but she'd seen him speaking to other nurses, maybe ones who knew she'd moved to a country practice but didn't understand that she wanted her new location to be kept secret.

'Damn,' Lara muttered under her breath, instantly feeling the scar on her head begin to throb. She drew a slow breath and pushed the letter firmly into her uniform pocket.

'Bad news?' murmured Mrs Hewitt.

She shook her head. 'No, not really, just irritating news.'

The housekeeper nodded. 'Well, I hope your day picks up when you get out on your visits.'

'I hope so too, Mrs H,' she sighed as she reached for the sheet of paper that detailed her work schedule. She spotted James Alston first on the list for a check of his newly sutured head following the fall he'd sustained yesterday. She hadn't seen Grace since the village dance so it would be nice to pick up on some of her calm good nature. Also, given all her visits were local, she would be able to ride her bicycle, so that gave her an extra boost.

Needing to nip into the post office to buy a stamp for the letter she wanted to send back to Fiona, she decided to wheel her bicycle. Seeing Herbert Threlfall's black horse and milk-cart passing by, she felt soothed by his cheery smile and the hand he raised in greeting.

'Morning, Nurse Flynn,' he called, and his horse turned its head as if it were also saying hello. Already, she was feeling more optimistic.

But instantly, her brighter mood was dispelled when she saw Vic Taylor striding towards her with a face like thunder.

Her stomach twisted with resolve; she'd dealt with aggrieved relatives before in Liverpool and she knew it was important to stay calm and show she was prepared to listen. But once he was up close, he scowled right at her, and he looked so hostile, she knew this was a very different scenario to anything she'd ever dealt with. She couldn't let him take the upper hand so even as he opened his mouth to speak, she cut him off. 'I know what you've been saying about me, Mr Taylor, so I'll make this clear. I followed all the instructions left by Nurse Wright regarding the dressing of your daughter's leg. Everything was done in the proper manner, and I was extremely shocked yesterday to see such a change in the wound.'

His eyes bored into her, then he snarled, 'So if you did everything by the book... strange then, isn't it, that my lass is so sick.' His tone was sarcastic, mocking, and it filled her with fury and already, she wanted to throttle him.

'I need to get on,' she said, 'but if you have anything else to say, I would prefer you to do it directly rather than spreading rumours around the village.'

'Well, how about this for being direct – I think you're a jumped-up city girl who isn't fit to be a nurse.'

Her chest constricted with fury; she felt like challenging him further but didn't want to get into a shouting match out here in the street.

'Goodbye, Mr Taylor. I hope Lucy's condition continues to improve.'

It took all her willpower to keep her voice steady and when he shouted back to her, 'If it hadn't been for you, Nurse Fancy-Pants, my lass wouldn't be in that hospital in the first place,' she mounted her bicycle and pedalled away so furiously and with such a tight grip on her handlebars that her knuckles turned white.

Once she was far enough away, she slowed down then pulled over beside the whitewashed shippon where she'd helped Tom Douglas deliver that calf on her first day. Still steaming with anger, she wondered if she'd done the right thing by staying on in Ingleside; maybe she should have followed her instinct that first day and got back on the train. But as she swiped away tears with the back of her hand and gazed out to the meadow where swallows dipped and dived, her steely, determined side rallied and she vowed not to let this issue with Vic Taylor drag her down. She was always scrupulous in her clinical practice, and she was certain she'd done nothing wrong in the management of Lucy's wound. It was the unfairness of his claim that was eating at her. And that's when it hit her; she was amazed she hadn't remembered it sooner... but that day when she'd found the bandage grubby, maybe it had something to do with the infection. But then, even if it were a factor, there was probably no way she could prove it. From a purely professional point of view though, it might offer an explanation as to why there'd been such a drastic change in a healing wound.

Feeling calmer now, she pushed off on her bicycle to cover the remaining distance to the Alstons' farm and as she steeled herself to go by chestnut corner, she glanced to where she'd found Marion after the crash. The grass had grown up already and apart from the deep scrape on the trunk of the tree, all trace of the accident had gone. Nature had done its work and restored the place and already Lara was beginning to feel more comfortable here.

With thoughts of Marion running through her head, she almost missed the turning to the farm, but she had it now and she was soon wheeling her bicycle up the farm track. That first time she'd visited to remove Mr Alston's stitches, hay time had been in full swing and as she'd walked back down, she'd met those two smiling young men with scythes over their shoulders. She'd been so hard-pressed since Marion's accident that she hadn't even noticed that they were moving through the summer season now and soon it would be September.

As she approached the farmyard, the angry black and white dog startled her when it barked aggressively and rattled its chain. Then Grace ran out of the house in her stockinged feet, her trousers cinched at the waist with that leather belt and her wild hair all over the place. 'Welcome back,' she called, and the warmth of her smile made Lara's heart squeeze tight.

'It's so good to see you, Grace. Sorry I had to run off like that at the dance.'

'No problem at all.' Her friend grinned. 'Not when there's a baby needing to be born. And from what I've heard, you made an excellent job of a very difficult delivery.'

'Oh, well, it's what we district nurses do.'

'Mmm, steady on with that, Nurse Flynn; credit where cred-it's due, hey.'

Lara couldn't help but smile and as she followed Grace through into the low-ceilinged kitchen, it almost felt as if she were coming home.

It was quiet in the farmhouse so clearly, Mr Alston was settled.

'He's sleeping right now,' Grace said, 'and it's all down to the increased dose of laudanum the doc has prescribed. So maybe we can have a quick cup of tea, give him a chance to have a bit more rest before you disturb him?'

It was on the tip of her tongue to refuse the tea and offer to go in there as quietly as she could. But when she saw Grace's warm smile and the playful tilt of her head, she couldn't resist.

Once the tea was brewed and Grace sat opposite, she said, 'I'm so sorry your dad keeps falling.'

'Not your fault, not anybody's fault. It's just bad luck he's got such nasty Parkinson's. I mean, I've seen older folk, mostly retired farmers, with a bit of a shake but nothing on the same scale as this. I know you understand because you've seen it, but his shakes are so violent, we're fighting with him.'

She nodded. 'I can't even imagine how hard it must be to manage this all day, every day. And you're running the farm as well.'

Grace shrugged her shoulders, heaved a sigh and when her voice came, it was weary. 'I just get on with it... but my dad suffering like this, it's tragic. And given there's nothing to hold it back, the disease just gets worse and worse. I'm sick of managing, sick of seeing him suffering, but we have to keep going. "One day at a time" is what Aunt Agnes often says, and she's right. There's not much point in trying to look too far ahead; it's the here and now that matters and if he's having a good day, so are we.'

'Still, it must be agonising.'

Grace pressed her lips together, nodded. 'It's strange, but sometimes, when I walk into the yard, I almost see him bobbing out of the shippon with that smile he always had.' She gasped then, pressed a hand to her chest.

'It's hard, it must be so hard,' Lara murmured, reaching across the table.

Grace forced a wobbly smile. 'Look at me getting all sentimental.'

'There's nothing wrong with talking about those feelings of loss, Grace. What you are going through now is a slow, agonising grieving process. And I'm ready to listen any time, you know that.'

'Yes, I do know. And I'm grateful for that,' she said, then forced a ragged smile. 'Hark at us two... if we're not dancing together, we're having an emotional heart-to-heart. We just seemed to click right away, didn't we?'

'We did, but I don't want you to think of me as just a friend. I'm your father's nurse and that means I'm here for you too.'

'That's good to know,' she said, her voice throaty. 'But there's no more time for talking right now – you need to see Dad then get on with your other visits. And I'll be in trouble with Aunt Agnes if I don't have the Aga stoked up ready and waiting for her to start cooking the dinner as soon as she arrives.'

Sensing Grace's agitation, she said gently, 'Let's just take a few moments to sit quietly.'

Grace gulped in air, nodded.

And as they sat quietly together, the fire in the stove gently spat and the ancient beams of the farmhouse continued to stand over them as they'd done for every decade of joy and sorrow they'd witnessed in this house.

Then, needing to move the moment on, Lara said, 'I want you to take time every now and then to walk around the farm and think back to how things used to be when your dad was fit and well. It'll feel hard but it's a way of trying to make peace with what's happened to him and to you.'

When Grace spoke again, her voice quavered on the edge of tears. 'I will. I promise.'

Lara reached out to give her hand a squeeze. Then as she pushed back her chair and stood up, Grace walked over and hugged her.

'Thank you... I needed that, and I'll talk to you again some-time if that's all right.'

Then as a cheeky hen ran in through the half-open door, Grace shooshed it back out and it was time for Lara to get on with her visit. But as she rose from the table, Grace raised a delaying hand. 'Just before you go in to see Dad, one of my workers told me this morning that Vic Taylor's been spreading horrible rumours about you. I just want to say I'm sorry to hear that and I'll wring his neck if I get hold of him.'

'Thanks for your support,' she said, then smiled. 'But it's not the first time I've had to deal with this kind of thing... except in the city, it didn't feel anywhere near as personal. This place is so small, everybody hears the gossip and it's intense.'

'What you've just said is a good summing-up of life in the country, especially the villages. I wouldn't ever move to Ingleside; if you so much as sneeze too loud, everybody knows about it... but if you need anything at all, you come to me. I've had a few run-ins with Vic Taylor and he's a nasty piece of work.'

'Thank you, I really appreciate that.'

'Anyway, Nurse Flynn... I am certain that what you need as soon as possible is another opportunity to dance. And if there's nothing doing at the village hall, I'll put my gramophone on here and we'll shimmy round the kitchen table.'

Lara giggled then as Grace performed one of her dances in her stockinged feet. Then she took her medical bag and made her way to Mr Alston's room to check his sutures. He was sleeping soundly in bed, the black cat with the white-tipped tail curled peacefully by his side. So ever so carefully, she made her checks without disturbing him, then quietly left the room.

Later, after she'd finished the rest of her visits, she headed back to the village for her final call to see Daniel Makepeace. The cottage was quiet as she entered and as had become her routine, she called out to him after closing the front door. And as the peace inside the cottage wrapped itself around her, she tapped on the bedroom door, then opened it to see Daniel propped against his pillows. Instantly, she noted how much paler and more breathless he seemed, and his brow was deeply furrowed. But still he smiled and raised a hand in greeting.

'How are you this morning, Mr Makepeace?' she asked, already palpating his wrist to check his pulse. It was pounding faster than she'd ever known it to.

'I'm fine,' he wheezed, then he spoke quickly. 'I've just had one of those cows that belong to the young vet with its head through the window. I'd have liked to get up to give it a stroke and a scratch behind its ears but I couldn't manage it. I'm out of breath with nothing these days.' He was gasping for air now just with the effort of speaking.

'That's your ticker I'm afraid, Mr Makepeace. It can't quite keep up with things.'

He still seemed agitated as he carried on talking. 'Well, at least I've still got the cows in the field, and I can hear them munching the grass.'

As she took hold of his wrist to recheck his pulse, he emitted a low groan and leant towards her. 'It's no use. I'll have to tell you because it's been making me feel bad... I've had Victor Taylor in here this morning and he's been saying all kinds of things about you.'

She felt his pulse skip a few beats and instantly, she was furious to know Vic had even been here to this poorly old man with his malicious talk.

She gulped her anger down, steadied her voice. 'I'm sorry about that. He's spreading all kinds of rumours... I think he's under a lot of pressure at present because he's hit rock bottom at the farm.'

'There is that, and I know his young lass is very sick, but he's always been a nasty sort of person. And I told him straight that you're as good a nurse as any we've ever had and just 'cos you were born and raised in a city doesn't mean you can't do a good job.'

Feeling increasingly agitated by the impact of this issue on her patient, she tried once more to soothe him, but still he carried on. 'I think the amount of beer he drinks is a big reason why he's like he is. There are other folk in the village who are scared of him, and I've no idea how his wife copes.'

'Like I say, please don't worry. It'll all get sorted out.'

He nodded then, reached out to take her hand. 'I wish my heart and lungs were up to scratch. I'd be straight up to that farm to see him and I'd sort him out good and proper.'

It heartened her to know that Mr Makepeace was on her side but the stress it was causing him was deeply troubling. She'd felt unsettled when she'd been confronted by Vic Taylor, but she was appalled at the thought of any of her patients, particularly the more poorly ones like Daniel, being caught up in this. And her fury built even more when she checked his pulse again and it was very fast.

'Take a slow breath, try to calm down now, Mr Makepeace. And just so you know, it means a lot that you are on my side.'

He opened his eyes wide. 'Well, it's true. I always speak plain... and I've known Victor since he was born, and he should be behaving much better... Fair enough, he might have had a rough upbringing but look at young Ed Cronshaw; his father served in the trenches and he came back gassed and blown-up and in a terrible state. And as a result, he was a violent, aggressive man who regularly beat and threw young Ed out of the house. I found him early one morning asleep in the doorway of The Fleece. It broke my heart to find a child cast out like that so I woke him up and brought him back here for some porridge and a hot cup of tea. After we'd warmed him up and fed him, he went off to school and once he'd gone, my

Martha cried her eyes out. But then she told me to check for him in the village every morning and that's what we did… He was back here for breakfast many a time with bruises on his legs and sometimes, he'd have a black eye or a busted lip but he always had a smile, did Ed, and he was grateful for our help…'

Lara felt tears prick her eyes, not only at the plight of Ed as a child but at the kindness and generosity of Daniel and Martha.

Daniel was lying back now against his pillows, ashen-faced, gasping for air.

To soothe him, she spoke softly. 'Thank you for telling me about Ed… and what you and Martha did was very special.'

He opened his eyes, smiled. 'I don't know if it was special as such… but it was the right thing to do and that's what my mother always told me – "Now Daniel… always try to do the right thing and you won't go far wrong in life."'

His breathing had begun to settle now and when she checked his pulse, it was steady. So she stood by him until he'd fallen asleep and then she picked up her medical bag and murmured a goodbye and for the first time since she'd been visiting him, he didn't raise a hand in farewell. She let her anger over Vic Taylor swell inside of her then and as soon as she was out through the door, she growled with agitation. Then knowing she was on view to the village, she reined it all back in.

It was busy on the street with villagers chatting and in and out of the post office. Mr Collins raised a hand in greeting as he climbed in his van farther up the hill and it made her feel for a fleeting moment that maybe most of the village was on her side. As she wheeled her bicycle up the street, she kept her expression neutral and from what she could see, the villagers were getting on with their normal day and barely paying her any attention. That was what she wanted: to blend in. And she was just beginning to relax when she spotted Miss Frobisher moving very quickly down the hill towards her with a fierce expression.

'Well, Nurse Flynn, you seem to have stirred up a heck of a fuss in the village,' the woman growled as she stood eye to eye. Then before Lara could reply, she spoke again. 'You stick to your guns, girl. Vic Taylor was a mean child when I was teaching him at school, and he's grown up to be a mean man. Don't let him get the better of you.'

Shocked, Lara stood open-mouthed as the woman turned then strode back up the street with her walking stick tapping at every step. As she followed in her wake, she met some frosty glances from other villagers who probably thought the school-teacher had been giving her a dressing-down. She held onto the moment she'd just had, and it was even more special because Miss Frobisher had been the patient who'd looked her up and down disapprovingly on her first day as she'd stood hot and exhausted from the journey in her white summer hat with its band of silk flowers.

21

An insistent knock on Lara's bedroom door in the early hours of the next morning woke her instantly. She scrambled out of bed and clicked open the door. 'Yes?' she breathed, seeing Mrs Hewitt in a white, frill-necked nightgown.

'Lizzie Cronshaw's gone into labour. Her pains are strong and close together; sounds like you need to get over there as quick as you can. I'll have some freshly brewed coffee waiting.'

'I'll be down as fast as I can,' Lara called as she clicked the door shut and went straight to the sink to sponge her face. Her uniform was waiting and her bag had been checked through last night. She would be ready to attend her third delivery since moving to the village in double-quick time. Hopefully, Lizzie's delivery of her second child would be far more straightforward than Rose Ryan's breech birth. Rose had been home from hospital for quite a while now and she was still pale and tired, but she had that glow that some first-time mums had, and the little red-haired girl who'd been delivered on a wing and a prayer that night of the village dance was thriving. Rose was lucky, she had good support from her husband Danny and right now as Lara thought of Lizzie in labour, she wondered how things would turn out with Ed being the father-in-waiting. But despite having been threatened by him on her first proper day in the job, she made every effort to withhold judgement. If her years of experience in Liverpool had taught her anything at all, it was to always expect the unexpected. Who knows, Ed worked with Danny Ryan at the sawmill and maybe some of his steady approach might have rubbed off, and now Daniel had told her the story of Ed as a child, she was far more inclined to be understanding. But as she caught a flash of Ed's snarling face that night Bingham took Sue to the hospital, she didn't hold out too much hope of being able to do that.

    As she slipped into her uniform, she was already revising Lizzie's antenatal history in her head. Little Sue had been a normal delivery ably attended by Nurse Beecham, and Lara had seen a note in her predecessor's bold cursive handwriting indicating that there'd been a bit more blood loss than normal but nothing to cause undue concern. She was glad of Nurse Beecham's attention to detail and the more of her notes she read, the more she felt their practice aligned. So, Lizzie was now a week overdue and when she'd seen her in clinic for the most recent check, the baby was small for dates, but foetal movements were lively and the heartbeat was strong. She'd noted how exhausted Lizzie had seemed though, and little Sue was fretful and clingy as she continued to recover from her scalds. On the surface, the antenatal detail was straightforward, but it was the outlying issues that gave her cause for concern, especially since Ed could be a violent drunk and he was a drinking companion of Vic Taylor's. At least it was reassuring that the Cronshaws' terraced cottage was just across the street from the surgery, and she knew for a fact that Mrs Hewitt would be listening out for any sign of a kerfuffle.

Sweeping up her medical bag, she walked briskly from the room and ran down the stairs. And after a few slurps of sweet coffee, she was out through the front door and across the street to Lizzie's cottage. Instantly, even before she reached the door, she heard the guttural sound of a woman in labour. She was about to knock when the door burst open and a startled-looking Ed, his hair standing on end and his sleeping daughter in his arms, stepped out. 'I'm taking Sue to my mother's just down the street,' he croaked. 'It won't be long before I'm back.'

Knowing how most of the men were when their wives were in labour, she took what he'd just said about coming back to the cottage with a pinch of salt. But it was a good sign that he wasn't still drunk from the night before. Hearing Lizzie upstairs as another strong contraction began to build, she walked quickly through to the small, darkened parlour. Glancing to the tiny kitchen at the rear, she was pleased to note the stove was lit and Ed had placed two big pans of water on to boil. As she climbed the narrow stairs to the bedroom, she heard that deep, guttural sound once more as Lizzie worked through another contraction.

'Hello, Lizzie, it's Nurse Flynn. That's it, breathe just breathe.'

Even as she spoke, she gently pulled back the twist of bedclothes where Lizzie writhed and laid a hand over the contracting uterus. 'Good, that's good, these pains are strong. We should see your baby soon.'

'I bloody well hope so,' Lizzie groaned, reaching out to clutch her arm as the pain reached its peak then began to recede. Then she gasped, 'I'm glad to see you, Nurse Flynn. I've been so upset with what some folks are saying about you, especially after what you did that day for Sue.'

'Don't you be worrying about any of that, Lizzie. We district nurses are made of strong stuff. I'm here to help you deliver this baby and we're going to get through it together.'

The woman nodded then, swiped at her eyes.

'You seem a bit hot, Lizzie. I'm just going downstairs to get some warm water so I can sponge you down. And I'll set up a bowl of soapy water in here for hand-washing.'

Her patient nodded as another big pain began to build.

As she decanted the water, Lara listened for any catch or change in Lizzie's labouring breath. The young woman was doing well. She would check with an examination but already she was sure the labour was progressing nicely. Climbing back up the steep stairs, she then sat by the bed on a wicker chair and as she did the necessary checks and gave encouragement, she became part of the rhythm of the labour. And as she held Lizzie's hand, sponged her face and rubbed her back, she developed a strong bond with her patient. When at regular intervals, she checked and recorded Lizzie's vital signs and listened to the baby's heartbeat, she felt buoyed up by the fact that she was doing all she could to ensure the safety of mother and baby. The rituals which made up this process were unique to every labouring woman and as each pain hit and Lizzie reached for her hand, she became a crucial tether that grounded her patient. And she felt this bond even more strongly given what had happened that day when Lizzie had run into the surgery with her scalded daughter in her arms. This felt like closing the circle for Lizzie and her family, but there was also something very personal about bringing new life into such a small community.

As time moved on with more contractions, she noted her patient's level of exhaustion. The pains were coming one on top of another now and when she examined, she knew instantly that Lizzie was very close to delivery. 'I need you to roll over onto your side,' she said gently. 'Baby's getting ready to be born and this will help.'

The labour moved up a notch then and she could see her

patient already pushing. 'Hold off, if you can, just a little longer. Let's get your baby's head right down.'

Quickly, she examined again and knew by the position of the head that this one would be born face up: a stargazer. Lizzie couldn't hold back now; she was pushing hard. And as she helped her over onto her back, Lara saw the head coming face up and in moments, the child was delivered.

'It's a boy, Lizzie, you have a son.' Feeling as always that lump of emotion in her throat.

'A boy,' Lizzie cried. 'Is he all right? Is he breathing?'

'Yes. He's a skinny one but he's perfect and he's already kicking.'

Lizzie was crying as Lara tied off and cut the cord.

'There you go,' she called, as she wrapped the child in a cot sheet. 'You can have a hold of him.'

That moment, the first time a mother held her child, was always special. And as she eased back to take it in, her heart was full of joy, and then she saw the first light of day strike through a gap in the curtains.

'Look, the sun's coming up... you have a new baby on a brand-new day.'

'Thank you, Nurse Flynn,' Lizzie called, tears streaming down her sweat-stained cheeks. And in the next moment, the baby boy emitted a hearty cry.

'Well, he might be a bit skinny, but he's got a good set of lungs on him,' Lara laughed.

'Like his dad, I think.'

Almost as if she'd summoned her husband, they heard Ed's voice at the bottom of the stairs.

'Can I come up?' he called, his voice thick with anxiety or excitement – it was hard to tell which was uppermost.

'Yes,' Lara shouted down. 'Come and meet your baby son.'

She heard him choke back a sob then he was bounding up the stairs.

She'd barely seen Ed without him being drunk, scowling, or looking for a fight, so to observe this other side of him was heart-warming. She knew he might revert once he had a drink inside him and no doubt as soon as the pubs were open, he'd be out in The Fleece or The Old Oak wetting the baby's head. But as he snuggled close to Lizzie and reached out with his work-roughened hands to stroke his baby son's tiny face, she couldn't help but feel moved.

Nurse that she was though, she noted the grubby bandage over the stump of his left index finger and remembered Angus being called out to an accident at the sawmill some weeks ago. The stitches should have come out well before now and she couldn't remember Ed having attended the surgery to have them removed. So if they were still in, they would be digging well into the flesh by now and might cause an infection. If she got the opportunity, she'd ask him if she could take a look at that finger.

'Have you any idea on names?' she asked gently.

Ed stroked the baby's face. 'How about Oliver, like Oliver Twist from that book about the orphan.'

'But he's not an orphan is he, you twit,' Lizzie laughed. Then she tipped her head to the side. 'Well, how about calling him after your dad? I know you didn't know him all that well, but it'd be nice, wouldn't it?'

He drew a sharp breath. 'No, not my dad. I don't think that would work.'

Lara realised that Ed must not have disclosed any of the abuse he'd suffered at the hands of the father who'd come home from the war physically and mentally scarred.

But Lizzie scrunched her brow and wouldn't let the name issue drop. 'So just out of interest, what *was* your dad's name?'

He couldn't speak for a moment but then a smile twitched at his lips. 'It was Algernon.'

'Crikey,' Lizzie giggled, 'I was thinking he'd been called William.'

'No, it was Algernon,' Ed breathed.

'Well I'm glad I don't like it, given that you don't want to call him after your father,' she said gently.

Ed thrust his shoulders back. 'Well, how about William? Given that's what you thought my dad was called.'

Lizzie gazed down at the baby boy who lay snuffling in her arms. 'Yes, that might work. I like the name, and he looks like a William.'

'How the heck can somebody look like a name?' Ed smiled, shaking his head. 'But William's a good name and we could always call him Bill or Billy.'

'So that's settled then.' Lizzie smiled as she reached down to gently stroke her baby's face. 'Hello, William, wait till you meet your big sister Sue.'

Later, after the clean-up following the delivery had been done and the bed had been stripped and made up with fresh linen, Lara took a few moments to observe her patient. Having been awake all night, Lizzie looked pale and exhausted, with dark smudges beneath her eyes, but as she fed her baby at the breast, she had that same glow about her that she'd noted in Rose. It seemed a far cry from how Lizzie had seemed that first time she'd met her, when she'd observed that shadow of a bruise on her collarbone. But the biggest change had come today from seeing Ed sober and ably playing his part as a proud father. She hoped this would be a turning point for him, but she'd seen enough similar cases in Liverpool to know it might only be a temporary respite. Even so, she savoured the moment of seeing Lizzie so content and already bonded with her baby son. It was a heartening image to be left with as she prepared to go back over the road to the surgery.

'I'll bob in later just to check on you again,' she called.

Lizzie smiled, raised a hand. 'Thank you so much for what you've done, Nurse Flynn. You are just as good at the job, if not better, than Nurse Beecham.'

Uh oh, there she was again, good old Nurse Beecham. But at least this time, she'd come out equal if not slightly on top.

As she descended the stairs, she heard Ed bumping around in the tiny kitchen as he prepared to go off to work and she remembered to ask about the dressing. 'Mr Cronshaw, I couldn't help but notice that bandage on your finger. Do you want me to replace it for you?'

He frowned, then he was shaking his head. 'No, Nurse Flynn, you've got enough to do. And you've been here most of the night bringing my son into the world.'

'It won't take a moment, and I'd like to check the wound so I can make sure it's properly healed.'

'Fair enough.' He smiled as he held out his hand. 'Who am I to argue with the nurse who's just delivered my son.'

'*Never* argue with a nurse, is my advice.' She laughed as she quickly unravelled the grubby bandage to reveal a stump that bore no sign of sutures. 'I don't remember you coming into the surgery to have the stitches removed. Was it one of the doctors who took them out?'

He grinned, then, 'Nah, we sawmill fellas have our own methods. It was my mate Colin who took 'em out with his razor-sharp penknife.'

'Ah, I see... well, on this occasion, it looks like your mate has done well. But if you need more stitches in future, please come back to the surgery to have them removed.'

He offered a single nod but the way he twisted his mouth let her know he probably wouldn't be doing that. But that was all right; whoever this Colin was, he seemed to have done an excellent job.

'You could probably leave the bandage off now, if you wanted.'

'Nah, I need to keep it on for the time being. It protects the scar, stops it getting sore when I feed the trees through the big, circular saw.'

'Ah, right, I understand... So if you want, I can rebandage it for you and I'll give you a spare so you can change it yourself.'

It took no more than a few minutes to bandage the stump, then she was offering more congratulations on the birth of the baby boy.

'Thank you very much, Nurse Flynn. I'm just nipping down to my mum's – she'll stay here when I go off to work. I'll only be a few minutes.'

'Well, I'm just off across the road to the surgery but I'll be calling back later to see Lizzie and the baby.'

After he'd gone, she checked her bag to make sure she'd collected all her equipment, and she was just raising a hand to open the front door when a heavy knock sounded and the door burst open.

She gasped, as did the man who'd just pushed his way into the cottage. It was Vic Taylor and by his dishevelled appearance and stink of strong alcohol, she strongly suspected he'd been sleeping rough in the village overnight.

'So,' he snarled, 'it's our new nurse yet again. What have you been messing up this time?'

Shocked, she opened her mouth to speak. But his eyes flashed and before she had any chance to defend herself, he grabbed her roughly by the throat and pushed her back so violently against the wall, she saw stars. His face was right there against her own. She saw his bloodshot eyes, smelt his stale breath and felt a spray of spittle as he tightened his grip on her throat and hissed, 'It's time you packed your little bag, Nursey. We don't want the likes of you round here.'

Gasping for breath, she kicked out, but he just laughed and tightened his grip on her throat.

In the next second, she heard Ed shout and Vic was dragged back, pulling her with him till he let go.

'What the hell are you doing?' Ed yelled, grabbing Vic by the collar and giving him a violent shake. 'Nurse Flynn has just delivered my baby son. My wife and child are up there now in bed, and you come in here like *that*.'

Vic growled, tried to speak, but Ed had his arm twisted up his back and he was marching him to the door. 'You bloody well stay away from here in future,' he shouted as he pushed him out into the street.

'What's going on?' Lizzie shouted down the stairs, sounding panicked.

Lara was still gasping for breath, but she was desperate to keep her newly delivered mother calm. She coughed, cleared her throat. 'It's okay, nothing for you to worry about. Just Vic still a bit drunk from last night.'

Ed came back into the cottage red in the face and violently shaking his head. 'I am so sorry,' he said, tears welling in his eyes. 'After all you've done for us and that man thinks he can come into my house and push you around. He's no friend of mine, not after that.'

She nodded, patted his arm. 'You look after your wife and that new baby,' she called back to him as she staggered to the door.

Out on the street, she attempted to walk across to the surgery but straight away, her head was swimming. In the next breath, she felt Ed beside her again, and he put a steadying arm around her.

His voice was so gentle, it almost brought tears to her eyes. 'You go easy there, Nurse Flynn. I'll make sure you get back safe and sound.'

'Thank you,' she breathed, not having any choice but to accept his help.

'What the heck's been going on?' Mrs Hewitt called as she raced up the tiled hallway to assist Ed.

'I'm so sorry,' he said, his voice breaking, 'Nurse Flynn has been with my Lizzie during her labour; she's brought my new son into the world. And that Vic Taylor's gone and attacked her.'

'What?' Mrs Hewitt spat. 'We need to call the police right now.'

'What's going on?' Angus shouted as he ran down the stairs two at a time. 'Lara, are you OK?'

She nodded. 'Yes, I'm fine, and really, I don't think there's any need for the police.'

'What's all this talk of police?' Dr Bingham called, emerging from his room with a white serviette tucked into his shirt collar and a piece of buttered toast in his hand.

'Nurse Flynn's been attacked by Vic Taylor,' Mrs Hewitt said, her voice breaking.

Lara felt her legs begin to weaken. This was all coming at her too fast, especially after being awake since the early hours with the delivery.

'Quick, sit her down,' Bingham called, and she felt herself being led to the sitting room.

She almost passed out but as Ed lowered her into an armchair, she came round.

As the whole group talked over each other about Vic, the assault, calling the police, she listened for a few moments, then she called out, 'Look, I'm fine. Honestly, I am. I need a cup of sweet tea, and I'll have to catch up on my sleep. But let's leave all the other things for now, shall we?'

'I still think we should call the police,' Mrs Hewitt said.

'Let's hold fast for the time being; I'm not up to answering any questions right now,' she croaked, her throat still throbbing painfully and feeling more exhausted by the minute.

'Yes, that makes sense,' Bingham offered, still holding his piece of toast.

'Right, then,' Mrs Hewitt called, clapping her hands. 'Let's all go back to our posts and let our nurse get some rest.'

Before he left the room, Bingham stooped down to speak quietly to her. 'I'll be back with my medical bag to check you over. And before you refuse, you have no choice. From what Ed told me, you got quite a whack to the back of the head. Also, you must take the rest of the day off. I'll cover your essential visits, including that first postnatal check on Lizzie Cronshaw.'

She opened her mouth to retaliate but her throat felt so sore, and she was suddenly so overwhelmed by exhaustion that all she could do was nod her head and murmur a thank you as she slumped back against the chair and closed her eyes. And as images of Lizzie and her baby boy and Vic Taylor's bloodshot eyes circled and scrolled through her head, she wasn't sure if she was sleeping or waking. But the quiet of the sitting room and the gentle tick of the clock on the wall helped to soothe her. And when Mrs Hewitt came back with some tea and toast and Tiddles the cat followed her from the kitchen to rub his soft back against her legs, she knew she had never felt so cared for, not in the whole of her life.

22

Lara woke the next morning with a dull, throbbing headache and acute pain in her neck. It puzzled her for a few seconds till she recalled exactly what had happened the day before. Reaching for the aspirin and the drink of water Mrs Hewitt had insisted on leaving by her bed, she swallowed them down and lay for a while longer until the pain began to ease. It brought back thoughts of waking up in the Liverpool Royal after her accident and she smiled wryly to herself, wondering if the incident yesterday might push the previous trauma out of her head. Or was it all going to mingle and stew and turn her into a jibbering wreck?

'Never,' she growled as she forced herself out of bed. They had so much work to get through given they were still a member of staff down, there was no way she could give in to what her body was telling her to do and lie in bed for the rest of the day. At least they had Nurse Greenwood helping in clinic this afternoon. Mrs Hewitt had summed her up as a delightful young woman and a very efficient nurse, and Lara also knew Bingham must be satisfied because otherwise, he'd have been chunnering about her. Angus was, of course, oblivious to Nurse Green-wood's charms because he was still obsessing over Ada Lightfoot.

As she walked to the sink in the corner of the room, she felt steady, and it was pleasing. But when she looked in the mirror and saw the navy-blue fingerprint bruises on either side of her neck, she gasped with shock.

'He really put some pressure on there,' she murmured to her reflection, not able to deal with thoughts of what might have happened if Ed hadn't come back. It made anger surge through her knowing Vic had attacked her with a newly delivered mother and her tiny baby just up the stairs. She'd been here before, inspecting her injuries in the mirror, and she knew she'd have to manage her feelings alongside the physical injury, so she'd have to go easy on her visits today. And by now, everyone in the village and the surrounding district would know exactly what had happened to her at the hands of Vic Taylor, and she wasn't sure if that made it easier or harder to go out bearing the marks of the assault. But one thing was very clear: she *would* go out and she would manage her visits to the absolute best of her ability.

At breakfast, she felt moved by Mrs Hewitt's heartfelt concern and even Angus put an arm around her shoulders and gave her a comradely squeeze.

'How are you doing this morning?' he asked, before throwing himself down onto his chair.

'I'm all right,' she offered.

'Mmm,' he replied, 'I suppose "all right" will have to suffice. But if that bastard comes anywhere near you again, I'll break his bloody neck.'

'Oi,' Mrs Hewitt called, turning from the Aga to point a wooden spoon coated with scrambled egg in his direction. 'I fully agree with the sentiment, but no swear words please at the breakfast table.'

Lara didn't feel all that hungry this morning but once she had Mrs Hewitt's porridge in front of her, she cleared the lot. Then as Angus jumped up from his chair muttering about getting the clinic room sorted, the housekeeper walked back into the kitchen and dropped a letter in front of her. 'Another one for you with a Liverpool postmark. Those friends and colleagues of yours in the big city must be missing you terribly.'

The moment she glanced at the envelope and clocked the bold flourish of Patrick's handwriting, she felt sick to the pit of her stomach. On top of everything that had happened yesterday, she knew she could not open it. Her chair scraped loudly on the stone-flagged floor as she rose abruptly. Startled, Mrs Hewitt switched round.

'Whatever is the matter, Nurse Flynn? Did the letter bring bad news?'

She hadn't had a flashback to her accident in ages but one came at her now and she felt a wave of nausea as her whole body began to shake. There was no choice but to slump back down in her chair.

'I told Dr Bingham it was too soon for you to be going back to work,' Mrs Hewitt said firmly, already by her side, putting an arm around her shoulders.

'It's not that,' she said, her voice cracking as she gripped the table with both hands and fought to wrestle back control of her body.

'Whatever is it then?' Mrs Hewitt asked, and the gentleness of the housekeeper's voice brought tears to her eyes.

'It's about this,' she said, lifting her hair to reveal the scar.

'Oh my goodness, whatever happened to you there?' Mrs Hewitt said quietly.

Feeling her body relax a little just at the sympathy in Mrs H's voice, Lara told the housekeeper exactly what had happened to her in Liverpool. It flowed out of her; she didn't hold anything back.

And when she was done, Mrs Hewitt slipped into the seat opposite and leant across to take her hands. 'I wish you'd told me about this sooner, but I understand every bit of the reason why you didn't.'

Lara nodded, then smiled weakly. 'I didn't tell anyone here because every time I thought about doing so, it brought back the shock of the accident and I didn't want to risk stirring it up and undermining the fresh start I needed.'

'I understand, I do for sure,' the housekeeper said, her eyes brimming with tears. And Lara felt a bat squeak of something then and knew Mrs Hewitt had her own secrets locked away.

'Please, Mrs H, will you keep this to yourself?'

'Of course I will.'

'It's just that with everything else going on, and then what happened yesterday...'

Mrs Hewitt was nodding. 'You can trust me with your life,' she said firmly, 'but you must talk to me again if you feel things are getting on top of you. It's doubly hard for you at present with Marion still in hospital.' She stopped then, snatched a breath. 'You had that as well, didn't you... Finding Marion after her accident.'

Lara nodded. 'Yes, but that's all part of the work, isn't it.'

'Not when you're attending a friend, it's not.'

She heaved a sigh. 'I hadn't really thought about it like that.'

Mrs Hewitt shook her head. 'It seems to me that you've jumped out of your Liverpool frying pan and into an Ingleside fire.'

'Good way of putting it,' she replied, reaching out to give the housekeeper's hand a squeeze. 'And thank you for listening. I hadn't realised till right now how much lighter I'd feel if I spoke out loud about what had happened to me.'

As she rose from the table, Mrs Hewitt got up with her. 'You must be made of tough stuff, Nurse Flynn, to keep going like you do. And just so you know, I'm proud of you.'

Lara gulped back tears. 'Thank you... but we just keep going, don't we. We have to, for our patients.'

'It seems to be what we were made for.' Mrs Hewitt smiled, then reaching into her apron pocket and pulling out a folded piece of paper, 'Speaking of which... here's your list of visits. But don't you be pushing yourself too hard. I want you back here for lunch in good time so you can have a proper break.'

The moment Lara pushed the list in her pocket, she felt the sharp corners of the letter from Patrick. It made her heart jump, but she left the letter right there until she was back in her room. Then pulling out the dusty trunk she'd stashed beneath her bed on the day she'd arrived, she threw the letter in beside the leather case containing the emerald necklace, banged down the lid and with a grunt of satisfaction, she shoved the whole thing back under her bed. She knew she needed to return the necklace but right now, she felt no urgency to do so and besides, it would mean she'd have to go back to Liverpool at a time when the surgery was snowed under with work.

Still feeling muzzy-headed and sluggish compared to her usual level of function, she took it slowly as she made her way to her first visit.

James Alston was number one on her list and as she cycled along the country lanes, the fresh air, the warm sun on her face and the glory of nature all around her was just the tonic she needed. And as she brushed by the grass and wildflowers at the side of the road, she noted ripe blackberries in the hedgerow and up ahead, a wild rabbit hopped out from under the hedge and lolloped across the road.

Arriving at Manor House Farm, she saw Grace in the yard and even before she'd parked up the bicycle, her friend was there, giving her a hug, telling her how sorry she was about what had happened to her at the hands of Vic Taylor.

'I'm all right,' she said, forcing a smile when Grace finally let go of her.

Then with tears shining in her eyes, her friend reached up to gently touch the dark bruises on her neck. But when she spoke, her voice was laced with anger. 'And that man did this to you?'

'Yes, he did.' She nodded. 'But I'm OK. Still a bit shaky, but there's no way I'm going to let anything he did stop me from working.'

'I'm so proud of you.' Grace gulped. 'I mean, you are a bit crazy... Most people would have taken more time off to get over something like that. So you go easy.'

'I will,' she said firmly, feeling and enjoying a strong sense of being a real part of this place and the people who lived here.

'Do you know what, though?' Grace smiled. 'It looks like you'll be needing that dance even more now.'

'Most definitely.' She smiled as she linked Grace's arm and walked towards the farmhouse. 'Now tell me about your dad; how has he been? Is he still taking the dose of laudanum prescribed by Dr Bingham?'

'He's very settled at present. The shakes are still violent when he's awake but he's resting much more and getting a lot of sleep. He's taking bits of soft food and as much fluid as we can get into him when he's awake, but it's very little compared to how much he was having before the most recent fall.'

Lara went straight in to see James and found him sleeping peacefully in bed with the black cat curled beside him. It was pleasing to see him so comfortable, but this change in his condition was more consistent now and she knew it might be the beginnings of further deterioration. It was too soon to open a discussion with Grace, so she kept her thoughts to herself, but she'd speak to Dr Bingham as soon as she got the chance.

'It's good to see him so much more comfortable,' she offered.

Grace nodded. 'Yes, and it's nice to know he's far less likely to fall and hit his head.'

'True,' Lara murmured, her sharp eyes inspecting the sutures and assessing the healing of the most recent head wound. 'It's looking good. A few more days and we can take those stitches out.'

As they were walking back to the kitchen, Grace heaved a weary sigh.

'How are you doing?' Lara asked gently.

'I'm okay. But I know there's a change in Dad... and I've nursed enough sick livestock to recognise he's slowly going downhill.'

It wouldn't be fair to suggest otherwise so Lara said, 'I think you're right... but we can't be sure just yet. Let's see how he goes over the next few days and of course, I'll speak to Dr Bingham about it.'

Grace nodded. 'I respect your honesty and I can take anything you or the doc have to say to me regarding Dad's condition.'

'Well, as you know, there is one thing about Dr Bingham – he'll tell you straight. In fact, he's brutally honest, maybe a bit too stark for some people's liking.'

'It wouldn't work for everyone, but I like that approach. When my mum was dying from her cancer, I wasn't much more than a teenager, but he made it clear to me what was happening, and it was hard to take but at least I had the truth.'

Lara nodded. 'And don't forget, you've got me as well, so don't be bottling things up... You can telephone the surgery and leave a message for me any time.'

Grace twisted her mouth. 'Well, I know you're always busy—'

'You ring if you need to.'

'Thanks for that.' She nodded then offered a smile. 'Oh, there is one more thing I need to ask before you go. It's not about Dad or any of the medical stuff... It's just that it's the village show on Saturday, and I was wondering if you wanted to accompany me. Aunt Agnes will be here to see to Dad and she's all in favour of me getting out whenever I can.'

'Show, what kind of show? Do you mean a play or some kind of performance?'

Grace cracked up laughing. 'Well, there's usually more than one performance when that lot get together. But no, it's the local agricultural show.'

Still it meant nothing to her and sensing her lack of awareness, Grace explained further. 'We have it every year at the end of August; it's where the local farmers show their livestock and win prizes. And there are tents with vegetables and cakes and poultry being judged for first, second and third rosettes.'

'How bizarre.' Lara laughed, still not able to envisage it. 'But it sounds intriguing. So yes, I'd love to come.'

'Excellent.' Grace grinned. 'It's held in the grounds of Ingleside Hall, so I'll cycle down to meet you somewhere... Maybe Tom Douglas's shippon, the one where you delivered the calf?'

'Yes, I know where that is. In fact, I'll probably never be allowed to forget what happened there.'

Grace pulled her close as they walked to the door. 'It's usually a good day out. But just to warn you, the villagers can get a bit merry in the beer tent. So be prepared.'

'I went to The Fleece with Marion before the village dance. So, I might have the measure of it... Anyway, I'll see you Saturday,' she called, still smiling as she wheeled her bicycle back through the yard.

As she progressed through her remaining visits, she needed more time at each stop to engage with the outpouring of sympathy regarding her assault by Vic Taylor. Her final visit was to Daniel Makepeace and his eyes instantly filled with tears when he spotted the bruises on her neck. 'I'm so sorry for what happened to you in our village,' he said, his voice almost breaking.

'Well as you can see, I'm absolutely fine,' she soothed.

He was still shaking his head. 'I've never heard of anything like this ever before in Ingleside, at least not involving the doctors or nurses. It's shameful, it truly is.'

'Please, Mr Makepeace, I'm absolutely fine.'

He heaved a sigh, patted her hand. 'Leo was here yesterday tending his cows and he was very upset about the whole thing. He said if he clapped eyes on that Vic Taylor, he'd give him what for.'

The strength of the vet's reaction surprised her but after being greeted all day with apologies and condemnation of her attacker, she was getting used to it.

'Most of all, Daniel, I don't want you being upset,' she said, already concerned by his increased blood pressure. To settle him, she began to ask about the village show, told him she'd never even heard of such a thing.

He was off then recounting stories of the shows long ago and the red rosettes he'd won for his cattle and the best Shire horse he'd ever owned. 'Beauty was her name, and she was eighteen hands high. A huge creature, but she was gentle as a lamb.'

'Do you think I'll see some Shire horses at the show on Saturday?'

'I'm sure you will. They're still used on most of the farms round here despite the newfangled tractors and machines the younger farmers have started buying. It goes against nature—'

'What does?' a voice called from the open window.

It was Leo, and as he brushed back his dark hair and offered his lopsided smile, for the first time since she'd encountered him in Tom Douglas's shippon, she felt truly glad to see him.

'I was telling Nurse Flynn about the Shire horses that'll be at the show on Saturday.'

'Beautiful creatures.' Leo smiled. 'But the new tractors also have their place.'

Daniel twisted his mouth; she could tell he didn't agree, but good-natured as he was, he didn't argue with the vet.

In the next breath, she saw Leo furrow his brow and she knew he was going to offer condolences over what had happened with Vic Taylor. It was nice, it felt supportive, but she'd had the same concerned glances, apologies and condemnation of the perpetrator at each of her visits this morning and every time, it brought back the trauma in some part, and she had to work to push it back.

'I need to get off,' she said with a polite smile, 'but maybe I'll see you at the show on Saturday?'

'I'll be there. Vets and agricultural shows go hand in hand.' He grinned.

She smiled, then turning to Daniel, 'Remember what I said, Mr Makepeace: I need you to stay calm. No getting worked up. It raises your blood pressure.'

'Right you are, Nurse Flynn. You're the boss,' he offered as he raised a hand in farewell.

'See you Saturday,' Leo called after her.

As she clicked the door shut behind her, she felt a little flushed, but after all, it was a warm day and she'd been busy with her visits. But somehow, as she pulled her bicycle from the stone wall and began to wheel it up the hill towards the surgery, she recognised it wasn't entirely related to the things she'd just rhymed off in her head. She smiled at the villagers who shouted hello to her, not all of them; some of them still scowled in her direction. But she was feeling more acceptance now and it made her feel much more at home.

This afternoon, she was out on mother and baby checks – Lizzie first with little William, then she'd be visiting Rose Ryan and her baby girl. And then she'd be setting out on her bicycle to see Mrs Haworth at Bridge Farm. The delivery of her baby girl had been her first ever as a country nurse and it had all taken place on the floor of a barn amid the hay and pecking hens.

She knew now that she hadn't been anywhere near prepared for how very different it would be to work out here. The sheer distance she had to cover to see the patients who lived outside the village for a start, then dealing with livestock and farm dogs and being fully exposed to all weathers. Knowing what she knew now, she wondered if she'd still make the same decision to work as a country nurse but instantly, she knew it was nothing to do with where she was working or the patients she was seeing. *The* reason, the only reason she'd chosen to come out here, was because of what had happened with Patrick and the accident resulting from it. But what was the point of going back over that? And if there was one thing she'd already learned from these straightforward, plain-speaking country folk, it was that difficult issues are best dealt with by an attitude of, *'it is what it is, you've just got to get on with it'*.

Still wheeling her bicycle, she was halfway up the hill towards the surgery when she heard many hooves heading towards her. *Sheep, it was sheep.* This time she didn't hesitate and set off at a brisk run, only just making it to the alley beside the surgery before the whole flock trotted down the street jostling and pushing one another. It gave her instant satisfaction because even if she'd learned little else about surviving village life, at least she'd worked out how to outmanoeuvre a flock of sheep.

23

It was the day of the show and thankfully, all Lara's Saturday morning visits were done and currently, she had no pregnant women close to their delivery dates. She'd hoped for one of those clear, blue sky, late August days, but the clouds had scudded in to obscure the sun and there was just the lightest nip of a cool breeze. Bingham had already warned her at breakfast to expect rain and he'd told her that over the years, he'd spent any number of shows up to the ankles in mud and needing to take shelter in one of the tents. Of course, Bingham always tended to make more of the gloomier side of life, so she hadn't taken all that much notice. But she'd still worn her old leather shoes, and she'd packed a macintosh in the small backpack Mrs Hewitt had issued her with, just in case the heavens did open.

Angus had already set off for his pre-show meet with Leo at The Fleece. He'd been playful and light-hearted as he'd gone out through the door in his new blue shirt with the sleeves rolled, his thatch of dark-blond hair neatly coiffed. She'd known he'd been excited not so much about the show but with the pub open early, he'd be able to spend even more time at the bar trying to chat to Ada. Lara still had hopes of matching him with Nurse Greenwood, but he only saw her as an efficient and dedicated nurse. And indeed, her help in the clinic had been crucial to them getting by without Marion. They'd had word that their colleague might be discharged next week, and the news had made Lara feel so relieved. She'd been desperate to get down to the Infirmary to visit her on the ward, but it had been impossible due to the sheer pressure of work. Bingham had of course nipped in to see her when he'd been visiting other Ingleside patients. Lara knew Marion was his favourite and it didn't bother her because she'd also fallen under her spell on that first day when she'd bounded in through the door, full of her stories.

Grace was already at the shippon and she waved a cheery hello. And as they stashed their bicycles down the side of the building, they walked together over the final distance to Ingleside Hall. 'I could have cycled up to the farm to meet you,' Lara said, realising her friend was going back over the road she'd just travelled.

'Oh, that's all right.' Grace smiled. 'Out in the country, we like to set folk on their way.'

Lara frowned; she'd never heard the expression before.

'It means when we're heading back from the show, we can take our time, have a chat. Then I'll turn round and cycle back up to the farm and you'll go back to the village.'

'Oh,' she said, still feeling puzzled and imagining the chaos that would ensue in the city if people did that.

'You'll see. It's a nice thing to do,' Grace said.

The noisy clamour and the strong smell of sawdust met Lara as they approached the high stone wall that surrounded the showground. White-coated, official-looking men stood at various points along the perimeter and there was a queue of people waiting to get in. Grace took charge. 'We need to go to the main gate to pay our admission, then we can get onto the showground.'

Once they had their tickets and they'd been ushered through by more white-coated attendants, she was in awe of the impressive façade of Ingleside Hall. The warm stone walls and mullioned windows, the tall chimneys and carved oak door set between two stone pillars, reminded her of the stately buildings in Liverpool. It surprised her to see such architecture out here in the sticks, but of course it was the Harringtons' country house and no doubt they'd have other property in one of the northern cities or in London.

As they walked by the Hall, Grace murmured, 'I need to be on my best behaviour today. Sir Charles and Lady Olivia Harrington are my landlords and even though our farm's been tenanted by generations of our family, my dad's always wary when it comes to rich folk.'

'Oh, I see,' Lara breathed, feeling a little daunted now by the grand façade.

Instantly, Grace chuckled mischievously and linked her arm. 'So let's go and have some fun. And once we've done a tour of the showground, we'll get ourselves into the beer tent and have a few bevvies.'

'Sounds like a very good plan,' she giggled.

The showground was packed out with farming folk and other working people, probably from the sawmill in Ingleside and the Ridgetown cotton mills. Gaggles of children were laughing, running, chasing one another through the lively, good-natured crowd.

'Oi, Tommy Slater,' Grace called as a rosy-cheeked lad with a mop of dark, curly hair crashed into her leg. Laughing, she grabbed him by the scruff of the neck, gave him a shake, then sent him on his way. 'He's the eldest of a family of six, next farm down the road from me. He's a little scallywag but no more than I was at that age.'

Being with Grace made her feel secure in this hectic environment and it was good to have some local context; as she began to settle among the boisterous crowd, her friend pulled her towards one of the white canvas tents. 'Come on, we'll go and have a look at the baked goods first before the buttercream starts to melt and those sponge cakes go on the slide.'

The tent was shaded inside but airless and hot and as she walked the length of a long trestle table displaying iced buns, sugar-dusted sponge cakes, plates of scones, ginger biscuits and shortbread, she marvelled at the meticulously presented entries. Even as she breathed in the sweet smell and stood for a few more moments to admire the baked goods on display, two middle-aged women with clipboards came to stand by each item and make notes.

Grace leant in to speak quietly. 'Those women are the judges... and if Alice Taylor's entered – though I doubt she will have, given what she's got going on – she'd win first prize hands down. I mean, Aunt Agnes is a good baker and she's won the red rosette here a few times, but Alice's cakes are divine.'

'What do you mean by the "red rosette"?'

'Oh, it's what's given for the winning entry, then it's blue for second, yellow for third.'

'Ah, right, I get it now.'

'As the judges move along the line of cakes, they score the entries and mark them up. Then they make their decision.'

'Sounds intense.'

'It is,' laughed Grace. 'Baked goods are a very serious business in Ingleside, especially on show day.'

When they walked out of the cakes and into the next tent, they wandered past neat displays of evenly shaped vegetables: four potatoes, six broad beans, one cabbage and then a line of giant marrows. A red rosette and a first prize certificate were already sitting beside a marrow.

Grace smiled, then she spoke quietly. 'The men are the ones who grow the vegetables, and they get very competitive. Last year, there was a fist fight over a disputed winner for sticks of rhubarb.'

Lara began to giggle; it all seemed so bizarre. But there was no disputing the freshness and the beauty of the home-grown produce on display. And after they'd moved on to the next tent and paid due homage to jars of jam and marmalade and Lancashire cheeses in their categories of creamy, crumbly, and tasty, they made their way to the needlework and knitting tent. Walking between tables, gazing at knitted garments with complex patterns, silk thread embroidery and tapestries fit to adorn any stately home, she was impressed by the items. Having struggled to pay attention to her own needlework skills and knowing from her late Aunt Matilda's delicate embroidery the level of practice it required to produce something like this, she was in awe of the workmanship on display.

'There's some beautiful work here,' Grace breathed. 'Not that I'm fixing to get cracking with my own needles any time soon. I could never sit still long enough to do anything like this, and I've always been happier mucking out the shippon anyway.'

Lara laughed and as they emerged from the tent, she glanced towards the show ring and saw Leo deep in conversation with a young woman sitting astride a fine-boned black horse with a neat stripe of white down its face. As the horse jostled and chomped at its bit and shifted from side to side, the woman sat comfortably in the saddle. Then as Leo stepped back, she pressed a hand to her black velvet riding hat, raised a leather-gloved hand in farewell and trotted away. Instantly, Lara admired the assured way she sat firmly in the saddle even as the horse danced and shied its way across the grass.

'That's Philippa Harrington,' Grace said. 'She's the daughter of the bigwigs I mentioned before who own the estate.'

'Oh,' she said, as she watched the lithe young woman deftly negotiate her way through the busy showground, raising a gloved hand here and there to those who called out a greeting. She didn't know exactly what to think about Miss Harrington but atop the horse in her immaculate riding habit, she looked as haughty as you'd expect from the daughter of a lord and lady of the manor.

Grace pulled her through a busy area packed with local folk jostling for position around the show ring. 'I just need to take a look at the penned livestock,' she said, 'then we'll come back to see what's happening in the ring.'

'Yes, that's fine.' Lara smiled, content just to be directed and bask in the energy of the gathering.

'This lot will've already been judged,' Grace said as they arrived by some wooden pens, 'but I just want to see who's come out on top this year.'

Lara watched as her friend moved along the line of pens and halted at each one to narrow her eyes, then run a hand along the back of the sheep or the cows and calves who were contentedly munching their fodder. Hearing the squeal of pigs from further down the line instantly triggered thoughts of the Taylors' farm and it shocked her a little. She pushed it back, knowing if she wanted to continue to practise out here, she'd have to make her peace with the pigs. It helped her in that moment to recall Bingham's response that first night around the table when she'd naively asked what a boar was. 'A boar is an uncastrated male swine.' She heard his voice in her head, and it made her chuckle.

Arriving back to the show ring in time for the Shire horses, she marvelled at the sheer size and beauty of the shiny-coated creatures with their shaggy legs and thick-set bodies. Seeing them out on the lanes pulling the farm carts with their drivers up top or in the fields at a distance, she hadn't realised how huge they were; their handlers seemed dwarfed by comparison. She smiled when she thought of how Daniel Makepeace had raved about these gentle giants.

'They're massive, aren't they,' Grace breathed. 'But look how gracefully they move. One of my earliest memories is being held up by my dad to stroke the muzzle of a Shire. And once I felt that velvet softness and smelt that special horse smell, I was hooked. They're at the heart of the farms around here and I can't ever see myself trading them in for one of those newfangled tractors.'

Next up were the Hereford bulls, and the creatures were led carefully into the ring by broad-shouldered farmers wearing white coats and peaked caps pulled low over their faces. Instantly, Lara could see the fellas had their work cut out to control the bulls, even with the thick halters and ropes attached to the metal rings through their noses.

Grace leant in and murmured, 'Last year, one of the handlers tripped and fell, and his bull shot off round the ring. It was like the Wild West in there when they were trying to catch it.'

'Sounds terrifying,' Lara murmured. She'd only seen bulls at a distance as she'd cycled by the fields. It was so much more unsettling to be up close to the muscular, snorting creatures. But she had to admit that these, with their curly, chestnut coats and bright-white faces, were so clean and impressive that she had to admire them.

'Do you have a bull on your farm?'

'We used to but now, when we need one, I borrow Tom Douglas's... that one there.'

When she pointed, Lara glanced at Tom and he acknowledged her with a brief raise of his cap as the bull tugged at the rope. It made her feel tense to see the raw power of the creatures and almost as if Grace had picked up on her anxiety, she leant in and murmured, 'Enough bulls for now. Come on, let's head to the beer tent for a pint.'

Grace moved boldly to lead her through a crush of spectators. Nodding a hello here, shouting a greeting there, it seemed as if Grace knew everyone. The impression Lara got was that her friend was very well-liked and there was so much care and concern in the way folk asked after Grace's father, it made Lara feel humbled.

As they approached the beer tent, Grace grabbed her arm and pulled her through the open canvas flap into a noisy, raucous space. The place was packed but as they entered, two elderly farmers wearing flat caps pulled low over their faces nodded a greeting and got up from their table. Grace nabbed it quickly and gestured for Lara to sit down.

'They don't have a big selection of beverages, so are you all right with a pint of bitter?' she called over her shoulder, already moving towards the makeshift bar at the far side of the tent.

'Yes, I'll have a go at that,' she called after her, realising she'd only ever drunk beer once before.

As she waited, she spotted Ed Cronshaw crammed in next to Angus and Leo in the far corner of the tent, close to the bar. They were laughing together, and it looked as if they'd already had a fair bit to drink. Angus's neat appearance from this morning had been wrecked. He now stood swaying at the bar, his hair dishevelled, and his new blue shirt stained with slops of beer. But at least he was still upright. However, it looked like Leo was also struggling and Ed wasn't much better. It worried her more than a little – after seeing the kind and gentle side of Ed when Lizzie had given birth and he'd been sober, she'd hoped he wouldn't lurch back to that angry drunk. It made her feel annoyed with Angus over the issue. Yes, she understood that steam had to be let off and of course, once they all started drinking, it was a spiral that soon got out of control. But Lizzie was her concern and despite how lovely Ed had been after the delivery, she hadn't forgotten that shadow of a bruise she'd seen on the young mother's collar-bone when she'd first encountered her in the waiting room of the surgery.

As soon as Grace returned with two glasses of ale and plonked them down on the table, she said, 'Sometimes, men can be so bloody stupid... Have you seen Ed Cronshaw and Leo over there with Angus? One of them has a newborn baby to look after and the other is supposed to be on call here at the show in case there are any veterinary emergencies.'

'Don't get me started,' Lara replied, shifting her gaze so she didn't have to look at them. Then raising her glass, she clinked Grace's and took a good slug. And although the beer was very warm, she loved the malty taste, and right then with the smell of the grass mingled with sawdust and warm canvas, it was a flavour that blended perfectly. She was thirsty too, so she soon had the glass emptied. And as Grace stood up to go back to the bar, Lara pulled some coins from her pocket. 'Let me buy these, please, Grace. I'm really enjoying this day out. It's so different from anything I've ever experienced.'

'You can say that again.' Grace laughed, nodding in the

direction of Angus and Leo, who were now dancing with each other in the middle of the tent.

Oh my God, what would Dr Bingham think?

Even as Lara thought it, she spotted Bingham propped at the bar with another man of similar age who was already swaying a little, and who then began shouting to anyone who would listen what good friends he and Dr Henry Bingham were, and how they'd served their King and country in the Great War. It intrigued her to have that information, but it troubled her that the senior doctor might also be inebriated. If that were the case, then that was their two doctors out of action, leaving her and Mrs Hewitt alone to manage any emergencies.

'I'm afraid this will have to be my last,' she sighed when Grace returned with two more glasses of ale. 'I've just seen Bingham at the bar and he's probably had more than a few too many already. So that leaves me to deal with anything that comes in.'

'Where is Bingham?' Grace shouted. 'Ah, yes, I see him. He's with Leo's dad, Arthur Sullivan. They're a strange pair, those two. Most of the year, they're having a go at each other; anyone would think they were sworn enemies. But on show day, this is what happens every year.'

'How odd.'

Grace scrunched her brow. 'It's strange, isn't it... and I'm sorry that on your first proper day out, you need to be the responsible one. And do you know what... I can never understand how or why the men of this world have so much power, given most of them are bloody idiots.'

It made Lara laugh out loud, and she raised her glass in a cheers.

Once their drinks were finished, she glanced towards the bar and saw Leo raise his glass unsteadily in her direction. Then

Angus waved and offered a bleary smile, and it looked as if he might try to stagger towards her.

Instantly, she shouted, 'It's okay, Angus. I'll see you back at the surgery.'

Then giggling like a schoolgirl, she grabbed Grace's hand and they ran out of the tent. As they stood catching their breath, still laughing, a rough voice shouted, 'Glad you've got summat to laugh about,' and she froze.

It was Vic Taylor, stone-cold sober, his face twisted into a nasty scowl.

She stood motionless, her breath trapped as Vic growled then lunged straight at her. In that split second, Grace jumped in front just in time to block the punch he was about to throw.

'What the hell are you doing?' Grace hollered, pushing him back with both hands. 'I mean, even if you were blind drunk, there would be absolutely no excuse. This lass still has the bruises on her neck from the last time you had a go at her.'

His eyes blazed in Lara's direction, but she could see his shoulders slumping now, particularly as some of the men from the rear of the beer tent had become aware of what was going on.

'Ease up there, Vic.' A young fella with strong arms and shirtsleeves rolled up to the elbow stepped in front of him. 'We can't stand by and watch you threaten this young lass. And she's a nurse serving our community.'

'Pah,' he spat. 'The bitch put my little lass in the hospital with her incompetence.'

The young man visibly bristled, stepped closer and was about to speak again when a louder voice emerged from the direction of the beer tent. 'You need to think very carefully about what you are saying, Mr Taylor.'

Dr Bingham stepped through the crowd right up to Vic and matched him, eye to eye.

'Why should I?' Vic growled. 'She damn near killed my Lucy.'

'You know that's not true,' Bingham said authoritatively, then glancing around the impromptu crowd that had gathered, 'And anyone here right now who doubts what I've just said, I want you to think very carefully. I am your doctor, I've served this community all my professional life, and I need you to know that Nurse Flynn is one of the finest district nurses I have ever worked with. Yes, she's not from round here and she's a city girl but she's extremely competent, well trained, dedicated, meticulous in her practice and most of all, through very difficult circumstances, she has worked tirelessly for the people of this community since she arrived.'

A murmur ran through the crowd, then voices began to shout, 'Leave the lass alone, Vic. If the doc says she's a good nurse, then let it stand.'

Lara felt the full beat of her heart; she hadn't ever expected to hear anything like that from Bingham, even if he was a bit tipsy. Then, as the murmur of the crowd strengthened and Angus pushed his way through and staggered over to put an arm around her shoulders, she felt tears prick her eyes.

'If any one of you comes for my coll... colleague, well, they'll have to go through me first,' he slurred.

She saw Vic's head drop. He knew he was beaten and as he turned and walked away, the whole crowd began to cheer.

'Looks like you've got full support today, at least from the beer tent.' Grace smiled and as Angus staggered, she grabbed his arm and began to lead him away. 'Come on, champ, let's go and find you a seat,' she said.

'D'you know Ada, the barmaid from The Fleesh?'

'Yes, I do. She's a lovely young woman.'

'Shall we go and shee her right now?'

'No, I don't think so, Dr Fitzwilliam. It's probably not a good time.'

'Come on Fitz, old boy,' Leo called, weaving out of the tent and linking Angus's other arm.

Grace glanced over her shoulder with a wry smile and then she steered the two young men back inside.

Seeing Dr Bingham still glancing around, perhaps checking Vic had definitely gone, Lara walked over to thank him.

'Oh, that's no problem at all. I'm not going to stand by and watch a valued member of my team verbally attacked by the likes of him.' He smiled then and patted her on the shoulder and made to walk away but then he stopped. 'Oh, and I didn't see you earlier, so I was unable to let you know... Little Lucy Taylor has been discharged from hospital. She's back at the farm with her mother and brother and Alice has called in her uncle Josh in case Vic turns up. He's a big bruiser of a fella who was a prize fighter in his younger years, so that feels more secure. And I was saving another bit of news as a surprise, but I might as well tell you now... Our Nurse Wright will be home tomorrow. She'll need to rest up for a while longer but she's eager to get back to work as soon as possible.'

'That's such good news, all of it,' Lara said, blowing out a breath to try and ease her still unsettled state of mind. But when Grace came back out of the tent and linked her arm, it tethered her. And once Bingham had made his way back in, her friend leant in and murmured, 'So, Nurse Flynn, I think we might need a whisky to steady our nerves.'

'Most definitely,' she sighed.

And as Grace pulled her close and they walked into the packed-out beer tent with its raucous crowd of country folk, she experienced a shift in how she felt as a newcomer within this close community. What had happened with Vic Taylor spreading his false rumours and attacking her had been distressing, but the reaction from these people, the strong support she'd had from her team at the surgery, and of course from her new friend Grace, had catapulted her to a place where even though she'd only been here a few months, she was beginning to feel accepted.

24

Mrs Hewitt had spent the whole of last evening sewing blue fabric letters reading '*Welcome Home Marion*' onto a strip of white cotton sheet. As the banner lay folded on Marion's empty chair at lunchtime, Lara could feel expectation laced with mild anguish bouncing between the older woman and Bingham.

The housekeeper had nibbled the corner of a ham sandwich, then sighed and pushed away her plate before pouring her third cup of tea. 'I think I might be needing a glass of sherry or something even stronger before she arrives.'

'We all need to calm down,' Bingham called, slightly too loudly. 'I've told you, Nurse Wright has a scar on her head, she's lost a bit of weight, but she is absolutely fine.'

Lara knew the senior doctor well enough by now to recognise the tension in the way he enunciated his words and then placed his china teacup down to its saucer with just that bit more force. 'Where the blazes is Angus?' he growled, picking up his cup and taking too big a sip of hot tea, then spluttering and fussing over what he claimed was a scalded tongue.

'I told you to be careful; the tea is freshly brewed,' Mrs

Hewitt tutted, 'and I also told you this morning, Dr Bingham, that Angus said he had an errand to run at lunchtime, so he'll be late to the table.'

'No change there, then,' muttered Bingham, risking a more cautious sip of the hot beverage.

Mrs Hewitt scraped back her chair and got up from the table. 'I'm putting a dash of brandy in my tea... Anyone else fancy a drop?'

'No thank you,' Lara said with a polite shake of her head, but Bingham pushed his cup across the table.

'Just a single shot please, Mrs Hewitt; it'll help cool the blasted tea down if nothing else.'

Once the brandy had been poured, they all sat quietly for a while longer. Then, abruptly, the silence was broken as a dishevelled Angus bounded in through the door. 'Sorry, Mrs H, that took a bit longer than I expected. But I've got it all sorted.'

'What have you got sorted?' Bingham growled.

'Oh, it's just a surprise for Marion... I hope she's going to like it.'

'What kind of surprise?'

'I can't say.' Angus grinned, getting stuck into the first of four ham and pickle sandwiches Mrs Hewitt had plated up for him. 'I think she might just love it, though,' he mumbled through a mouthful of bread.

Lara wracked her brain to think what the surprise might be, but beyond a bottle of champagne – which would not be an appropriate gift for a patient recovering from a head injury – she had absolutely no idea.

'Well, I hope whatever it is, it's not going to be a shock for the girl,' Mrs Hewitt said firmly, both eyebrows raised in Angus's direction.

'I don't think so; it should be fine.'

The use of 'should' and not 'will' was an instant alarm bell for Lara, but she didn't want to pursue it any further because given Marion was due back in half an hour or so, it was way too late to offer any useful advice to Angus.

Five minutes later, Mrs Hewitt was asking for help with the banner and as Angus jumped up to get the ladder from the garage, Lara went round to the front of the surgery to advise on where to position it.

'We'll use those hooks there.' Mrs Hewitt pointed to either side of the door. 'The ones we had last year for the late King's Silver Jubilee.'

'Sounds like a good plan,' Lara offered. Then when Angus arrived huffing and puffing with the ladder over his shoulder, she put a foot on the first rung to climb up it.

Instantly, Mrs Hewitt was shaking her head. 'Thank you, Nurse Flynn, but I will do it. I'm not into my dotage just yet. Your job is to tell me if the banner is straight.'

'Righto,' Lara called as Angus shifted the position of the ladder and held it firm as Mrs Hewitt clambered nimbly up it to hook the banner first to one side, and then to the other.

'It looks perfect,' Lara declared, beginning to feel the first flutter of excitement as one or two villagers began to arrive to welcome Marion home.

'What about your thing, your surprise?' Mrs Hewitt asked Angus.

He tapped the side of his nose. 'All will be revealed.' He grinned.

By the time the ambulance turned onto the cobbled street, there was a good crowd of people waiting to greet it.

'She's coming!' Mrs Hewitt shouted as she ran back into the surgery. In moments, Bingham shambled out, slightly breathless.

Glancing around the group, Lara noted Sam Collins the butcher in his blue and white striped apron standing next to Miss Shaw the postmistress, and Lizzie Cronshaw and Rose Ryan were there with their babes in arms. At the last moment, Miss Frobisher joined the group and then Ada from The Fleece and Ted, the landlord from The Old Oak down the street. There were other villagers that Lara hadn't got to know yet and at the last minute, Leo and his dad ran up from the vet's surgery.

As the back door of the ambulance opened and Marion stepped out assisted by a uniformed attendant, the whole group cheered, then shouted a welcome. Lara saw Marion dab at her eyes, then she beamed a smile and called, 'It's so good to be back,' and the crowd cheered again. It was a shock, though, seeing Marion; she'd lost weight, her face was pale, and worst of all, her black, wavy locks had been cut right back, leaving tufts of hair sticking out untidily at the margins of her bandage. With the plaster cast on her arm, she was still very much a patient, but her eyes were bright, and Lara felt satisfied at the recovery she was making.

Mrs Hewitt was already hugging Marion, then Bingham patted her shoulder as he wiped his eyes with a large polka-dot handkerchief. Lara stepped forward then to give her a hug and that's when she felt her stomach twist with a flashback to seeing her friend lying helpless in the grass. Her throat constricted with emotion, but she managed to croak, 'Welcome back. I've missed you so much.'

Marion was crying freely, and she sobbed, 'Thank you, Lara. Thank you for what you did that day.'

'You would have done the same for me.'

'Maybe not quite as efficiently,' her colleague said, then staggered as she began to laugh. Instantly, Lara grabbed hold to support her.

The gathered villagers were now singing 'For she's a jolly good fellow,' and that's when Lara saw that Angus was missing.

It must be the surprise he's been going on about, she thought. And then, in the moment she saw him coming around the corner of the surgery wheeling a motorcycle, her heart twisted. She was sure Marion would not want to be confronted by such a hefty reminder of the accident so soon. And it was the same bike, her beloved Norton. He must have paid to have it repaired; there was no other explanation.

She saw the shock on Marion's face and her gut tightened with anxiety. By this time, Angus was also looking uncertain. *And quite rightly*, she thought.

As Marion stepped forward and ran a hand over the leather seat of the motorcycle, then grasped a handlebar, the waiting crowd were subdued. Lara could feel the collective held breath and she was desperate for this to be all right – not just for Marion but for Angus, who must have been so excited to see this moment, but now looked stricken.

Marion glanced up, tears welling in her eyes. 'Gloria, it's Gloria. I never thought I'd see her ever again.'

Lara was about to walk over to support her but then Marion smiled and turned to give Angus a hug.

'Thank you,' she croaked. 'Thank you for knocking my bike back into shape. Even if I never ride her again, it's amazing to have her restored.' She furrowed her brow, seemed to falter. 'My brain seems to have blocked out what happened that day. All I remember is waking up in the hospital. But it's so good to be back with all you lovely folks here to welcome me. I never expected this. Thank you.'

The villagers were cheering and Angus was grinning ear to ear.

Relief flooded through Lara; she couldn't stop smiling, but this could have gone horribly wrong.

Angus puffed out his cheeks as he blew out a breath and when he caught her eye, he drew the back of his hand across his forehead and mouthed, 'Phew.'

Phew indeed, she thought, still feeling the full beat of her heart. And then she saw Marion falter, just briefly as she walked towards the surgery door. She was straight there beside her, even though her colleague tried to say she was fine, just fine.

Once Marion was safely in the charge of Mrs Hewitt and making her way into the surgery, Lara was about to follow when she noted an anxious glance from Angus.

'Are you okay?' she mouthed. He nodded but he didn't look right. She walked straight over to check on him.

'I really got the jitters there, when I saw her face,' he muttered. 'I thought she was going to have a very bad reaction.'

'It was probably a bit overwhelming for her to see the motor-cycle, but it turned out well in the end,' she offered. 'But if there is a next time – and touch wood I hope there never will be – maybe run it by me or Mrs H first.'

'Roger that.' He nodded. 'But as you say, hopefully, we won't ever be in another situation where we're greeting an injured colleague back from hospital.'

'Hear, hear,' she breathed. 'And like I said, it turned out all right in the end... even though she might be having flashbacks for the rest of her life.'

He gasped, then frowned.

'I'm only teasing, Angus.' She laughed. 'It's probably a good thing for her to see the motorbike restored. I had a bump on my trusty bicycle just before I moved here. But when I got back to work, it had been scrapped and used for spares. I think I would have loved to have had it put back together again.'

He seemed to relax, but then he shot her a concerned glance. 'Were you all right? Did you get injured?'

'Oh, honestly, it was just minor,' she lied, definitely not wanting to go back over any of that, not now that she was feeling much stronger.

'Gives you a jolt, though,' he breathed, then he was immediately distracted by a shout from Leo.

She turned to go back in the surgery but saw Alice Taylor coming up the street holding Robin's hand, with a tall, muscular man with close-cropped grey hair next to her, carrying Lucy as if she were no weight at all. The fella was thick through the chest and sported a snake tattoo on his forearm, and he had to be the prize-fighting Uncle Josh that Bingham had told her about at the show.

'Hello, Nurse Flynn,' Alice called. 'I'm sorry, we seem to be a bit late to greet Nurse Marion, but I need to speak to you as well.' Her face was sheet-white, she had dark shadows beneath her eyes, but she looked brighter and more confident than she'd ever done before.

Leaving the two children with her uncle, she murmured that she needed to speak privately and beckoned for Lara to follow her down the alley at the side of the surgery. As she stopped, she placed a hand against the solid stone wall to steady herself and Lara could sense how tightly wound she was by the rasp of her breath.

Then she heaved a sigh. 'There's something very important I need to tell you, Nurse Flynn, and I'm so sorry I've not been able to speak out before now. It's gone against all I've ever stood for, to keep quiet about such an important thing.'

Lara reached out a hand, seeing how hard this was for Alice.

'So, Nurse Flynn, you need to know that what happened to Lucy with the infection in her leg was absolutely nothing to do with you or your dressings. You took over from Nurse Marion and followed her instructions to the letter.'

Of course Lara already knew that, but it was such a relief to have her own understanding of the events leading up to Lucy's hospital admission confirmed.

Alice cleared her throat and when she continued, her words were deliberate, spoken with emphasis. 'It was Vic who put Lucy at risk. He'd been out drinking during the day and he came back steaming drunk and nasty-minded, and he went upstairs and pulled Lucy out of bed. He was careful with her even though he was drunk, but when I saw him heading to the door, I begged him not to take her outside. You and Nurse Marion had drilled into me about keeping her dressing scrupulously clean. But he pushed me aside and staggered out with me begging and trying to make him stop. He carried her down to see the pigs, of all things. Then he slipped and fell by the shippon with her in his arms. By the time I'd managed to pull her up, the bandage was unravelling, and her leg was smeared with dirt. I did my best to clean it, but it was still grubby, so it was a poor attempt. I wanted to tell you about it so you could be even more vigilant, but he swore me to silence, said he'd hurt me so badly, I wouldn't be able to look after the children if I even breathed a word.'

'Oh, Alice, I'm so sorry,' Lara murmured, reaching out to her.

'There's no need to apologise to me; none of this is your fault. And Lucy could have died from that infection. When I rang the hospital from Mrs Hodgson's phone, the surgeon I spoke to told me that they were on the verge of amputating the leg just to hold the blood poisoning at bay.'

Tears were streaming down Alice's face now and she could barely speak. 'I have nothing but the deepest gratitude for everything you did for Lucy, and I will be sorry for the rest of my life because of the way my so-called husband treated you. He's gone now. I couldn't bear to have him in the house. And if he ever dares to threaten you again, come straight to me and I'll set Uncle Josh on him.'

Lara felt stunned but instantly, she was so much lighter for having the truth about what had happened at Fell Farm. 'Thank you so much for coming here to tell me this,' she gasped.

Alice offered a nod. 'I'll be seeing you again soon, Nurse Flynn. We're moving to the village in due course and I'm setting up a bakery in an outbuilding attached to the cottage we'll be renting behind The Old Oak. The landlord there, Ted, he's been very supportive of my proposal to start my own business.'

'That's good… and, my word, you've certainly not wasted any time getting yourself sorted.'

'It's in my blood; I come from generations of hill farmers and we're a tough breed. And although it goes against the grain to sell the farm that's been in my family for generations, I know it's the right thing to do. Times have changed; it's much harder to make a living from hill farming, especially if you have children to support. And not only that; I need to make the most of this modern world we're living in, with its motor cars and telephones and women who run their own businesses.'

'I'm so proud of you, Alice, and I think you'd do well with any business, but I've heard on the grapevine that you're an excellent baker so this sounds like a very good move.' Then knowing she'd soon be required for the afternoon clinic, she linked Alice's arm and walked with her back to her family. 'If you want to see Nurse Marion, I'm sure it would be fine for you to nip into the surgery for a few minutes.'

'No, that's okay. Tell her we'll catch up with her when she's had a chance to rest. And I need to go in to see Ted at The Old Oak anyway to talk through some of the arrangements for the bakery.'

'Nurse Flynn,' Lucy called, 'I've still got that caramel toffee you gave me that day I went to hospital. It was my good-luck charm. I kept it in my locker and every time the nurses needed to do my dressings and it was a bit sore, I held it in my hand and squeezed it very tight.'

'Well, I'm so glad it was such a help. I'll have to remember that in future, write a caramel toffee into my plan of care.'

As the family group said their goodbyes then went down the street, Lara turned to walk back up and saw Angus and Leo leaning against the surgery wall, deep in conversation. The moment she made to go back inside, Angus glanced up, offered a nod, then walked ahead of her. Leo was still against the wall and he smiled at her, just smiled, and she had to fight the giggle that was forming in the pit of her stomach.

'Don't you vets have any work to do?' she offered playfully over her shoulder before she went in through the door.

'No.' He grinned. 'No work at all. Not since the district nurses are doing it all for us. I mean, it started one day when a nurse helped deliver a calf, and now it's spreading through the villages, out into the farms, and even up to the fells.'

She couldn't hold back that giggle now and as they shared the moment, she stepped forward instinctively and kissed him gently on the cheek. His skin tasted of salt, and she wasn't prepared for the frisson it gave her. But for some reason, the gesture had felt perfectly natural and as she drew back, she saw him smile and then he was laughing and shaking his head.

It made her chuckle as she stepped through the front door and walked down the green-tiled corridor towards the kitchen. After nodding a hello to the patients waiting for the afternoon clinic, she heard Mrs Hewitt, Bingham, Angus and Marion all laughing together around the kitchen table. And just in that moment, she recognised the sense of completeness it offered, and for the first time since she'd come through the door in her summer dress and white hat with its band of silk flowers, she felt as if she were fully a part of something that mattered. Here, within the thick stone walls of a village surgery that had been serving this community for the best part of a century, she was finally beginning to feel properly at home.

ACKNOWLEDGEMENTS

I am indebted as always to the stories that inspire me, and for this first book in my *Diary of a Country Nurse* series, these connections are personal and very satisfying. Having grown up close to the Bowland fells amid the glorious Ribble Valley, the people and places I have created are very close to my heart. Revisiting that special time of a childhood spent on my grandfather's farm has been a joy and I look forward to developing this connection throughout the series.

I'd like to thank my agent, Judith Murdoch, for her continuing support and advice. Also, my editor – Francesca Best – and all the lovely team at Boldwood Books who have given me such a warm welcome.

As ever I would like to thank my family for their love, enthusiasm and for believing in me; and, despite the relentless progress of my husband's Parkinson's disease, his sharp wit regularly buoys me up.

Finally, I need to mention my lovely Mum who died following a long battle with dementia just as I began to write the first draft of this novel. Her lightness of being, sense of fun and glorious farmhouse cooking are at the heart of this series. I have so many happy childhood memories of laughter and conversation around the kitchen table, back in the days when it felt as if the sun was always shining and the green fields and babbling brook were right there waiting to be explored.

ABOUT THE AUTHOR

Kate Eastham is the author of heartbreaking wartime historical fiction. Before this, she was a trained nurse and midwife, and spent 20 years working in palliative care. During this time she had the privilege of listening to stories from patients of all ages and backgrounds, many of whom were veterans of the world wars.

Sign up to Kate Eastham's mailing list for news, competitions and updates on future books.

Follow Kate on social media:

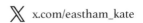 x.com/eastham_kate

Sixpence Stories

Introducing Sixpence Stories!

Discover page-turning historical novels from your favourite authors, meet new friends and be transported back in time.

Join our book club Facebook group

https://bit.ly/SixpenceGroup

Sign up to our newsletter

https://bit.ly/SixpenceNews

Boldwood

Boldwood Books is an award-winning fiction publishing company seeking out the best stories from around the world.

Find out more at www.boldwoodbooks.com

Join our reader community for brilliant books, competitions and offers!

Follow us

@BoldwoodBooks

@TheBoldBookClub

Sign up to our weekly deals newsletter

https://bit.ly/BoldwoodBNewsletter

Printed in Great Britain
by Amazon